PRAISE FOR

THE EXTRA

"Stuart Schoffman's rendition of Yehoshua's Hebrew prose is a delight, and Noga is a compelling contemporary heroine ... Yehoshua's writing chops are undiminished and his content fearlessly topical." — *New York Journal of Books*

"[A] finely etched new novel ... A marvel of a book." — *Haaretz*

"Thoughtful ... Yehoshua seems to be hinting that, 'in a country that never ceases to be a threat to itself,' peaceful deadlock is a small but genuine victory." — *The New Yorker*

"Rich in reflection and personal truth. Yehoshua's masterful portrayal of a female musician at a pivotal moment in her life is deep, unpredictable, and, in the end, surprisingly suspenseful." — *Kirkus Reviews*, starred review

"Award-winning Israeli novelist Yehoshua gives moral force, even grandeur, to the inevitable push-pull of one family's life." — *Library Journal*, starred review

"[*The Extra*] movingly portrays a woman's struggle for independence amid familial expectations and obligations ... Readers who enjoy delving into the intersections of art and literature, or who are interested in the difficulties of controlling one's trajectory while simultaneously remaining responsive to friends and family, will appreciate the ideas put forth in Yehoshua's latest piece." — *Jewish Book Council*

"Engaging ... Yehoshua is a master." — *New York Times Book Review*

Books by A. B. Yehoshua

The Lover

A Late Divorce

Five Seasons

Mr. Mani

Open Heart

A Journey to the End of the Millennium

The Liberated Bride

A Woman in Jerusalem

Friendly Fire

The Retrospective

The Extra

THE EXTRA

A. B. YEHOSHUA

Translated from the Hebrew by Stuart Schoffman

MARINER BOOKS
HOUGHTON MIFFLIN HARCOURT
BOSTON   NEW YORK

First Mariner Books edition 2017

Copyright © 2014 by Abraham B. Yehoshua

English translation copyright © 2016 by Stuart Schoffman

www.hmhco.com

Library of Congress Cataloging-in-Publication Data
Names: Yehoshua, Abraham B.
Title: The extra / A. B. Yehoshua ; translated by Stuart Schoffman.
Other titles: Nitzevet. English
Description: 1st U.S. edition. | Boston : Houghton Mifflin Harcourt, 2016. |
Originally published as: Nitzevet.
Identifiers: LCCN 2015043035 (print) | LCCN 2015048954 (ebook) |
ISBN 9780544609709 (hardback) | ISBN 9780544715936 (ebook)
ISBN 9780544944428 (pbk.)
Subjects: LCSH: Musicians—Fiction. | Domestic fiction. | Jewish fiction. |
BISAC: FICTION / Literary. | FICTION / Jewish.
Classification: LCC PJ5054.Y42 N5813 2016 (print) | LCC PJ5054.Y42 (ebook) |
DDC 892.4/36—DC23
LC record available at http://lccn.loc.gov/2015043035

Book design by David Futato

Printed in the United States of America
DOC 10 9 8 7 6 5 4 3 2 1

First published as *Nitzevet* by Hakibbutz Hameuchad, Tel Aviv, 2014

For Ika, my beloved, my partner

ONE

A T FOUR IN THE MORNING the cell phone rings, its alarm forgotten from the day before, yet she doesn't turn off the wistful melody planted in the gadget by an elderly flutist who wanted to be remembered during her long visit to Israel. Nor, when quiet is restored, does she curl up under her parents' warm quilt to resume her interrupted sleep. Instead she tugs lightly on the levers of the electric bed and elevates its head, so that while still lying down she can scan the dawning Jerusalem sky, in search of the planet for which she was named.

When she was a child, her father told her to look for that planet before sunrise or just after sunset. "Even if you don't find yourself in the sky," he said, "it's important to look up now and then, at least at the moon, which is smaller than your planet, just as your brother is smaller than you, but seems bigger to us because it's closer."

And so, on this visit to Israel—perhaps because of her forced unemployment, or else her temporary job as a movie extra, which sometimes requires working at night—she often lifts her eyes to the Israeli skies, less hazy than those over Europe.

On her brief visits to Israel in the years before her father's death, she would stay with old friends from the Academy of Music rather than at her parents' home. Contrary to what her brother, Honi, thought, this was not out of distaste for the new Orthodox neighbors who were turning the neighborhood "black." Actually she, who in recent years had kept her distance from Jerusalem and enjoyed the secure and liberal milieu of Europe, found it easy to believe in respectful, tolerant coexistence with a minority, even as it showed signs of becoming a majority. After all, in her youth, when she practiced her music on Shabbat, the neighbors did not protest.

"In the ancient Temple they would play the harp on religious holidays,"

Mr. Pomerantz, the handsome Hasid who lived one floor above, once told her. "So it's nice for God-fearing people to know that you're now practicing for the coming of the Messiah."

"But will they also let girls like me play music in the new Temple?" demanded the young musician, red-faced.

"Also girls like you," affirmed the man, gazing at her, "and if, when the Messiah comes, the priests won't let you because you're a girl, we'll turn you into a handsome lad."

Even this minor memory strengthens her belief in a local climate of tolerance, and unlike her brother, who fears his mother's besiegement by the ultra-Orthodox, Noga watches their bustling lives with no grudge or complaint, merely with the amused eye of a tourist or folklorist who welcomes all the songs of the world to sing out in full color.

After her marriage, she had lived in Jerusalem for a few years with her husband, Uriah, but after leaving Jerusalem, and subsequently her husband, she preferred, on her occasional Friday night visits, to return after Shabbat dinner to Tel Aviv. Her parents' intimacy, which only deepened in old age, made things harder for her, not easier. They'd said nothing about her refusal to have children, had even made their peace with it, and still she sensed that it was a relief for them that she not spend the night in their space. That way she would not intrude on a couple fiercely faithful to their ancient, narrow wooden bed, where they would snuggle together in serene harmony. If one of them was alarmed by a strange dream, or woke up over some fresh worry, the other would immediately wake up too and continue a conversation that apparently took place while they were sleeping.

Once, on a stormy Friday, lacking transportation back to Tel Aviv, Noga stayed over and slept in her childhood room, and during the night, between whistling winds and flashes of lightning, she saw her father walking with tiny steps from room to room, his head bent submissively and hands pressed to his chest, Buddhist fashion.

From the double bed, a voice of gentle exasperation: "And what's the matter now?"

"The lightning and thunder turned me all of a sudden from a Jew into a

Chinaman," the father explained in a whisper, nodding his head graciously at the masses of Chinese who had come to wish him well.

"But the Chinese don't walk like that."

"What?"

"They don't walk that way, the Chinese."

"So who does walk like that?"

"Japanese, only Japanese."

"Then I'm Japanese," her father conceded, shortening his steps and circling the narrow double bed, bowing to the bride of his youth who lay before him. "What can I do, my love? The storm blew me from China to Japan and turned me into a Japanese."

TWO

T HE SINO-JAPANESE MAN was seventy-five when he died, amiable and funny to his last breath. One night his wife woke up to complete a thought she'd had before falling asleep, but was met with silence. At first she interpreted the silence as agreement, until she grew suspicious, tried shaking her husband and, while shaking him, realized that her life-long companion had left the world with no pain and no complaint.

During the mourning period, as she grieved with relatives and friends, she spoke with amazement but also resentment about his silent and rude exit. Since her husband had been an engineer, the supervisor of the water department of the city of Jerusalem, she joked that he had secretly engi-neered his own death, blocking the flow of blood to his brain the way he had sometimes blocked the water supply of ultra-Orthodox Jews who re-fused to pay their water bills to the Zionist municipality. "Had he revealed to me the secret of an easy death," she complained to her son and daughter, "I would spare you the ordeal of mine, which I know will take longer and be harder for all of us."

"We'll manage the ordeal," her son solemnly promised, "on condition that you finally leave Jerusalem. Sell the apartment—its value goes down by the day, thanks to the Orthodox—and move to a retirement home in Tel Aviv, near my house, near your grandchildren, who are afraid to visit Jerusalem on Shabbat."

"Afraid? Of what?"

"That some religious fanatic will throw stones at the car."

"So park outside the neighborhood and walk with the children, it'll be good exercise for all of you. Fear of the Orthodox is unbecoming, in my opinion."

"It's not exactly fear . . . more like disgust."

"Disgust? Why disgust? They're simple people, and like anyplace else, there are good ones and bad ones."

"Of course, but you can't tell them apart. They all look alike, and even if they're all angels, they're not going to look after you. So they should stay where they are, and you, now that you're alone, should come and live near us."

His sister kept quiet, not because what he was saying wasn't logical, but because she didn't believe that their mother would consent to leave Jerusalem—that she'd agree to give up an apartment, old but comfortable and large, where she had spent most of her life, to imprison herself in a tiny flat in an old folks' home, in a city she considered inferior.

But Honi pressured his sister too. Now, after their father's death, it would be hard for him to look after his mother. "If you've left the country to escape responsibility for our parents," he accused his silent sibling, "at least help the one who stays on duty."

Now she took offense. She had not left Israel to escape responsibility but because she had not found a position with any of the local orchestras.

"You would have been accepted by many Israeli orchestras if you hadn't insisted on playing an aristocratic instrument instead of a democratic one."

"Democratic?" She laughed. "What's a democratic instrument?"

"Flute, violin, even trumpet."

"Trumpet? You'll regret it."

"I regret it already, but before you leave the country again, help me convince Ima to leave Jerusalem. That way, you can stay in Europe with your mind at ease till the end of your days."

Despite their gripes and acrimony, mutual trust and affection prevail, and when he teases her, she retaliates with embarrassing episodes from his childhood—telling everyone how she'd be summoned from her class in grade school to her brother's kindergarten, where he played pranks on his friends and had to be confined to the bathroom until his sister arrived to walk him home as he bawled the whole way from the Street of the Prophets to their apartment on Rashi, while she tried to calm his stormy soul.

Now Honi is thirty-six, with his own media company, producing documentaries and commercials, a man struggling and mostly succeeding to sustain himself and his staff with new ideas. But his life is not easy. His wife, whom he adores, is an artist who enjoys a modest reputation among cognoscenti, but her works are too intellectual and complex, and buyers hard to find. This may be why she raises their three children with a certain bitterness, which has led to attention deficit in the older boy and chronic crying in the younger girl. And so, when Honi again urges his mother to leave Jerusalem and move to assisted living near his home in Tel Aviv, it's not for economic reasons, but because he demands of himself, especially after his father's death, that he be a devoted and helpful son, without making his already hard life harder.

THREE

S HE TILTS THE BED downward with a soft electric buzz, hops nimbly to her feet and, with small steps reminiscent of her father's on that stormy night, heads for the big living room window to watch for the golden planet through its iron bars. An erudite friend, a violinist in the Arnhem orchestra, on learning the origin of her Hebrew name, Noga, explained to her that in mythology, Venus is not only female but satanic, but could provide no additional information. In the quiet deserted street, a young woman in an impressive blond wig leads a sleepy schoolboy by the hand, his pale sidelocks dangling from his little black hat. She watches the two intently until they round a corner, then goes into the old "children's room," where her two suitcases lie wide open, as if yearning to return to Europe. In the corner, wrapped in oilcloth, rests a musical instrument that Honi had taken down from storage so she could decide what to do with it. When she graduated from elementary school her father had surprised her with this instrument, something between a harp and an Oriental oud, which he found in an antique shop in East Jerusalem. It had twenty-seven strings, some broken now or missing, and those that remain wobble at the slightest touch. On one of her previous visits to Israel, she considered taking it to Arnhem and finding a young European musician eager to tackle the historic instrument, but she knew that even in such a cultured Dutch city as hers, situated not far from the German border, she was unlikely to find someone so inclined.

At the start of her current sojourn in Israel she greatly missed her music. Even if she were to replace the strings on her childhood harp, it would not satisfy her passion for the rich timbre of a true harp. A week after her arrival, she attended a concert of the Jerusalem Symphony Orchestra, and during intermission introduced herself to the harpist, a young woman of Russian origin, and asked if she could practice on the orchestra's harp when it was not in use. "Let me think," said the young woman, studying the middle-aged emigrant from Jerusalem, wary that she might be plotting to return to Israel and take her job. "Leave me your phone number," she said defensively, "and I'll get back to you." And as expected, the woman has not yet finished thinking about it, but in the meantime Noga's passion for playing has subsided. In another ten weeks the trial period in assisted living will be over, and she will return to the harp that awaits her in the basement of the Dutch concert hall, ready and willing for the rehearsals of Berlioz's *Symphonie Fantastique.*

For now, she makes do with plucking the levers on the bed, whose electrical mechanism crouches underneath in a dusty black box. This bed, an alien creature amid the old furniture of the Jerusalem apartment, was a welcome addition after her father's death, consolation and compensation for the man of the house who had vanished from the world in silence. Indeed, only after the man's demise could it establish residence here, in place of the narrow, worn-out double bed—such a sophisticated bed, crafted by Yosef Abadi, a young and talented engineer who had worked with her father at the municipality and remained friendly after his retirement. During the week of shiva, Abadi and his wife came daily to visit the mourners, bringing them meals and newspapers and offering help with any problems arising from the sudden death. It occurred to the widow to ask Yosef to help her dispose of the old double bed, which might be of use to a young couple in Jerusalem, Jewish or Arab, since with her husband gone she felt an urge to create more open space in the bedroom and would do fine with a simple single bed. But the young engineer protested. Why simple if you can enjoy a sophisticated bed? A year earlier, in his small home workshop, he had upgraded a hospital bed for his elderly aunt, adding an electrical mechanism controlled by levers and pedals, and now suggested installing a similar bed for the widow. This bed would have a variety of movements but be easy to operate. It could lay a person down or tip her out of bed. It could elevate the head to suit the owner's eyesight and soothe aching legs by tilting them to a comfortable angle.

Since no one understood at first what this was all about, the gracious offer was not declined, and when the shiva ended, workers from the water department removed their former manager's wooden bed and replaced it with an electric bed, and the young friend promptly taught the surprised widow how to make her life easier at the flick of a finger.

"But why didn't you tell my husband about this bed?" she asked. "You could have built one for him. He would have enjoyed it before he died."

The engineer laughed. "No, he would never have given up that old double bed of yours."

"That's true," said the widow, blushing girlishly. "You knew him maybe better than I did. No wonder he loved you."

And with an air of victory she challenged Honi, as he too lay down on the bed to test its capabilities: "See, there's no reason to exile me from Jerusalem. A smart bed like this will take care of me all by itself"

But the firm response came at once: even a smart bed cannot do it alone at an hour of need, but if the bed also moves to assisted living, it will be a helpful partner.

FOUR

THE PREVIOUS DAY, BEFORE DAWN, Noga had waited for her ride at the intersection of Yeshayahu Street and the Street of the Prophets. Ultra-Orthodox men from Geulah and Kerem Avraham strode silently toward the center of town, taking care not to come near the lone woman. But across the street, beside what was once the Edison movie theater, a large figure sat immobile at a bus stop, the face concealed by a hat. Was it a living person? Noga suddenly trembled, for her father's final slumber of half a year ago still weighed on her. Hesitantly, fearfully, she crossed the street, and despite the likelihood that this was merely a huge *haredi* who had stopped to rest, she dared to reach out and nudge the hat to look directly into the reddened blue eyes of an elderly extra waiting for the same ride.

This man is a former magistrates' court judge, now a pensioner, and because of his height and girth he is in great demand as an extra. For many years he sat passively on the judicial bench, and is delighted to spice his later years with new and unusual roles throughout Israel. Despite his considerable experience as an extra, he has no idea where and for what role he has been summoned today. The producers, it turns out, are reluctant to reveal the destinations to the extras in advance, for fear they will back out at the last minute. For example, not everyone is fond of performing in commercials. People are pleased to take part, even in a small and marginal way, in a fictional story, but shy away from serving as meaningless extras in a quickie commercial, sometimes of a dubious nature and unworthy of the participants.

"And you, your honor," Noga gently asks the older extra, "are you also averse to commercials?"

It turns out that the retired judge is not afraid to appear in commercials that advertise unreliable products or subjects. His son and daughter are embarrassed, it's true, but his grandchildren are excited to see him on the television screen. "I have no enemies to ridicule me," he jokes. "As a judge I preferred to impose fines rather than send people to jail."

A yellow minibus pulls up, with one male passenger, about sixty years old and swarthy, who apparently recognizes her, for after the judge and Noga climb aboard, he hurries to sit next to her, and in a friendly tone mixed with a slight stutter, says, "G-good that you returned from the d-dead."

"From the dead?"

"I mean, from the m-murdered," he clarifies, and introduces himself as one of the extras from that night a week ago when the refugees landed on the coast.

"Really," she says, surprised, "you were also in the old boat? So why don't I recognize you? We sailed and landed three times."

"No, I wasn't in the boat with the refugees. They had me up on the hill with the p-police who shot at you. It could very well be"—he laughs with embarrassment, his stutter more pronounced—"that it was m-m-me who killed you three times, even though I felt s-sorry for you."

"Why sorry?"

"Because in spite of the darkness and the rags they gave you to wear, you looked sweet and interesting even from a distance, and I hoped that the director would let you climb up so we could k-kill you at short range."

"Ah, no," she sighs with a smile, "the director didn't have much patience for me, and every time we came back for a landing, he killed me off quickly, told me to lie still, on my belly and then on my back, so the camera could document your cruelty."

Noga studies the extra sympathetically as he bursts into a hearty laugh. His face is narrow, sharply lined, but his gaze is soft, kindly. His childlike stutter is intermittent and unpredictable. For a moment she considers telling him that she actually enjoyed the long moments of playing dead. The spring skies shone with stars, and the sand retained the warmth of the sun. The tiny shells that pricked her face reminded her of the beach at Tel Aviv, where she and her former husband used to stroll at night.

"What did you do after you killed all of us?" Noga asks.

"We quickly changed clothes and became farmers who sh-sheltered the heroine."

"Heroine? There was a heroine among us?"

"Of course. She was with you in the boat, a refugee whom the script spared from death and allowed to escape to a village. They didn't tell you what the story was? Or at least the scene on the beach?"

"Maybe they did, but apparently I didn't pick it up," she apologizes. "That was the first time in my life I was an extra, and it was strange for me to surrender to other people's imagination."

"If s-so"—his stutter gets stronger—"it's no s-s-surprise they decided to k-kill you off e-early on."

"Why?"

"Because apparently you, as an extra I mean, weren't a natural, and probably stared at the camera. But how did you get to us, anyway? What d-do you d-do in life? You're not from Jerusalem?"

Though the questions are friendly, she is not quick to reply, and only after a long silence she says, "Why don't you introduce yourself first?"

"With pleasure," says the man. "I am such a veteran extra that they don't hire me much anymore, because viewers will recognize me from other movies. For years I was a police c-commander, but when my little stutter, which you probably noticed, got worse, I took early retirement, and now I can make a living from my p-passions. But today, not to worry, there won't be any shooting or deaths. Today we will sit quietly as members of a j-j-jury and listen to a trial, until one of us announces the verdict."

"A jury?" interjects the judge, who had listened to the conversation from his seat in front of them. "Are you sure, Elazar? Here in Israel we don't have juries."

"True, but maybe the scene is about someplace else. These days in Israel they also sh-shoot foreign films, and anyway, sometimes there are dreamlike scenes, like in Bergman or Fellini, so why not a jury?"

The minibus picked up speed on the downhill highway from Jerusalem, but soon exited at the suburb of Mevaseret Zion. There, waiting at the bus stop, were ten or so men and women of various ages.

"Look," said Elazar, "you can count. Including us, it's twelve members of the jury plus one as a backup, in case somebody gets tired or quits. But why don't you want to tell me how you ended up with us? Is it a secret, or just complicated?"

"No secret," the harpist says with a smile, "just a little complicated."

FIVE

IN MIDWINTER, TWO MONTHS after the death of their father, her brother sent her an e-mail:

My Noga,

I'm writing you an e-mail, not phoning, as I fear that on the phone you will cut me off as you usually do. I therefore ask you to read this calmly and carefully before any knee-jerk reaction.

I'm well aware that you don't believe Ima will agree to leave Jerusalem and move to assisted living near me in Tel Aviv. But just as I can't dispel your disbelief, you can't disprove my belief that this is possible. Therefore we should both submit to a reality check.

Two weeks ago Ima came down with a bad case of flu — maybe you could hear it in her voice in your weekly phone conversations, or maybe not. She almost certainly tried to mask this with you, just as she tried to hide her illness from me. It's true that flu isn't life-threatening, not in a strong woman of 75, an age that in light of the amazing performance of our elderly president seems downright youthful. But one of the neighbors, whom Ima asked at the height of her illness to bring her milk, was alarmed by her condition and phoned me.

I canceled a day of work, rushed to Jerusalem, found Ima weak and burning with fever. I called the doctor, bought medicines and decided, despite her objection, to stay the night at her place, to take advantage of her condition to weaken her resistance to the idea. And indeed, by pleading and scolding I succeeded the next morning to get her to agree to try out the assisted living in Tel Aviv for a few months.

I know you don't believe anything real could come of this trial period. I know you're convinced it would be a futile exercise. But I'm willing to cling to the imaginary, because sometimes life has a way of making the imaginary into something real. It's not unreasonable to assume that in assisted living, with devoted care and proper supervision, she will come to understand that this option is preferable to living alone in Jerusalem, where she is increasingly surrounded by strangers, and every illness or accident becomes a threat to her and to me as well, amounting to a test of my responsibility.

And therefore from a moral point of view (forgive the melodrama) you must not only encourage and strengthen me from afar, you must also be a supportive partner not only in words but in deeds.

To be specific:

Abba is gone, and you have chosen an unusual musical instrument that forced you to go far away from home. This is your right. But in so doing you've left me alone with Ima. Maybe I'm an old-fashioned worrier, but I can't help it.

I've found assisted living near us. A small flat has become available there, on the ground floor, with an adjacent garden. The management is willing to let her try out the place for three months in exchange for the maintenance fee alone, with no deposit or commitment in advance.

I took her there, she looked the facility over carefully, and with goodwill and an open mind, she visited the unit they are offering, was impressed by the garden, and having brought with her the measurements of the electric bed, realized there would be room for it. At the end she took an interest in the identity of the last occupant and even requested a description of his dying days. Then, suddenly, she spoke proudly of Abba's silent passing. Her words were so beautiful that for a moment I choked up with tears.

True, I don't know what she feels in her heart of hearts. You, who resemble her more, can probably guess better than I can.

In any case, Ima promised to undergo the experiment with a positive outlook, but on one condition. And this condition, my sister, is addressed to your conscience. A condition imposed by Ima.

Because only after Abba died, and maybe as a result, she thought it right to divulge to me (maybe in the past they had been embarrassed to do so) that they had never owned the Jerusalem apartment, that it was a rental, under the old key-money system. In other words, many years ago, when they moved from Kerem Avraham to Mekor Baruch, the apartment on Rashi Street was acquired for key money alone, which in those days was a convenient arrangement for those who could not afford to buy. The key money was intended to protect the tenant from eviction for life, and also to bequeath that right to his spouse, in exchange for a fixed rental payment which in its day was reasonable but over the years, with inflation, became ridiculously low.

The original owner of the apartment died long ago, and his son and heir died as well, and his widow, who went to live abroad, entrusted the apartment to the care of an elderly lawyer, to whom Abba in recent years would pay the rent every six months. Something totally absurd, like 800 shekels a month or less. Obviously, even an elderly lawyer was aware how absurd this was, so after Abba died, and since the lease was only in his name, the lawyer saw it as an opportunity to take over the property and return it to the inheriting widow. From then on he has been staking out the apartment, waiting for Ima to die or to leave, for only then would he have the legal right to regain control in return for a paltry sum, a portion of the original key money, which had become part of the overall absurdity.

It is therefore of great importance to Ima that during the trial period we maintain our presence in the apartment—in other words, that of an immediate relative. Under the terms of the key-money agreement, we're not allowed to sublet the place.

Beyond the stalking lawyer, Ima is worried about the apartment itself. The front door and lock are in bad shape, and replacing them in this interim period makes no sense, especially since it's easy to slip into the apartment from the floor above and the floor below, through the utility porch or the bathroom window. You may ask who would want to break into such an old apartment. What would they find there anyway? So let's go back to Pomerantz, the nice Hasid who promised when you were young to permit you to play the harp in the Holy Temple if you turned into a handsome lad. The middle son of the Pomerantz family, Shaya, the one who was friendly with you, became a religious fanatic and moved to Kerem Avraham, and of course has countless children, and the two oldest often come to visit their grandparents and loiter in the stairway. Once Ima secretly invited them to watch a children's show on her TV, and they immediately became zealous devotees of the tube. Ima quickly realized her mistake and refrained from ever inviting them again, but they found a way to get in uninvited, and maybe managed to make a copy of her house key. In any event, when she's not at home they apparently go out through Pomerantz's bathroom, shimmy down the drainpipe, enter Ima's apartment through the bathroom window and turn on the TV, and not only to children's programs. Ima caught them once, but took pity and kept quiet, maybe because she has no grandchildren of her own in Jerusalem, but the little bastards look no pity on her, and soon enough she caught them again. Sometimes they break into the apartment at night when she's sleeping. The lust for television drives them mad, and it's a good thing she warned them her kitchen isn't kosher, because otherwise they might raid the refrigerator.

And for this reason too, during the trial period (of only three months) someone responsible must stay on the lookout, and we have nobody other than you.

As a practical matter I see the situation as follows: I understand that you used your annual vacation at the time of Abba's death, and now you can only take a leave of absence without pay. And we thought, Ima and I, how this could be done without causing you financial damage, which I will get to in a moment.

But first the fundamental question: can your orchestra make do without a harpist? You once explained to me that your job consists of two parts, playing the harp and serving as an orchestra librarian, as not every musical work requires a harp, including, oddly enough, the big symphonies by Beethoven, Brahms, Mozart, Schubert and Haydn. Am I right? You told me that the inclusion of harps in orchestras happened later, with such Romantics as Berlioz, Mahler, Bruckner, Tchaikovsky and others. Am I right? After all, from the age of three I learned to internalize everything you told me. Yes, Nogati, yes.

And if this is the case, would it not be possible to plan your orchestra's repertoire in such a way that in your absence they would play classical works that do not require a harp, and to postpone the more modern works till after your return.

Don't get angry—you know your brother and his manipulative imagination. I make a pretty good living from it.

Now, as to the economic side of things. Neither Ima nor I wants this experiment to cost you money, and would in no way approve your dipping into your savings to fund your leave of absence. I know you live frugally, and I also know, of course, that you have no legal right, or desire, to sublet, for such a short period, your rented studio apartment, the charming little flat we saw when we visited you in Arnhem.

Which leads us to the question of your Israeli finances. The Jerusalem apartment, of course, is yours free; electricity, water, gas and phone bills are deducted monthly from our parents' account. I will set up an open account for you at Rosenkrantz's grocery, so you'll have a full supply of staples. But you will doubtless have other expenses. Transportation, dinners out, theater, concerts. So we were thinking, Mother and I, to place at your disposal 8,000 shekels for the three months. And if you need additional funds, there'll be no problem.

I'm nearly done. I suspect you are someplace between shocked and furious. But Abba is dead, Ima is left alone, and I, Honi, your little brother, am trying to find a good solution for her, so we will not agonize, I and maybe you too, with guilt over abandoning her, albeit as a result of her own free will and stubbornness, leaving her alone in an old Jerusalem apartment, dependent on the kindness of strangers and weirdos.

I await your answer — if possible, reasonable and practical — preferably by e-mail, not phone, so we won't cut each other off.

Your loving brother, Honi

SIX

A ND INDEED HIS SISTER did not phone, but replied by e-mail.

My very dear brother,

Let's leave the subject of the repertoire of the Arnhem Philharmonic to the orchestra's management. By the way, Mozart wrote a concerto for harp, flute and orchestra, and I am to be the soloist, but lucky for you, it's not scheduled yet.

Regarding the experiment you have imposed on Ima — since you've defined my thinking on the subject so well, who am I to deny it?

Nevertheless, I will not abandon you to deal alone with the obligation you've undertaken. Let's get through the experiment as you've planned it and to which Ima has agreed. If it ends successfully, all well and good — I too will be reassured and happy. If not, we will both hang our heads in humility, and reconcile ourselves to her desire to end her life at the same place Abba ended his. You will be absolved of any guilt before God and man. That way you can also forgive me for leaving Israel.

In short, I agree to live in the Jerusalem apartment for three months, but I totally reject the insulting suggestion that you and Mother pay me a "per diem." Let me be clear: I will not take a penny from you and Ima. I don't need to. I have my own resources, and even if I take a small loan from my bank in the Netherlands, no problem. I'm in my prime, I have a job, and can cover any expenses.

Even so, if by chance, and only by chance, any idea for my employment should arise in your fertile and manipulative imagination, I'll be happy to consider it—not to earn a few pennies, but so as not to be bored. That's it in a nutshell.

Your loving and loyal sister, Noga

SEVEN

"No SECRETS, YOU SEE, just a slightly complex explanation of how I landed in this line of work. My brother, who has connections with movie and TV production companies, as well as advertising agencies, offered it to me—so I don't get bored during the three months I'm protecting my parents' apartment in Jerusalem, and to earn a little money. Also, it's an excellent opportunity for me to reconnect with forgotten places and experiences, and discover things I didn't know existed. And at the same time get to know all kinds of old and new Israelis and realize that they can be nice, like you, Mr. Elazar."

The extra gallantly takes her hand in his, touches it to his lips and laughs.

"You being paid a d-decent wage?"

"I don't know. My brother gets the money and transfers it straight into my old bank account, which we resurrected."

"You're not m-married?"

"I was."

"And children?"

"I didn't want any."

"Didn't want or couldn't have?"

"I could have, but I didn't want to."

He peers at her appreciatively. Her frankness is appealing, and he would like to continue his investigation, but she gracefully turns to the window, as if trying to figure out where they are going.

The minibus had turned left from the highway onto a side road winding toward the broad wadi that runs from Ein Kerem to the Valley of Elah. From there the minibus climbed toward the Jerusalem corridor villages of Nes Harim and Bar Giora, finally arriving at a regional school, transformed that day into a film location. And as the extras stretch their legs and are treated to coffee and cake with other crew members and actors too, one of the crew turns to Noga:

"If you're Noga, how come you forgot to do what they asked you to do?"

"Who asked, and what did I forget?"

"I told your brother to tell you to come today wearing red—a dress, pants or sweater—because it's important for us to film the jury in a variety of colors."

"I didn't forget, because I didn't know, and next time, ask me directly. My brother is a brother, not an agent."

A young, pretty woman who overheard the rebuke undid a red wool scarf from her neck and draped it around Noga's shoulders. "Here," she whispered, "give it back at the end of the day, and if you forget—no problem."

From there the group of thirteen was led inside the school, whose students were off for the Lag b'Omer holiday, and down a corridor to the gym, where ladders and other equipment were wrapped in black cloth that lent a somber, mysterious air to the courtroom. Twelve extras were asked one by one to sit in two rows of chairs behind a low plywood divider—the backup thirteenth extra took a coffee break—and Noga now noticed that they varied not only in age and ethnic origin, but in the style and color of their clothing.

She was put in the front row, and Elazar, the veteran extra, was exiled to the end of the second row. Was this because of his perennial visibility, his years of gliding from film to film, plot to plot? And yet the mighty figure of the retired judge, so familiar from tacky TV commercials, was selected for a conspicuous spot in the front row, perhaps because they had pegged him from the start as the one who would read out the verdict.

And as the film crew unwinds electrical cables and sets down a track for the camera, she pulls the woolen scarf to her neck, inhales its pleasant scent and closes her eyes with fatigue. In Arnhem, she plays music at night and goes to bed late and wakes up late. The camera had not yet entered the gym, but instructions were already given. "You are here to listen," a young man explained, "but sometimes, when we give you a signal, please whisper something to the person next to you, doesn't matter what—we won't record the whisper and don't need it, all we need is your lips moving. We're filming without sound. And because this is meant to be a long and important trial, taking up about twelve full minutes of screen time, which is a lot in a two-hour movie, we will shoot you in different kinds of light—morning, afternoon, evening, to convey through you the sense of time passing. For this reason, we'll film you separately, with no courtroom, without the prosecution and defense lawyers or the woman defendant. In any case, you must show attention and interest—you're supposed to pass judgment on a serious accusation. In the screenplay there is no text of your deliberations, but we'll take you to a room and shoot you from a distance, talking and arguing, without sound."

"Excuse me, young man," asks the judge, "are you aware that in the Israeli justice system there are no juries?"

"Obviously we're not that ignorant. This trial takes place in a foreign country. The movie is a coproduction."

"Which foreign country?" insists the judge. "Maybe there are no juries there either."

"It hasn't been decided yet. We're considering three countries. It also depends on funding. The world today is global, sir, and so also modular. In a film today you can move countries around like Legos."

EIGHT

THE LITTLE APARTMENT at the assisted living facility was already vacant, but its management had to agree to schedule a three-month trial period that would suit the orchestra in the Netherlands. Although the harpist had been granted permission to take a leave of absence to help her mother in Israel decide where to live out her life, the performance date of the Mozart Concerto for Flute and Harp remained an open question. Noga implored the orchestra's managers that the part of the soloist, which she knew by heart, be reserved for her until she returned, but had not been given unequivocal assurance. It was thus important to ask Manfred, the orchestra's first flutist, to look out for her interests in her absence.

"If not Mozart," consoled the aged flutist, on occasion her discreet lover, "then together we shall play the *Fantaisie* by Saint-Saëns," referring to a work for harp and violin where the violin part is sometimes played by a flute. "Only as an encore," cautioned the harpist, "only as an encore. No fantasia can be a consolation for the Mozart."

Honi was privy from afar to these deliberations, but hid them from his mother, so as not to upset her with the thought that the experiment might hamper the advancement of her daughter's career.

Finally the date was set: after Passover, at the beginning of summer. Late one evening Honi arrived to pick up his sister at the airport, and when he saw her wheeling two suitcases on her cart, not just one as on previous visits, he hugged her tight: "Thank you. Thank you for coming. I know you don't believe in our experiment, but even so, she's your mother too."

Plainly exhausted, his face pale but eyes glinting happily at the sight of his sister, he pushed her cart and talked of the previous day's move to the garden flat, and of their childhood apartment in Jerusalem, now awaiting her.

"We threw some stuff out, then more and more. I was surprised Ima was more into it than I was. She had no mercy on Abba's clothes and possessions, or her own for that matter. It's a good thing the *haredi* charities are so efficient. They take everything, even furniture that's falling apart. But Ima left a few old things of yours, so you could toss them out yourself."

"Old things of mine? What are you talking about? I moved out years ago and didn't leave a thing."

"Oh yes you did, plenty of stuff, believe me. You'll see for yourself—old toys, school notebooks, even clothes. And the little harp that Abba bought you, I took it down from storage. Go through everything and get rid of things—Ima and I threw out and gave away stuff with great enthusiasm, which is a sign, for me anyway, that the experiment you believe will fail will in fact succeed."

"One hopes," she whispered wearily, unaccustomed to the Israeli heat. Suddenly she stopped.

"Where are we going?"

"To the car."

"You're not planning to take me to Jerusalem."

"Why not? To help you with the suitcases, to show you what hasn't yet been tossed, and on the way there, to finalize our arrangements."

"Absolutely not. You're wiped out, and none of this is urgent. I'll take a taxi, you'll give me the key and go home to your wife and kids. What makes you think I can't manage by myself in the house I grew up in? Just do it."

For a moment he tried to protest, but she quickly got into a taxi, and Honi gave in and paid the driver, but held on to the open door. "I have a few ideas for you," he said with a confidential smile.

"Tomorrow. It's not urgent."

But he pressed on.

"I also have something to tell you, something about your concerto."

"My concerto?"

"The Mozart. I bought the CD and listened to it. Interesting, but—"

"But not now."

He thought himself knowledgeable about music, and though she regarded his knowledge as spotty and superficial, she persisted in trying to edify him.

"And most important, lock the door securely, and the windows too."

"The windows?"

"I mean in the bathroom, because the kids—"

"What kids?"

The taxi now needed to move.

"Okay, not now. We'll talk."

It was nearly midnight, but the Mekor Baruch neighborhood, which in her youth had been stone silent at such a late hour, was still whispering nervously, in search of sleep.

The apartment door opened easily, as if by the mere touch of the key, and when she switched on the light she was struck not only by cleanliness and order, never strictly enforced in her parents' home, but by the new emptiness.

Honi was right, a great many things had been removed, including furniture, and the living room was shockingly bare. She went into her childhood room to deposit her suitcases. Her bed was neatly made, and a clean-smelling bathrobe was laid on it. Her heartbeat quickened as she entered her parents' room, and to her surprise, the new electric bed, which she'd heard about from her mother, was also made up, as an alternative for sleeping. She opened her parents' closet. Her father's side was empty, his clothes were gone, but one suit, black and elegant, remained hanging, presumably because no worthy recipient had yet been found, and beneath it a pair of shoes sat waiting, with socks lying on top, as if the father or his successor were about to walk in. She pressed her tired face to the thick fabric to sniff a familiar scent, then mischievously took down the suit jacket and slipped into it, checking herself out in the mirror. Though her father had shrunk slightly in his last years, the jacket was wide and made her shoulders look bulky and square, and the sleeves swallowed her hands. With a little smile she slowly raised her arms and imagined herself conducting, with graceful rounded gestures, the harp and the flute in Mozart's concerto.

The ringing of the telephone cut short the imaginary performance.

Honi couldn't fall asleep, had to know if she'd arrived safely, if she appreciated how much stuff was discarded from the apartment in her honor.

"In *my* honor? Why? I didn't ask for anything."

But excited by the experiment that was becoming a reality, he wanted to talk at this late hour about his specific plans for his sister. "Not now, it's bedtime," she protested, worried that from here on he would try to manage not just her mother, but her as well, and she hung up and unplugged the phone.

In the refrigerator there was food her mother knew she liked—hard cheeses, herring in cream, grilled cauliflower, potato pancakes. She eats a light supper, checks the bathroom window and lies down in the bed in her childhood room. After three hours of sleep she wakes up and walks in a daze to her parents' room, sinking into her mother's electric bed. But as dawn approaches she again feels drawn to her childhood bed, and the nocturnal shuttle between two beds promises to be an enjoyable experience for the duration of the trial period.

She reconnects the phone at ten in the morning, so her mother won't worry. Sure enough, it rings at once, but it's not the worried mother calling, it's the brother, whose patience has run out and he cannot wait to present his sister with a surprising offer.

"A movie extra?" She laughs. "What? I'm not an actress!"

"You're not supposed to act, but to be . . . just be . . . try it. What have you got to lose? Nowadays there's a boom in film and television in this country, and many opportunities come up, and you'll also meet new people, be part of other people's stories and make a little money, which you're unwilling to take from us. What else do you have going here in Israel? To keep chasing after music? Really, Noga, doesn't music also deserve a break from you?"

NINE

T HE DAY DWINDLES SLOWLY, the jury still sitting in two rows at the back of the gymnasium. Sometimes the camera closes in on their faces, sometimes it pulls back, at other times it seems to disappear entirely, though it is always there. "Please don't be upset we're keeping you so long," a cameraman apologizes, "but this trial is important to the film, and the changing light outside, which in the film changes within minutes, will indicate that you've been here all day, listening carefully, and only in the evening are you supposed to deliberate and render your verdict."

Other extras, not from Jerusalem, are scattered around the gym along with actors, from scenes that have been shot and scenes that will be, but the judge, the prosecutor, the defense attorney, the witnesses and the woman defendant are not yet present, presumably still rehearsing.

"Do you know anything about the content of the film?" she asks the retired magistrate, who sits next to her in the first row.

"Just in broad strokes. At the booking agency they are stingy with information, maybe for fear of people dropping out at the last minute. Because extras, not being actors, sometimes confuse the imagination of others with the reality of themselves."

At dusk, two additional lights are set up opposite the jurors. A procession of robed figures enters — the prosecutor and defense lawyer and judge, who disappear into a classroom that is now the courtroom. Two burly men in indeterminate uniforms march the handcuffed defendant past the jury, back and forth. Noga recognizes her as the pretty young woman who in the morning had given her the perfumed red scarf. Her makeup gone now, her face is pale, her eyes ringed with black circles. Her clothes are gray and her walk slow, contemplative, as if she is lost in thoughts of her crime. She scans the jurors, and when she sees the red scarf on the neck of the extra, she nods her head and stops in front of her as if about to say something, but no lines have been scripted. Yet the anguish in her eyes is so credible and persuasive that Noga fearfully tugs the scarf tighter around her neck, as if this were not an actress standing before her, but a despondent fellow traveler from her past.

"What did she do?" she whispers to the retired judge after the accused is gone.

"Murdered her husband."

"Why?"

"You'll know when you see the movie," he answers ironically, "if it actually gets done."

All the actors in the trial have vanished into the classroom-turned-courtroom, but the camera refuses to let the jury go. The time has come to announce the verdict of the trial that has not yet begun.

And as determined ahead of time, the portly magistrate rises from his seat, and with a look of satisfaction pronounces the answer to the question that has not yet been asked.

"Guilty."

His pathetic pleasure displeases the director, who asks him to do it over. Yet the veteran extra cannot suppress the joy of a tiny speaking part.

The director then turns to Noga and asks her to stand and announce the same verdict.

"Guilty," she says, simply and softly.

The director appears satisfied and asks if she can also say it in English.

And again she pronounces the word, softly and sadly, this time in English.

The producer whispers something in the ear of the director, who asks Noga if she knows other languages.

"Yes, Dutch and a little German."

"Then please, in Dutch and German as well."

At first she is confused, but regains her composure and reiterates the guilt in the other languages.

TEN

S HE HAD INTENDED TO VISIT her mother two days after arriving in Israel, but Honi tried to delay it. "You came for three months, not a week, so rest, get acclimated. In two days the retirement home has sched uled an excursion for the residents, and it would be good for Ima to join them. Wait another two, three days, let her get acclimated too, and I'll try to pick you up from Jerusalem."

She realized that the experiment on which he hung his hopes required his constant vigilance, not only regarding his mother, but her as well. But after four days in Jerusalem, she decided to elude his control and go down to Tel Aviv without his knowledge.

When she entered the gleaming lobby of the facility she was told her mother was at a concert. At first she stood by the closed door and listened to an amateur string trio, then grew impatient, silently opened the door and stood in the back of a small, dark hall, where perhaps twenty elderly residents were concentrating on their friends, a violinist, a violist and a cellist in a wheelchair, who played a trio by Schubert, missing more than a few notes as they fiddled vigorously together. The musicians noticed as she entered, and it seemed that her stately presence made them slightly anxious, but her mother, tranquilly enjoying the musical bonus of assisted living, did not yet see her.

Finally, she too noticed the extra woman standing in the back, and urgently wished to join her, but Noga signaled her to wait, and sat down so as not to offend the musicians.

At the end of the concert her mother introduced her to one of the old women.

"This is my daughter, a musician, but she lives in Holland . . ."

The visitor liked her mother's experimental one-room apartment, which though located on the street level was attached to a private patch of ground, with flowers and bushes abutting a grassy lawn. The furniture was modest but new, and the bathroom was spanking clean.

"Would you believe, Noga," said her mother, "that I as a tenant have to water the flowers?"

"And you don't like that?"

"The watering I like, but not the obligation. In Mekor Baruch nobody has flowers anymore."

"Don't exaggerate."

"And besides," sighed her mother, "if Abba could have imagined that after he died I'd end up in Tel Aviv, he wouldn't have left the world so peacefully."

"But you're not in Tel Aviv, you're in assisted living."

"Assisted in what?"

"In tolerating Tel Aviv."

Her mother laughed. "In the six days I've been here, some nice old women have befriended me, one of them from Jerusalem, who remembers me from kindergarten and insists I haven't changed a bit, not my looks or my mind."

"So you already have a good friend."

"Yes, it's easy to make friends here, but to create a solid connection you have to provide stories of illness and other misfortunes. So many amazing stories here about exotic maladies, so vividly described you imagine catching them right then and there."

"And you don't have a disease you can spread in return?"

"None, my child. You know I'm healthy. Also, Abba's death was so easy and simple, people are jealous."

"Then talk about family problems."

"We don't have any. We were always a normal and stable family."

"Normal?" Noga laughed. "What about me?"

"What about you?"

"A woman no longer young, whose husband left her because she refused to have children."

"If you refused, what's the problem? If you were unable, I could look for sympathy or pity. I'm not going to turn you into a problem to satisfy some old lady here."

"Then at least provoke a little anger at me."

"Why anger at you? If the experiment succeeds and I move here permanently, what will I gain from other people's anger at you? Your father didn't get angry, and he didn't allow us to get angry either. 'We have to honor Noga's wishes,' he said. 'Childbirth can have complications, even cause death.'"

"Even death? That's what he said?"

"He not only said it, he thought it."

"Good Abba, he couldn't think of another way to justify what I did."

"That's how he tried to explain it."

"I didn't connect my decision to any death."

"Of course you didn't. I don't think you connected it to anything at all. You didn't want to, and that was it. That's also how I put it to Abba. But he stuck stubbornly to his explanation. So I said to myself, if Noga's imaginary escape from death calms him down, who am I to deny it?"

The back door leading to the porch and garden was open, and Noga noticed that the room faced the western sky, bathed now in a reddish glow.

"It's nice here, so pleasant. Honi found you a good place. By the way, I was amazed to see how many things you threw away. All of Abba's clothes . . ."

"Not just Abba's, mine too. Honi was impressed how easily I emptied out the closets. If the experiment here doesn't succeed, I'll at least return to an apartment that's light and airy. If you had been with us, we would have convinced you to throw out things of yours that were still there."

"Not much is still there."

"True, not much, and you can throw the rest out yourself."

"In any case, you left Abba's black suit."

"It was so beautiful and new, a shame to give it to charity."

"Maybe you're saving it for a new husband," teased Noga, and her mother laughed.

"You know me, Nogaleh—do you see me with a new husband?"

"Or at least a lover," the daughter insisted.

"A lover, fine, but he'd have to be Japanese or Chinese, as Abba used to joke with me at night, but they're so small and thin the suit wouldn't fit them. I thought of offering it to Abadi, but I worried he would be embarrassed to wear a dead man's suit. So let's keep thinking. If you want, we can give it to our neighbor Mr. Pomerantz. He's still a handsome man and dresses well."

"But without the shoes and socks, because that would be insulting."

"Shoes and socks? What are you talking about?"

"The shoes and socks you left below the suit. It almost looked like you were waiting for Abba to come back."

"That's right, Noga, I am waiting for him to come back, but if the shoes and socks bother you, then you should throw them out right away."

"We'll see. It really is lovely here, and the residents seem quite cultured."

"The ones you saw. There are others in frightful condition who barely get out of their rooms. But if the experiment succeeds, it will be a relief for Honi, who won't need to travel to Jerusalem, which he hates more by the day. That's why he's so pleased I'm here."

"He's really attached to you."

"Too much. Drops in several times a day to see how I am, even joined me twice for meals in the dining room. Yesterday he brought the children for me to look after. Good thing there's grass here where they can run around, because my room's too small for their energy. I thought they'd be picked up in two hours, but Sarai showed up after four hours. I said nothing, she's an artist after all, and her sense of time is rather vague. If I can be useful once in a while, why not? Now it's dinnertime, come join me."

But Noga didn't get up.

"Take it slowly, Ima. We'll do it next time. Today I have no strength for interrogation by your old ladies."

The mother went off to the dining hall, and Noga sank into the small armchair, fixated on the remains of sunlight. After a while she stood up and went out past the porch to the darkening lawn. How did this grow here? she wondered. This old folks' home is a building among other buildings on an ordinary street, and suddenly it's like Oxford or Cambridge, where you open a plain door to find an ancient cathedral with great expanses of grass.

She strolls across the lawn to figure out where it goes and how it ends, and in the violet twilight she can make out, beside a bench, a little old man in a wheelchair covered in a blanket, a thin scarf around his neck, dozing or perhaps unconscious, a shriveling intravenous bag connected to his arm.

A forgotten resident, not brought in for dinner? Or perhaps the IV is his meal?

She is careful not to wake him, and sits on the bench to ensure his safety in the gathering darkness. But soon, in the warm evening air, she is intoxicated by the serenity of her napping neighbor and closes her eyes — and suddenly an unknown hand clutches her neck.

For a moment she is terrified that the man with the IV has risen up to strangle her. But the old man is gone. Apparently someone has quietly wheeled him back inside. And behind her, the laughter of her brother.

"You better watch out," she says. "At age forty-one my heart can't handle your jokes."

"Your heart is the same as ever," Honi says, holding her wrist as if checking her pulse. "A young heart, a strong heart, a heart of stone, as Uriah used to say."

"He complained about me to you too?"

"Yes, out of desperate love for you. And how's the home I found for Ima? The lawn lets her look after the kids while sitting in an armchair."

"And this will be her final apartment, if she wants?"

"This one, or maybe a better one, providing you don't weaken her resolve."

"I didn't come to Israel to weaken any resolves, yours or hers."

He nods in gratitude.

In the room, a fruit platter assembled by the new tenant awaits her two children, and the three of them now sit, six months after the father's death, in the peaceful setting of a posh old-age home, light years away from the blackening neighborhood in Jerusalem, discussing the experiment just begun, and the arrangements for the Jerusalem flat under Noga's care.

"Wait a minute," Noga says. "Those children, Pomerantz's grandchildren . . . what do I do if they come into the apartment again?"

"They won't come in," decrees her brother, "and if they try, don't let them. Even if they beg, no mercy. Don't repeat Ima's mistake. And make sure the bathroom window stays locked. They managed in the past to climb down the drainpipe."

"From the third floor down the drainpipe? How old are they?"

"The older one," says the mother, "is eleven or twelve, the younger six or so. The older one is Shaya's son. You remember him, Noga? Pomerantz's middle son, the handsome boy you sometimes ran into on the stairs or in the street. After you got married and left, they arranged for him a bride among the most extreme ultra-Orthodox in Mea Shearim, and though he is more or less your age, he's already fathered ten or maybe eleven children —I think even his mother gets confused how many. And that younger one is a cousin, and as it happens in these huge families, one of them always turns out retarded."

"That's not a nice word, Ima," scolds Honi.

"If not retarded, then strange, a space cadet, but sweet, nice-looking. And because he is hyperactive, they send him with Shaya's son to let off steam at grandma's house. But how much can Mrs. Pomerantz keep him occupied? She's not a well woman. They don't have a television, of course, just a radio tuned to some religious station, so it's no wonder the kids get bored and run around on the stairway, up and down, over and over, making noise and yelling. And this little one, the retar— 'challenged' one, he sometimes makes these blood-curdling screams. So to keep them quiet, I invited them to watch a little television, children's programs, because they don't allow television."

"And you got permission from the grandma?"

"I didn't want to put her to the test, get her in trouble with Shaya, who has become a total fanatic, but I'm sure she knew, or at least guessed and looked the other way. It brought her peace and quiet. The Pomerantzes were always a respectable family, not extreme. When you played music on Shabbat, Nogaleh, they didn't get angry."

"Well, bottom line, what am I supposed to do now? Not only keep watch on the apartment, but also deal with crazy Orthodox children?"

"No, not at all. Don't let them in, period," says Honi. "Ima took pity on them, that was a mistake, but you don't need to do that. Just take the key away from them."

"Key? What key?"

"They apparently walked off with my spare key," the mother says defensively.

"Then you should call the police."

"Police?" The mother is taken aback. "How can you talk that way, Nogaleh? These are Pomerantz's grandchildren, Shaya's unfortunate kids. We should call the cops to lock them up? What's wrong with you?"

"Not lock them up, just take away the key."

"We'll take the key, don't you worry. Honi will phone Mrs. Pomerantz, she'll take the key from them. Just lock the bathroom window at night, that's all. It's not so hard."

ELEVEN

H ONI DROVE HIS SISTER to the bus station, but when he found out there'd be a long wait for the next bus, he offered to drive her to Jerusalem.

"What's going on?" she again protested. "Go back to your wife and children. You're addicted to this experiment. You've fallen in love with it."

"So don't ruin it."

"Why would I ruin it?"

He took out a few bills from his wallet.

"Here, for the time being, just for now."

"Don't you dare . . ."

"But you won't be able to last for three months without additional income. That way you'll trip me up with your stubbornness and pride. Ima is also worried."

"I have my own money, and if I run out, you said you could find me work."

"Very good. So what I'm giving you now is an advance on your first paycheck. Please don't say no. I won't be able to rest easy if I know you're going back to Jerusalem without enough money."

She hesitates. In the evening darkness, by the desolate bus station, her brother grows older by the minute. His hair has gone gray, and though no one ever said he resembled his late father, the old man's look has begun to flicker in his eyes.

She sighs and strokes his arm.

"It's strange to come back home and be an extra. Where do I go, anyway? Who do I talk to?"

"Nobody. I'll take care of everything. They'll be in touch with you and work it out. I heard about a movie about foreign workers or refugees, and they need a lot of extras there. I'll handle it all."

Aboard the bus, racing along the highway to Jerusalem, her anxiety surfaces: the orchestra will perform the Mozart double concerto without her. I should have asked for clearer assurance that they will not forget me, she says to herself, gently extending her arms to the seat in front, as if it were the harp she will clasp to her breast when the conductor gives her the sign.

A taxi takes her to Rashi Street, but the driver seems hesitant. "You sure this is your address?"

"For now," she says blithely, and hurries out.

The hour is late, there are few cars in the street, a human presence prevails. People exit and enter the apartment buildings.

By the gate of their building an old man stands in the dark, waving to her with his hat.

"Are you Noga?"

He pronounces her name softly, though they have never met. She reckons this is the lawyer who lies in wait to liberate the apartment.

"For now," she answers cheerfully.

"But you live abroad, in Holland."

"For now," she repeats, liking the sound of it.

"Because even if you came back to Israel," the man continues, "you should know that your mother cannot transfer the apartment to you, and you may not even rent it from her."

"Why is that?"

"Because this is a key-money flat with only your father's name on the contract. After his death, your mother was granted, out of pure kindness, the rights of a protected tenant, but not the right to rent it out."

"You're the owner?"

"I am their emissary. I am their legal eagle."

"How nice."

"The neighbors say your mother left, went into a home."

"For now."

"So please tell her Attorney Stoller sends his regards. I had good relations with your late father. He would bring me the piddling rent money twice a year. As long as he was alive, we expected nothing. But now, tell her from me that to live in a home near her son and grandchildren is wonderful and important. Why should she live alone among people whose poverty turns them into strange fanatics? Also, we want to get rid of this apartment, and we have buyers. So give your mother my very best regards. If I were able to get into assisted living in Tel Aviv, I would have done it a long time ago."

"Are you Orthodox?"

"I can be Orthodox when I want, but so far I haven't found the Orthodoxy that suits me."

"And if I decide to stay here as the daughter of the family?"

"Without your mother, you can't. You have no legal standing for tenant protection. Besides, what do you want with an apartment like this? It needs a lot of repairs. You don't want to go back to your Dutch orchestra?"

"You've even heard about that?"

"I know a lot about your family. Your father, of blessed memory, used to jabber in my ear about you all. What do you do in the orchestra? A drummer?"

"A harpist."

"That's better. More dignified."

"Every musical instrument has its own dignity."

"If you say so. You undoubtedly know."

And he tips his hat and bids her farewell.

The apartment's bathroom light was left on by mistake, though the window is closed.

She undresses, but before deciding in which bed to start the night, she sits in front of the TV, watching a concert with the orchestra on a stage in the middle of a forest, and a crowd of twenty thousand enthusiastic Germans sitting on the grassy ground, listening to popular classics. The camera lovingly caresses the bare shoulders of the women musicians. Until two years ago, she too performed with her shoulders bare, but they grew thicker, and compared with the magnificent shoulders of other female players, they suddenly seemed to her ungainly. So she decided to cover them, though Manfred, the first flutist, found no fault with them and kissed them with passion and joy.

TWELVE

I N THE MORNING Noga phones Manfred in Arnhem and asks him to nail down the promise given her regarding the Mozart concerto. "Not to worry," he assures her, "the Concerto for Flute and Harp is meant for the two of us, and I will not play it with any other harpist." Meanwhile, as the keeper of the key to her little flat in Arnhem, he casually mentions a faucet left running in her bathroom, a result no doubt of her hasty departure, but promises all will be dry by the time she returns.

She wonders if he is only looking after the apartment or also using it, but the distance between the Middle East and Europe dims her concern, and when Honi calls about tomorrow's work as an extra, she makes jokes as she jots down the details in her father's old notebook, where he would faithfully record every errand assigned him by his wife or children.

At lunchtime she cooks herself a real meal, then enters her parents' darkened bedroom, takes off her clothes and adjusts the electric bed, but her sleep is soon punctured by footsteps scurrying up and down the stairs and an occasional wild, piercing scream, as if a small predatory animal were fighting for its life.

Silence finally returns, a breeze compels the dozing woman to rearrange her blanket, and as sleep takes its time to settle in, there are two soft taps on the apartment door.

Noga smiles. These must be my mother's TV children, she thinks, doing her best to ignore them. But the tapping, soft and rhythmic, goes on. To hell with them, she says to herself, and waits, and it stops, permission now granted for blessed sleep, for Noga to burrow into the pillow and be carried to a place she's never been, a crowded city street in a ghetto, where someone is giving a speech in a faint but familiar voice full of eloquent indignation. Can she have traveled so far in her dream only to hear that voice again? She flings off her blanket, wraps herself in a bathrobe and silently opens the living room door.

The TV is on at low volume. Sitting cozily in the two faded armchairs that survived her mother and brother's purge are two boys with sidelocks, clad in black, hats perched on their laps, the *tzitzit* fringes of their ritual undershirts dangling on their thighs. The older boy senses her presence and looks up at her seriously, brazenly, with a tinge of supplication. In the other armchair nestles a beautiful, golden child, twisting his right sidelock into a curl as his light blue eyes stare at the speaking prime minister.

"Who are you? How did you get in?"

"Your mother said," the older one answers, "if she's not home, I'm allowed to calm him down with the television."

He points to the little boy.

"She couldn't possibly have said something like that."

"I swear it. You weren't in Israel, that's why you don't know."

"What's your name, boy?"

"Yudel ... Yehuda ... Yuda-Zvi."

"You be careful, Yuda-Zvi, I know all about you two. You're Shaya's kids."

"Just me. This is Shraga, he's a cousin, the youngest son of my mother's sister. But you got to know only my father, not my mother."

"Right," she answers. "I never met your mother and I don't want to meet her. Now turn off the television. Where's the remote?"

"I don't have it. He has it. He picks out for himself what and who calms him down."

"Like the prime minister, you mean," she says with a smile.

"Yes, he can relax him, depending on what he says. And this one, if he doesn't get a little TV every day, he runs up and down your stairs and everyone goes crazy, including your mother."

Noga bends over the little boy, who has still not looked at her, and searches for the remote under the hat on his lap. Then she removes him from his seat and rummages in the depths of the armchair. But the child doesn't mind; his eyes are glued to the screen, and the remote is hidden the devil knows where. She gives up on him and unplugs the TV, and the child attacks her with a wild scream, tries to bite the hand that silenced his prime minister, and when she shakes him off, he curls up on the floor and bitterly weeps.

"You can't take him away from the TV like that," Yuda-Zvi explains, sitting peacefully in his armchair.

"Like what?"

"All of a sudden."

"Enough is enough," she says. "What's with this kid? What's wrong with him? Where's his mother? Where's his father?"

"His father is always sick, and my aunt has no more strength for him, so my mother asks me to take care of him. Because he—you may not know this—he is not an ordinary boy but an important boy."

"Important?"

"He's the great-grandson of the Rebbe, the *Tzaddik*, the righteous one. And if other children in that family die, he might someday have to be the *Tzaddik*, when he's a hundred and twenty."

But she is unimpressed by the *tzaddik* wailing on the floor.

"Does your grandmother upstairs know you're breaking into an apartment that isn't yours?"

"Grandma doesn't know much of anything anymore," the boy answers truthfully. "But even if she did know, she wouldn't care, because she understands that only television can help his pain. And I promise you, Noga" —he speaks her name matter-of-factly—"your mother also doesn't care if I calm him down with her television. She even gave me a key."

"A key!"

"Yes. Because she knows that if I take him in through the bathroom window, he could possibly, God forbid, fall and be crushed."

"And where is the key now?"

"Why?"

"Where's the key?"

"It's here . . . I have it."

"Give it to me."

"Why? You don't have a key to the apartment?"

"Give it to me right now, or else . . ."

As the little *tzaddik* looks up at her, his eyes gleaming with tears, the older boy unbuttons his shirt collar and hands her a string with the key that her father had put on a red ring, to tell it apart from his many other keys.

She opens the front door and quietly says:

"That's it, boy. That's it, Mister Yuda-Zvi. This is the last time . . . and I will speak to your grandmother and your grandfather."

"Just not Grandpa," says the terrified boy. "Please, not Grandpa," he begs, before she slams the door on them both.

THIRTEEN

A FEW NIGHTS LATER, on the ride back to Jerusalem after the jury shoot, with the actress's red scarf still wrapped around her neck, Noga casually tells Elazar about the two boys.

"Even if you took away their key, don't be so sure they won't come back," he says. "The little b-b-bastard probably made a copy, so don't be surprised to find them again in front of your TV."

"So what am I to do?"

"The n-n-next time, don't kick them out and don't argue. Act friendly, get in touch with me, and I'll put on my old police uniform and make sure that the little *tz-tzaddiks* won't b-b-bother you again, forever."

"Forever?" She laughs. "I'm only staying in Israel for another couple of months."

"So wh-what? You're still entitled to p-p-peace and quiet."

The stutter is annoying, but also charming in its way, with an element of surprise. Entire sentences flow smoothly, and just as she has forgotten that he stutters, an ordinary word or a modest preposition, which might carry some hidden implication, becomes a psychological impediment, and then, instead of simply repeating a word or syllable, he gets stuck on a certain sound and prolongs it. In the dark minibus making its way to Jerusalem, she senses his attempt to draw closer to her, not only because he likes her, but because she is free and unattached, without a husband and children, with no desire to have children, and also because her time in Israel is limited and there's no risk of getting emotionally involved, which could hurt him or someone in his family.

And since he knows about future projects of the agency that hires the extras, he tries to win her over during the drive by urging her to take part in them as well.

"I don't need that much money," she says.

"It's not just m-m-money," he protests, "but to be a participant without any effort or ob obligation in the stories of all kinds of characters, and perhaps also be engraved in the m-m-memory of the audience. Tonight, for example, you announced the verdict very well. When this movie is completed, if it ever is, there will doubtless be viewers who will remember how softly but c-c-confidently you pronounced *gu-il-ty*, as if you were not talking about the killer, but about y-y-yourself."

The retired judge, sitting silently across the aisle, apparently dozing, turns his head. "Yes, madam, Elazar is right. These days a court is expected to announce a grim verdict in a personal tone of voice, even with mild hesitation. I am still used to declaring a verdict with dramatic force, which is why they passed me up."

At the bus stop near the former Edison movie theater Noga and the judge get out, and Elazar suddenly decides to join them. "I'll see you home so I know where to come q-q-quickly if you want to chase away the boys." But Noga points to her building from afar, lest he attempt to escort her upstairs.

FOURTEEN

ELAZAR WAS UNDETERRED. The next day he phoned and asked her to join him in the late evening at a bar, where a scene was to be shot for an Israeli film requiring several middle-aged extras to supplement the regular younger crowd. This was no more than a pleasant evening on the town, he added. The scene would be simple, not long, and would be shot without fancy direction or cinematic effects, the extras would blend in anonymously, the camera would be hidden. The extras would be asked to act naturally like the rest of the crowd, drink, listen to the music and chatter away to their heart's content. They would not be paid. The production would cover the cost of drinks; the night on the town constituted the pay.

They made plans to meet on the street, near her building, but he arrived early and came up to the apartment on the pretext of checking out the bathroom window and testing the strength of the drainpipe that the boys had used to enter the flat. Then he checked the front door and offered to come back and install an interior bolt, and also to put a new lock on the bathroom window, but Noga was reluctant to make improvements in the Jerusalem apartment before the resolution of the Tel Aviv experiment. She put on simple high-heeled shoes, donned the red scarf—her new favorite —and hurried him out the door.

To her surprise, he said that the bar was just around the corner and suggested they walk over. "You don't mean," she said, "there's such a place in my *haredi* neighborhood." A mysterious smile crossed his lips. He said, "You'd be amazed what one can discover not far from home." He led her into the nearby *shuk*, the Mahane Yehuda market, its alleys and passageways washed clean, the shops and vegetable stalls silent and shuttered. The smells of smoked fish, spices and cheese lingered in the night air along the route to a structure flanked by two torches of friendly fire, with a nighttime crowd gathering inside, and no telling who was a regular patron and who a mere extra.

"You ever go to the *shuk* at night?"

"Not by day or by night. My brother set up an open account at the grocery near the apartment so I wouldn't have to elbow through the *shuk* to find cheap tomatoes."

"Cheap tomatoes?" he said, feigning umbrage. "Kindly do not condescend to the *shuk*. It's much more than cheap tomatoes. This bar, for one, is a wonderful restaurant during the day."

They went down some stairs as music rose from underground, a former storage cellar tastefully made over with small tables and banquettes, and in a rear alcove, an accordionist belting out old favorites.

Now, as they sit close together, partly in the role of extras and partly as themselves, she is aware of the man's desire to succeed where previous men have failed. And though this stammering policeman has a wife and grown children, even a small grandson, and has no need for another child, he will not give up on the pretty, dimpled harpist, and tells her about upcoming jobs, such as a television series set in a hospital, complete with doctors, nurses, administrative staff, labs and of course patients, requiring many extras to supplement the professional actors, who suffer and agonize, die or get well, depending on the plot.

The accordion lets fly a Gypsy tune. Even if most of the assembled are strangers to one another, a breeze of intimacy blows among them.

"Can you tell, based on your experience, who here is an extra, who a customer, and who an actor?"

"No," he admits. "Even with my experience, it's hard, because I don't know where the camera is, so I can't tell who's aware of it and who's not."

She smiles, understands, slowly sips her beer and says softly:

"I must say, you're really something."

"So what do you say about the hospital show?" he asks, encouraged. "It's a long series, so they'll need some chronic extras. I'm already signed up, and if you extend your stay in Israel, you could make a fair bit of money."

"I didn't come here to make money, only to enable my mother to try out assisted living, and I have no intention of extending my stay longer than necessary. The Mozart Concerto for Harp and Flute is waiting for me in Arnhem, and my fingers are trembling with desire for it."

He cautiously places his hand on her fingers as if to feel the desire, and his stutter breaks out:

"S-so if not the hospi-pi-tal, maybe someth-thing else, short and special."

"That sounds better."

"Where they need extras with m-musical f-f-feeling."

"That's me."

"It's a production of *Carmen,* d-down in the d-desert at Masada, and they need extras to be G-G-Gypsies, but it would be without pay."

"Meaning what?"

"Meaning there's transportation, and staying in a g-good hotel, and of course seeing the opera for free three times."

"It sounds attractive. And you'll be there?"

"No, because for this opera they need only f-f-female extras."

"Then it sounds even more attractive."

"Why?"

"Because sometimes I get weary of men."

Crestfallen, he turns silent.

"What now?" she ventures.

"What now what?"

"*Carmen*—"

"Tell your brother to sign you up," he interrupts, and says nothing more.

After a long while the production assistant rescues them from awkward silence, informing them that their job as extras has ended but they are free to stay until closing time.

"Excu-cuse me," says Elazar, grabbing the young woman's arm. "Now you can tell us where the c-c-camera is hiding."

She smiles. This is a deep secret, but the need for secrecy has expired. She points at the ancient domed ceiling, and perched up above, like a strange bird of prey, is a black camera with a big shiny eye.

"You needn't walk me home, I know the way," says Noga as they leave the Mahane Yehuda market, which at this late hour is already showing signs of awakening. But the defeated extra doesn't stop. As either an escort or a follower he keeps walking, watching her heels strike the silent pavement, until her steps halt a fair distance from the building, signaling the final boundary of the shared evening. He hesitates, his humiliated desire still stinging, and suddenly he looks at her and wants to know how many strings her harp has.

"My harp?" She is taken aback.

"Yours . . . or in general."

"Why?"

"To know y-y-you better."

She laughs, then explains that a concert harp has forty-seven strings, with a range of six and a half octaves, almost as many as a piano. Thus it is possible to play pieces on the harp that were written for the piano, and vice versa.

"So the whole difference is that the piano is lying d-down and the harp is standing up?"

"That's the small, unimportant difference. The essential difference is in the sound."

"Why? They both have the same strings, from the guts of animals."

"Not necessarily. Some strings are made of nylon or metal."

"Metal . . . ," he mumbles.

"Of course," she says, spurred on by his late-night curiosity. "Besides the strings, the harp also has seven pedals."

"P-p-pedals? Why?"

"To produce additional tones and halftones."

"How many?"

"A hundred and forty-one altogether."

He is lost in thought, as if digesting the great number, then studies the harpist with a mixture of wonder and compassion, and declares, "You need to be very coordinated."

"Yes, coordination, that's the word. If I miss the right string or pedal, the whole orchestra will notice the mistake."

"And how long have you been playing the harp?" The former policeman continues his interrogation.

"From quite a young age."

"And because of the music, you c-c-couldn't have children."

"I couldn't?" She recoils. "Who told you that? I could have, but I didn't want to," she says, firmly repeating what she had told him when they first met.

"How do you know you could have?"

"Because I know. I know. My former husband also understood, which is why he left me."

Darkened streetlights surround them. The moon is gone. No one to be seen. It is the hour of deepest sleep, even in this neighborhood.

"I understand," he whispers, nursing his humiliation. "I-I understand y-you . . ."

And still he refuses to leave.

"So would you like me to come tomorrow and install the bolt, so the children—"

"Thank you," she interrupts. "For now there's no point in investing anything in that old apartment, and I'll control the children on my own."

By now the pain of rejection is turning into anger.

"If you never had ch-children, how will you know how to control them?"

"Precisely because I didn't have children."

His laugh is short and bitter, and as he disappears into the darkness, she fears that his fondness for her has come to an end.

In the apartment the bathroom light is on. Did she forget to turn it off, or did the little *tzaddik* slip in during the night to relax in front of the TV?

FIFTEEN

T HAT NIGHT SHE SLEEPS fitfully and migrates from bed to bed. In the morning she phones her mother at the retirement home, and is surprised to have awakened her.

"Yes, I get much more sleep here than I need at my age, and more than suits my personality. I was afraid that Tel Aviv would upset me, but instead I feel serene."

"And the experiment?"

"The experiment keeps experimenting."

"You think you can complete it, come back to Jerusalem and decide about the future from here?"

"No, Noga, we have no right to stop it. It's not fair to Honi, who made such an effort, and certainly not fair to this facility, which gave me such a lovely room without requiring a commitment. No, we mustn't stop in the middle."

"But I know you, and you won't stay there."

"Don't be so sure. We have another nine weeks, and despite the tiny distance between here and Jerusalem, by European standards anyway, I'm getting a new perspective on myself, because here I am free of old obligations and superfluous memories. Now I'm fully entitled to sleep deeply, so I'll also have a chance, like Abba, of taking my leave from you without any long illness or cause for worry."

"Not a chance."

"Not a chance? You, with your cruel honesty, may be right, though I get the impression that my experiment is hard for you. You're already bored in Jerusalem? But unlike Honi, you love the city and are tolerant of our pious neighbors. Honi also told me that you enjoy the little roles he finds for you —that they killed you at night on the beach and you enjoyed lying on the sand and looking at the stars, and that you condemned a young woman to death—"

"I didn't condemn anyone, I just said she was guilty. That's all."

"And you enjoyed it?"

"A little. What can I do, Ima? I'm trying to pass the time until you decide where you want to stay for the rest of your life."

"And I will decide. I'm not just dawdling, I'm weighing the pros and cons. And you, Noga, please don't put pressure on me, don't begrudge me the three months, and then you'll be able to fly back to the bosom of your orchestra . . . What's bothering you the most?"

"Those children."

"Which children?"

"The little religious ones you made into television addicts."

"But Honi said they returned the key I lent them."

"I had to take it from them by force, but they had apparently made a copy, and they come in whenever they feel like it, and it's annoying, even scary."

"Scary? You're exaggerating. These are little kids from huge families, and so they're a little lonely and depressed, sometimes a little crazy. After all, they are Shaya's kids, that handsome fellow you used to talk to on the stairway when you were young."

"Only the older one. The other one, the little one, the strange one, is his cousin, some kind of *tzaddik*."

"*Tzaddik?* How so?"

"Not important. But to change the lock would mean changing the whole front door, which is falling apart, and that should wait till you make up your mind."

"Yes, you're right, till I make up my mind."

"But in the meantime let's put in a bolt to lock the door from the inside. So I'll at least know that I'm safe when I'm in the apartment."

"Exactly. I'll ask Honi to put in a bolt for you on the inside of the door."

"You don't need to drag Honi to Jerusalem for that. I'll find someone in Jerusalem."

"Yes, that's possible. For example, Abadi, Abba's friend. This man, so polite, he and his wife brought food every day to the shiva, and after you left, he was the man who put in the electric bed. He'll install whatever bolts you need, not just willingly but with love."

"The devil only knows why you gave those children permission to come in."

"Right, Nogaleh." Her mother sighs. "Exactly. Only the devil can explain why I did such a foolish thing, but where do I find such a clever devil?"

SIXTEEN

ABADI ROSE QUICKLY to the occasion. Having stayed in touch with the family, he knew about the experiment and even hoped it would succeed, but had not understood why they needed to summon the daughter from Europe. "No reason to worry about the empty apartment," he said. "I'll be happy to stop by every so often to see that all is in order. What's left there to steal? Everything is old, nothing to tempt a thief." They had to explain to him that what they feared was the elderly lawyer looking for any excuse to liberate the apartment, and if a stranger like Abadi were to start dropping by, it would only strengthen his claim.

Now Abadi walks through the apartment and is astonished by its emptiness. "It's bold of your mother," he says, "to get rid of so many possessions without being sure she was leaving Jerusalem for good."

"She'll come back," says Noga to the gentle, melancholy man, whom she recalls as a passing shadow among the many visitors during the week of shiva. "I know her well. We're soul mates."

"So the experiment, bottom line, is just for Honi?"

"Yes, so he can be reassured that he has no choice, that till my mother's final day of clarity he'll be tied to the city that makes him very angry."

"And you?"

"I love Jerusalem, but I don't come here much."

"That's an easy way to love."

"Easy and successful. But come see, Mr. Abadi, how you can support this love, because the little *haredim* are driving me mad."

"I'll help on one condition—that you call me Yosef and not Mr. Abadi."

"Yosef. There, I said it."

And he goes to the front door, whose lock had seen better days. But in order to replace it with a reliable lock, one would have to replace the entire doorpost. It would therefore be best to wait until the experiment in Tel Aviv is resolved, and in the meantime the Jerusalem apartment will be protected by an ordinary bolt. Abadi, at home in this house, makes for the kitchen, opens the father's tool drawer, takes out a folding ruler, screwdriver and pliers, and returns to the front door to remove rusty nails before taking measurements.

From there he goes to the bathroom and stretches nearly all of his flexible body out the little window into the black of night, to estimate the distance to the drainpipe and the gutter. And again, since the window lock has disappeared entirely, and since only if Tel Aviv loses the experiment will it be worth hiring a carpenter to build a new window, all she needs now is a simple hook, which admittedly could be pried open from outside with a screwdriver, which would be a criminal act, not just a prank by kids who slide down the building's drainpipes for fun and accidentally land in their neighbor's bathroom.

She follows him around the apartment, studying him with appreciation. His movements are unhurried, his words level-headed, practical, and it's clear why her father liked him. After all, he is the talented inventor of the electric bed.

"You know, I myself sleep in it part of the time."

"Why only part of the time?"

"Because sometimes, in the middle of the night, I miss my childhood bed."

"Are you aware of all the possibilities offered by this electric bed?"

"I should hope so. I have the quick fingers of a harpist, and your bed doesn't have forty-seven strings or seven pedals."

He laughs. "Not quite. But I do think it has a few possibilities you haven't discovered. This was originally a hospital bed designed for gravely ill patients, designed to meet many needs, but so a healthy person could also enjoy it, I installed an upgraded electrical mechanism. Come on, I'll teach you, because I'm not sure you're aware of all the options."

"What I know is enough for me. I'm only here for a short time."

"Even so, it's a shame you won't enjoy it more."

His excitement is almost childish, but was apparently appreciated by her father, who had appointed him as his successor at the water department. And so, after writing down the measurements for the bolt and the hook, Abadi strides into her parents' bedroom, sheds his shoes, sprawls on the bed and begins to jiggle its controls, elevating and lowering its sections, activating internal vibrations, raising the whole bed levitation-like and finally tipping it over like a canoe, ejecting the recumbent man, who lands on his feet.

"You see?" he says, his eyes sparkling. "You didn't know it could do that!"

"True," she admits.

"So come here and I'll show you how."

It's hard to say no to such enthusiasm, and she too removes her shoes and carefully lies down on the bed, and he bends over her, and she can feel his steaming breath, which steams not for her but for his machinery, and he gently takes her hand and guides it to a hidden lever, slick from machine oil. But when she pulls, nothing budges, and a furious gargle emanates from the engine box.

"The machine is rejecting me."

"Impossible." He places his hand on hers, to pull harder, but still nothing moves, and the same furious gargle is heard. He then slides under the bed to patch a frayed connection. But something goes awry: there is a sharp pop and the apartment is plunged into darkness.

"Be careful," she says softly.

"It's okay," he assures her, and springs nimbly to his feet. "Don't move. I know where to find the fuse box."

And he goes to restore the light.

The bedroom windows are open to the clear summer night. The moon is late to appear, but stars are shining. The electric lights in the neighboring windows are dim, frugal. Her eyes can make out the objects around her, though she has yet to rise from the bed. She is waiting for the light to come back on. But Abadi is finding it difficult to replace the fuse in total darkness. "Your mother doesn't have any candles?" he calls out to Noga, who remains as immobile as the electric bed she lies on.

"What for? She doesn't light Shabbat candles. But the upstairs neighbor has a million candles. Maybe you should go up there."

"What's her name?"

"Mrs. Pomerantz. She's the grandma of the little bastards. I have no strength for her right now."

He walks out but does not even try the light in the stairway, despairing of that one too. She sits up in the bed but can't bring herself to leave it. A light begins to flicker on the stairs. Abadi descends, carrying a candle of majestic proportions. She hurriedly gets up to greet him and sees he is not alone. The two boys are following him down with lighted Hanukkah candles in their hands. Brazenly they enter the flat through the open door and stand at attention before the dark, silent TV screen.

"That's it." She laughs. "No more television."

"It'll come back," the older boy says quietly, and the little *tzaddik* turns his angelic face to her, adding, "With God's help."

SEVENTEEN

I N THE MORNING she goes to the bank to check her balance, which is noticeably higher than expected. She phones her brother to clarify if by any chance he might be giving her money she's not entitled to. "You're entitled to all of it, sister," he jokes. But is it possible that she had made that much for four jobs as an extra? "Apparently you were outstanding," Honi says, "and they gave you a bonus." Finally he admits that yes, here and there he "rounds upward" the amounts paid to her. "Please," she objects, "don't round anything, the experiment is already costing you enough, and I have only seven weeks left and want to live them with integrity. I lack for nothing. I even enjoy running the apartment," and she tells him about Abadi's visit.

"Fine. And if you need more repairs in the apartment, don't hesitate to call on him. He'll do it all happily. He was close to Abba and he also owes us — Abba promoted him and made him his successor. During the thirty mourning days, after you'd left because of an 'urgent' concert, Abadi and his wife insisted on bringing us meals, which got out of control, but of course we couldn't offer them to the *haredi* neighbors since we weren't sure if the food was kosher enough. And, of course, the electric bed . . ."

"What's his wife like?"

"Pleasant and polite like him, and kindhearted."

In the early afternoon Noga goes to Mahane Yehuda and heads for the bar that in the daytime becomes a restaurant. The little nighttime tables have been joined together into long ones covered with checkered oilcloths, and the customers sit in rows, facing one another, all of them male, for some reason — *shuk* people, greengrocers and butchers, workmen and porters, who satisfy their hunger quickly with large, identical servings of warm hummus with mashed hard-boiled egg, plus a red meatball garnished with whole chickpeas and fresh parsley.

She pushes her way among the sturdy patrons, and the moment she sits down and looks for a menu, a plate of the standard meal is plunked down in front of her, with two piping hot pitas tossed alongside and a bottle of soda water with a black straw. She turns to the elderly customer who sits across the way, sizing her up. "What is this," she asks, "a restaurant or a military base?" He smiles. "A restaurant, but only for believers." "Believers? In what?" "Believers in the holy trinity of hummus, egg and meatball," he says, motioning for the waiter to give her more hot chickpeas, which in his opinion are the pinnacle of this dish.

The taste of the hummus surprises her, and she scoops it ravenously down to the last scrap of pita, to the delight and fascination of the elderly man, who resists yielding his seat to waiting clientele.

"And what do you do in life?"

She is wary of replying "Harpist," and instead simply says, "Musician, a player in an orchestra."

"An orchestra I could go hear?"

"No, it's an orchestra far from here, very far," and she tilts her head back and waves a hand to indicate how far away her orchestra is, and suddenly sees, up on the ceiling, the camera with the big shiny eye, still nesting like a black bird of prey. What's going on? What's the truth? Was a film really shot that night? Did it have a plot? Or is this actually a security camera? She wants to ask the elderly diner, but he is gone, apparently rebuffed by her faraway orchestra.

The meal and the afternoon heat make her drowsy. And since Abadi's hook and bolt will not arrive until tomorrow, she blocks the front door with two chairs, locks the bathroom door from the outside, lets down the blinds and puts on a nightgown, ready to dive into sweet slumber in her childhood bed.

But the ringing of her mobile phone persists. She answers and hears a voice she recognizes at once, spoken from a great distance. Manfred, her loyal friend and occasional lover, inquires as to her welfare, and her mother's, and even the welfare of Jerusalem, but his tentative tone suggests he is about to impart painful news.

Yes, she is much missed at the orchestra, especially at the music library. The young violinist filling in for her there made an embarrassing error at the last concert, mixed up the scores of two Haydn symphonies, and only at the last moment was disaster averted. Everyone said that with "our Venus" this would not have happened.

"So far, anyway."

"Correct."

"But the repertoire is the same as scheduled before I left?" she asks cautiously.

"As much as possible," sighs the flutist, "but not entirely. We've had some issues. The Japanese or Chinese virtuoso, I can never get her name straight —the one who was supposed to play the Mozart Second Piano Concerto next week—played tennis in Berlin and broke her arm, and since it's impossible to find a pianist of her caliber on such short notice, we had to replace her Mozart with a different Mozart."

"It has to be Mozart?" asks the harpist fearfully. "Surely it can be something else."

"Impossible. We've advertised it and made the commitment that at every concert this season there will be a work by Mozart that the orchestra hasn't played recently, following the complaints that our repertoire is too repetitive. You know this—you were at the general meeting."

"I don't always understand everything you say in Dutch."

"That's that, Noga. We had to find a work by Mozart that hadn't been played in some time, and we thought—"

"No, no," she cuts him off with sudden horror, "don't tell me."

"Yes," he mumbles, his voice trembling. "No choice, because we haven't played the Concerto for Flute and Harp in C in the last ten years."

"But it's my concerto . . . mine and yours . . . ours . . ."

"Of course, ours. I even said that to everyone: Let's wait for Noga, for our Venus, I promised her, and she knows the score by heart and is ready at any time . . . And if this were just one concert, it might have been possible to ask you to come back for a few days, but this is a whole tour, ten concerts for our subscribers in the Netherlands, Germany and Belgium. How can she—this is what management said—leave her mother, who must decide within three months where to die, Jerusalem or Tel Aviv."

"To die? Why die? How can you talk like that?"

"Sorry, sorry, not to die, but of course to live. To decide where to live, Jerusalem or Tel Aviv, as you explained to us when you requested this long leave of absence."

"But how did you find another harpist who could do this concerto?"

"We found one. Admittedly not at your level, but we found her. Christina van Brienen from Antwerp. She has played the concerto in the past and happens to be available."

"I never heard of her. How old is she?"

"Your age, maybe a bit younger. She teaches at the conservatory there."

A long silence.

"Noga?" the flutist whispers. "Are you with me, my dear? Are you listening?"

"You betrayed me, Manfred. You are an immoral person."

"What?"

"You betrayed me, Manfred. You promised and I trusted you, and now you're stealing what is precious to me and giving it to another woman."

"But it's not me, Noga. Why me? It's all because of that stupid Japanese pianist who irresponsibly played tennis. Have you ever heard of a pianist playing tennis?"

"It's not the pianist, it's you. You. And I'm miserable now because I relied on you. You're the first flutist of the orchestra, you've been there a long time and have status. You could have told management that you will not play the Mozart concerto with anyone other than the harpist of our orchestra. You betrayed me, Manfred, just like all the Dutch did."

"Did what?"

"Betrayed the Jews."

"The Jews?" He is shocked. "Where did that come from, the Jews? No, Noga, don't be angry with me. It hurts you, and it hurts me. The members warned me: Don't tell her now—when she gets back it'll be a thing of the past. But I didn't agree, because I'm an honest man and I have to tell the truth, and after all we will play again in the future, other works, maybe more modern, something wilder, there will always be new pieces for flute and harp, it's such a special combination."

A long silence.

"Noga?" He calls her name, concerned that she may have hung up.

But she suddenly challenges him.

"And if I agree to come right away to Arnhem and commit to all ten concerts?"

She immediately senses the confusion of the flutist, who stammers uneasily: "Right away? How? And without any rehearsal? And what will we do with Christina, who became available just for us? No, my Venus, it's too late."

EIGHTEEN

NOT UNTIL THE EVENING did she manage to collect herself and call her brother to tell him about the loss of her concerto. "But please," she warned, "don't start cursing the Japanese pianist, she's not the guilty one. I'll deal with the actual guilty party, and you, Honi, just help me with a small compensation—say, Georges Bizet in place of Mozart."

"Georges Bizet?"

She tells him about the production of *Carmen* to be staged at the foot of Masada, for which, she has been told, female extras are needed, women not necessarily young who know how to listen and respond to music. This job comes without pay but provides a hotel room by the Dead Sea, and of course the enjoyment, three times over, of the opera itself—the singing, dancing and marvelous music. Yes, the Jerusalem apartment will have to remain empty for three days, but if Ima is worried, she can take her place. Three days in Jerusalem will do her good.

"No," Honi says firmly, "she absolutely must not go back to Jerusalem, not even for three days. The experiment must maintain its integrity. Every day in the assisted living facility is important. Returning to Jerusalem might set her back. Don't worry about the apartment, but rather about yourself, and I will arrange the job at the opera, and you'll enjoy the job as well as the hotel and the desert. And we, Sarai and I, will buy tickets and come and see you. And even if Shaya's little *haredim* sneak into the empty apartment, it's not the end of the world, you know. Sure, let them watch as much TV as they want, forbidden shows, let them see sex and violence, maybe that way they can break free of their father's Hasidism."

"Listen to yourself," Noga scolds him, half seriously.

The next day, in the early evening, Abadi arrives with a large tool chest. First he takes care of the front door. He removes it from its hinges, planes and straightens it, so the new bolt can do its job properly. And lo, the job she had thought would be simple is not so simple. She stands beside him throughout, to hand him tools and to be amazed by his manual dexterity. "I thought you were just an engineer, but I see you're also a carpenter," she says fondly.

Once the big bolt is in place, she offers him something to eat, though not at the level of the meals his wife had brought during the shiva—just a simple sandwich she had prepared beforehand.

Abadi wonders whether she had really eaten any of the food his wife had brought, for he doesn't recall seeing her when the gravestone was unveiled at the end of the thirty days. Or perhaps his memory fails him.

No, his memory is fine. It's true, she didn't stay for the full mourning period; after a few days she had to return to Europe. The sudden death came while her orchestra was touring, and because the program included two works with important parts for the harp, and no substitute could be found, she was forced to leave her mother and brother during the thirty days.

But something is bothering Abadi.

"Excuse me, in which works of music is the harp so vital? I usually don't hear its sound."

"You apparently don't really know how to listen," she chides the engineer. "But if you were to remove the sounds of the harp from a symphony by Mahler or Tchaikovsky, it would totally flatten the tone and resonance."

He absorbs the correction graciously and seeks to express interest:

"How many strings did you say in a harp?"

"Forty-seven, and they create a hundred and forty-one tones."

"So many? How is that possible?"

"Because a harp also has seven pedals."

"So that's the thing . . . the secret . . ."

He keeps chewing politely and gathers sandwich crumbs with the tips of his fingers. He is her age, and has already inherited her father's post. He's a nice-looking man with smooth black hair, in contrast with the baldness or shaven heads of many of his peers, and his chin sports a tiny bohemian beard, not typical of a municipal engineer. He looks at his watch and wants to continue the job, but Noga stops him:

"Just a minute. Tell me, did my father ever mention me?"

"When?"

"Whenever, the way people talk about their families."

"Yes."

"And you didn't detect a certain tone of criticism or disappointment?"

"Disappointment? Why?" The word disturbs him. "Disappointment over what?"

"That I didn't want children."

He seems taken aback. He stands up and carefully drops the remains of the sandwich in the trash and says, "Now we'll attach the hook to the little window."

But the small window in the bathroom refuses to comply. The frame is swollen and rotted from years of steam and moisture, and refuses the grip of any screw. Moreover, the light in the room is too dim. Abadi goes to the parents' bedroom, takes the reading lamp from beside the electric bed, connects it to an extension cord and hands it to Noga, so she can assist him in the battle against the rebellious window. He ingeniously nails two pieces of wood to the window and screws in the hook, which he admits will function more symbolically than practically to protect her from the little invaders from the upper floor.

"This will do until you go back to Europe, but the new tenant will have to replace the whole thing."

"There will be no new tenant," Noga says quietly, lighting Abadi's face with the lamp. "Ima will return, and nothing will come of the experiment."

And she turns off the light.

NINETEEN

S HE WATCHES HIM CLOSELY as he gathers his tools, detaches and winds up the extension cord and returns it to his tool chest. Then she follows him into her parents' bedroom, where he puts the reading lamp back in place. And before he takes his leave, she says:

"How can I repay you?"

"Don't be silly."

But she insists:

"I'm not being silly. You barely ate my sandwich, and the carpenter is entitled to some sort of gift."

Even as he waves his hands in refusal, she opens her parents' emptied clothes closet and shows him her father's new suit, and the shoes and socks below.

"Ima gave away tons of clothes, my father's and hers, to the neighborhood charities, but she felt sorry for this suit, and rightly so, because he hardly wore it. Honi is unwilling to wear his father's clothes, so before this good suit also flies away to some religious creature, you take it. Knowing that it's you wearing the suit would please him."

"Please who?" He is shocked.

"Abba." She laughs. "If he's still interested in his suits wherever he is now." She removes the jacket from its hanger with a flourish. "Try it on, don't be shy. What can happen?"

She expects him to resist, but Abadi, as if hypnotized in the gathering dusk, slips his arms into the sleeves of the jacket, which is too wide for his shoulders, and studies his reflection in the mirror with a mixture of concern and satisfaction. She then grips him by the shoulders and pulls the jacket tighter from behind, to demonstrate how it might be altered to fit his narrower frame.

And though Abadi is embarrassed by the demonstration, he is not averse to the surprising offer. "Yes, maybe, if no one else wants it."

"There's no one else."

"If that's really so, then rather than have the jacket go to a total stranger, I'll take it to the tailor and wear it to remember him by."

"Yes, to remember him by," she happily exclaims. "But also the pants, because it's a suit."

"The pants?" He laughs uneasily. "No, the pants are undoubtedly too short."

"Says who? At least try. It's not right to separate the two."

Now he is upset. This he didn't expect. Aware of her power, she firmly insists. "Why not? We won't know if you don't try them on." Now he smiles slightly, his embarrassment giving way to comprehension, even excitement, and, still wearing the jacket, he bends over and sheds his shoes, undoes his belt, removes his pants and puts them on a chair, and takes from her the trousers of a man of seventy-five, who a year or two before his death indulged a desire to own a tailor-made black suit of the finest wool gabardine, perhaps to blend in with the black-suited Orthodox of the neighborhood. Although it's clear that the trousers will be short on him and too big in the waist, Noga persists, and as if she were an artist of needle and thread as well as the harp, she gets down on her knees and shows him how the surplus fabric in the cuffs can be used to lengthen the legs, and then pinches the extra cloth at each of his hips. And deliberately or otherwise, she can feel that her fingers, the strong, precise fingers of a harpist, also know how to arouse desire.

"Here, it can be made narrower. It would be a shame to separate them . . . a shame to give it away . . ."

Unnerved by his erection, Abadi seeks a quick getaway. "No, it won't work," he mumbles, and wriggles free of her hands, climbs out of the trousers of his beloved late mentor, tries to conceal his tumescence as he hurriedly puts on his own pants and tosses the suit jacket on the electric bed. "No, not this either," he says, blushing, and picks up his toolbox and says goodbye without a look. And she knows he won't be back, even if the bolt and hook fall off and the electric bed falls silent.

TWENTY

In the morning she went to buy food at the corner grocery and inquired, for the first time since her arrival in Jerusalem, about her monthly account. "You don't owe us anything, Nogaleh," said the owners, an elderly couple who have known her since childhood. "Your brother left his credit card information, and what you buy is immediately paid for. Rest easy, sweetheart, and in the future, don't hesitate to buy things you didn't dare buy till now, because your credit here is unlimited."

This unlimited credit makes her angry, but since she doesn't want to annoy her brother, who for good reason has begun to fear for the outcome of his experiment, she simply decides that from now on she will purchase with her unlimited credit only basic necessities, and anything else, despite the distance, she will bring home from Mahane Yehuda in her mother's old shopping cart.

After lunching on a few delicacies from the *shuk,* she prepares for the television temptation of the little boys. She lowers blinds and draws curtains to darken the apartment, takes off her clothes and puts on a light robe, alert to the clatter of the shoes that now begin to scamper up and down the stairs, accompanied by the wild chortling of the dizzy little *tzaddik.* Soon, she knows, the boys will silently approach the front door and listen closely to determine whether or not the tenant is home, or perhaps asleep.

After the last invasion she wanted to go upstairs to the Pomerantzes and protest the shenanigans of their grandchildren. But then came a plea from the assisted living facility: "No, Noga, don't go up there. Mrs. Pomerantz is very ill, barely knows who she is, and Mr. Pomerantz can't control the situation. Most days he comes home only at night. Let's give Abadi's bolt a chance to prove itself."

Indeed, the bolt installed by Abadi passes the test. Snug in her childhood bed, she hears the key enter the squeaky lock and turn the tongue, but when the handle is pulled, the door won't open. The young intruder rattles the door in confusion, but the bolt steadfastly bars his way as the tiny *tzaddik*, lusting for television, wails desperately.

Noga wraps herself in her blanket and silently curses Shaya, who is presumably swaying over his useless books while he neglects the children, who now have no choice but to resume their crazy clambering on the stairs, their footsteps finally muted by the delicious onset of sleep.

And yet, for all its sweetness, the sleep is not long, and when Noga wakes up she first confirms the silence of the television, then removes the robe and walks naked into the bathroom, whose window is locked shut by its hook. She fills the bathtub, its iron feet like talons of a bird of prey, and pours blue bath salts into the water. And as she sinks with pleasure into the foam, she thinks she can see, beyond the steamed-up windowpane, the sad eyes of children whose path has been blocked.

In early evening Honi phones from Jerusalem. A dinner that was supposed to follow a meeting has been canceled, and he would very much like to share his hearty appetite with his sister. "So come to the house," she suggests, "and you can also see Abadi's bolt and hook." "No," he insists, "the bolt and hook you're in love with don't interest me, and our parents' home just gets me angry. No, you're entitled to compensation and consolation for the concerto that was stolen from you because of me. Hurry up, I'm at the table looking at the menu, and the chef is waiting just for you."

In the heart of downtown Jerusalem, in a truly superb restaurant, he tries to win his sister over with delicious food. Between courses he updates her about the job at the opera that will be staged at the foot of Masada. Members of the chorus are supposed to serve as extras, but additional women are needed for background. There are many eager applicants, but he has fought for his sister, so that during her stay in Israel—a stay he imposed on her—she will be involved in live music, if not as a performer, at least as an extra. Yes, he sighs, the loss of the Mozart concerto still tugs at his conscience, but what can you do? He is a good son who is not prepared to have his mother live out her life in the midst of the barren fanaticism of their childhood neighborhood. But recently he has noticed a hesitancy on his mother's part, and he therefore pleads with his sister to desist from romantic European notions of ancient cities and to stand with him in support of the move from a blackening Jerusalem to the White City, where she will be near her son, daughter-in-law and beloved grandchildren, and be able to find, at the assisted living facility, interesting friends and, just maybe, a new companion.

"Companion?"

"Anything is possible, Noga, and everything is permitted. Abba's death didn't weaken her or age her, and her loyalty to him for all those years surely makes her entitled. Don't you agree?"

"If you say so."

After dinner he takes her back to Rashi Street, but he has no time or desire to go up to his childhood home. "I saw enough of it in my life," he says, "and I miss it not at all. The time has come for a final break."

As she climbs the stairs, she wishes he'd have come up with her, because outside the front door he would have heard strange voices and the sounds of war, and as they entered he would have seen who was sitting in their father's chair: a bare-headed boy in a white shirt, remote control in hand, *tzitzit* fringes scattered about, long black sidelocks framing his face like a billy goat; and his charge asleep at his feet, his angelic face glowing, his sidelocks golden.

Abadi's bolt doesn't secure the door when she's out of the apartment, she recalls. Now she is shaken not only with anger but despair. She thinks about her small, orderly apartment in Arnhem, feels sorry for herself. And before she can speak a syllable, the older one launches into his refrain:

"Really, Noga, believe me, your mother used to let us watch war movies on TV."

"'Your mother,'" she says acidly. "Listen, boy, I am not my mother, and I'm sick of these games. So get out right now and go back to your grandparents and take this *tzaddik* with you, and I'll come up later to tell them what's going on here."

"It won't do you any good," he answers softly, sadly. "Grandma upstairs doesn't know anymore that she's a grandma."

"So I'll tell your grandfather. He'll know what to do with you."

"How will he do that?" he wonders, his voice still calm. "Grandpa comes home at night with no strength left and goes straight to sleep. But listen, Noga, I swear on a stack of Bibles, your mother would invite us in so the television would calm us down. She took pity on a poor child."

And as he speaks, he switches stations, from the History Channel to the Fashion Channel, and she again angrily attacks the television and disconnects it from the electric socket, and with a powerful hand grabs the boy's white collar and yanks him from the armchair.

"Listen, what did you say your name was?"

"Yuda-Zvi."

"Listen, Yuda-Zvi, you will not sneak in here anymore, because the next time I'll whip you, you hear me? You and your *tzaddik,* watch out."

But Shaya's son coolly picks up the yarmulke tossed on the chair and puts it on his head, straightens out his rumpled shirt and asks, with a little smile:

"You have a whip?"

"I have one. I always had one." And with the tip of her shoe she nudges the gold-sidelocked boy, who struggles to wake up, and says, "I'm a harpist, and I have a mighty hand, so beware of me."

TWENTY-ONE

T HAT NIGHT, IN BED, she wonders with a smile where on earth that whip came from. Was it the sound of the word that enchanted her, or the whip itself? In any case, why not? If the grandma upstairs doesn't know who she is, and grandpa drums Torah into students at night, and Shaya, that beautiful guy, has been abducted by an extremist cult, why not a whip to impose order? An actual whip that can be waved in the air and snapped to induce fear from afar. Because clearly this smart-ass kid won't give up his TV, and so in the remaining weeks of the trial period she will protect her privacy not merely with a bolt, but with a whip, not symbolic but real.

She falls asleep with this bizarre notion, and wakes up with it too, and after breakfast she goes for a walk among the stalls of Mahane Yehuda, where she might not find a whip but can at least inquire about one. But so that an elegant, cultured woman won't arouse laughter or suspicion by asking the vendors about a whip, she approaches an Arab porter who waits next to a fruit and vegetable stand with a big wicker basket on his back. The Arab is not shocked by either the question or the questioner, but cannot imagine that any of the Jews in the market still own a horse or donkey requiring a whip, and recommends that she look for one in the Old City.

"How do you say 'whip' in Arabic?"

"Why Arabic? Speak Hebrew—everyone in the Old City will understand you."

"Still, how do you say it?"

"Say *kurbash,* madam. Just *kurbash.*"

"*Kurbash,*" she pronounces with satisfaction. "Lovely word."

She is excited to have found a practical reason to go to the Old City, which she hasn't visited for many years, even before the job with the Dutch orchestra that took her far from Israel. To enhance the experience, she chooses to ride on the elegant light rail line, which deposits her near the Damascus Gate, and she is soon swallowed up in the shadowy marketplace. She doesn't rush to find what she seeks, but wanders through the narrow alleys, buffeted by shoppers and tourists, pausing by various shops, examining beads and copperware, even purchasing an unusual pipe for the administrative director of the orchestra, who allows himself a smoke backstage during concerts, the aroma of his tobacco sometimes complementing the music.

Finally, in a colorful souvenir shop she asks about a whip, using the Arabic word, but it turns out that in the overflowing market of the Old City it's difficult to get clear directions to a place where a whip may be found, and she is sent from one merchant to another, and they ask whether she wants a whip as a wall hanging or a real one.

"A real one," she clarifies, "and long, if possible." "How long?" the Arabs ask with a smile. "Two meters at least," she says, extending her arms wide. "Two meters?" They are astounded. "Two meters is a whip to train a wild horse. Does the lady have a horse?"

"No horse," she jokes, "but a husband as wild as a horse."

The vendors like her answer, and the laughter echoes from shop to shop, and one young man, whose headgear seems a hybrid of a turban and a Hasidic skullcap, offers to take her to a place where she might find the whip she desires. He leads her past the Western Wall and beyond the Old City walls, and there, on the road near the tour buses, crouches a group of gaudily decorated camels, poised to carry tourists, and the young man explains to one of the camel owners what the lady is looking for, and the owner is puzzled: Why a whip? What for? Is it even allowed?—as if she were seeking a dangerous weapon. At last he consents, and consults with an old Bedouin sitting on the curb, who gets up without delay and approaches one of the camels, burrows into an embroidered saddlebag and produces two whips —long and longer.

The harpist, who has never held a whip before, examines the two and considers one versus the other. These are clearly whips that in their day have prodded camels, trained horses and struck donkeys. Their leather lashes are tattered and cracked and emit a strange smell. Now she brandishes the longer of the two, and as it whistles in the air, a nearby camel rises to its feet.

She chooses the shorter one and asks its price. This is a question for the camel's owner, who thinks hard before declaring, "One hundred dinars."

"Dinars? What's a dinar?"

"He means dollars," explains the turbaned young middleman.

"Dollars? Why dollars? We're in Israel. Tell me in shekels."

"If it's shekels," says the young man, "he will have to charge value-added tax."

"VAT?" She laughs. "This Bedouin does VAT? What is he, a licensed contractor?"

"Why not? I can even write you a receipt in his name."

"Too much." She smiles. "A hundred shekels is plenty. It's an old whip."

"But genuine. You won't find one as strong and good in the whole Middle East."

They finally compromise on two hundred shekels, and everyone is happy. And she knows that the seller and the broker find her attractive, though she is neither young nor a virgin. She has not borne children, yet radiates womanly charm and sensuality. Thus even the Bedouin camel drivers, who doubtless have any number of wives, are in no hurry to part from her, and they take the whip from her on the pretext that it needs to be prepared, cleaned, oiled and bathed in a pungent liquid so that whoever is whipped will smell the lash and long remember it. Then they wrap the whip in a Jordanian newspaper bearing a photo of the king, and tie it with a linen cord. The young man in the turban, Yassin by name, who has learned Noga's name and its celestial connotation, and has translated it for her into Arabic, insists on walking with her to the place he brought her from.

On their way back, as they pass the Western Wall, Yassin stops and says obligingly, "If you want, Venus, to pray and cry a little at your wall, I can wait for you on the side." "No praying or crying, young man," she says with slight irritation, "but you can definitely let me go now," and hands him a twenty-shekel bill as an escort fee.

She decides to enjoy another ride on the light rail, which takes her near her neighborhood, and as she climbs the stairs to her parents' apartment, she secretly hopes to catch the ultra-Orthodox boys fixed on their television elixir, so she can crack her newly purchased whip and possibly land a blow.

But the apartment is silent. Can it be that the older one has finally been sent back to his Torah school and a new chaperone assigned to the little *tzaddik?*

She lays the wrapped-up whip on top of the television, as if to confirm its existence, but after she gets undressed, puts on a light bathrobe and consumes a full bottle of water, she moves the whip to her parents' closet, setting it on a shelf above the black suit that has yet to find its suitor.

TWENTY-TWO

S HE STAYED HOME for two full days, but the children didn't arrive. She undid the bolt and lay in wait, but they didn't come. Finally she left the apartment and went to a rehearsal of the Jerusalem Symphony Orchestra, hoping the children would take advantage of her absence, all in vain. It was as if they had learned, in some mysterious way, of the whip that awaited them on the shelf above her father's suit, a Jordanian newspaper spread out beneath it. Had she bought the whip for nothing? She considered this, though not with dismay. She knew she would take the whip with her to the Netherlands, where it might please the conductor of the orchestra.

She speaks with her mother every morning, but it's impossible to deduce what the decision will be. "I'm not hiding anything from you children," she says apologetically. "I'm truly ambivalent, still wavering. When I drink coffee and chat with a lovely resident who tells me entertaining stories, I say to myself, You're a widow, from now on this is where you belong. But when we're joined by another woman who keeps trashing everything and everybody around her, and I can't get a word in edgewise, even to get up and leave, I say to myself, Why on earth am I here? People are all well and good, insofar as you have control and you can turn them off or on as you want. But here, you're not allowed to bolt your door, either literally or metaphorically—you can lock it, but the management has a key to open it. And if you say, Nogaleh, there's no difference between a bolt and a lock, because nobody will enter the room without knocking—still, you know, if you wish to die, the bolt is better protection against anyone intervening at the last moment."

"You're joking, Ima."

"Not always."

The mother goes on:

"In the dining room, looking at the lavish buffet, I say to myself, Yes, madam, this is where you belong, where you can be calm and contented. Here you don't have to eat leftovers from yesterday or the day before, or something iffy just so as not to throw it out, waste it. Then I go back to my little flat in peace, but I'm also afraid of being bombarded with visits by unwanted guests, like one old woman who has had a lung and half her liver removed but is still amusing and lively as a sparrow. This woman has taken a shine to me, won't leave me alone. She apparently wants to encourage me regarding my future health, but what she does is plant anxiety, and all kinds of organs I've never heard of are starting to hurt."

"But Ima, now the grandchildren are close by."

"The grandchildren are darling and sweet, maybe also geniuses, though I have to be careful not to beat them at checkers or bingo or they get irritable and depressed. It's true, we've grown closer since I came to Tel Aviv, and the tension and annoyance they would pick up from Honi when they came to Jerusalem are gone. Also, they're much freer with me, sometimes they bring friends, whom I also have to feed. There's a big lawn here in the summer, but what happens in the winter? My one-room flat is tiny."

"But you love children . . ."

"Who told you that?"

"What about the two boys you would invite to watch television?"

"Who said I invited them?"

"They said."

"I didn't invite them, I felt a little sorry for them. When they grow up and face life, they'll be lost and won't understand the new world around them."

"They're not interested in a new world, Ima, they get along fine in their old world."

"You think so? Maybe you're right. But tell me, why are we talking on the phone? Why don't you visit me more often? It seems you came back and fell in love with Jerusalem."

"There's not much to fall in love with. I'm simply taking care of the apartment so no one will suspect you've given it up."

"Still and all, come visit me. Because if you think I need to move to the retirement home, come and reinforce that decision. More than Abba and more than Honi, you know how to speak to me heart to heart. Even if the road you've chosen in life is totally different from mine, I'm still a lot like you, or you're a lot like me, whichever is the way to put it."

"Okay, tomorrow lunch."

"Perfect. That way you can see for yourself what it's like here."

The next day she joins her mother for lunch, samples many of the dishes laid out on the buffet, rates their pluses and minuses. Her presence arouses interest in the dining room, and two elderly men in light summer suits come over to introduce themselves to the pretty daughter who has come from afar.

"Not so far," explains the mother. "At the moment from Jerusalem. She is keeping an eye on my big apartment there until my experiment here is over."

"And how will the experiment turn out?"

"Still a mystery, and my daughter is here to help me solve it."

"In which case," implore the old men, "help Mother decide in favor. There are not many among us like her, willing to listen patiently to other people's troubles."

"Maybe because I have no particular troubles of my own."

"Even if, God forbid, you should have some," the old men persist, "you would still listen with patience and good humor. We benefit from how you listen."

When they return to the room, Noga says, "You've been here seven weeks and you already have two charming admirers. Maybe you should invite them, just like the two little boys, to watch TV with you?"

The mother smiles.

"I know you're blaming me, but I wasn't the one who started the romance with the two children. It was your father, believe it or not, a few months before he died. At night, when he would go outside to smoke with Mr. Pomerantz, he got interested in the children who run wild on the stairs and how to calm them. And then he learned that the little one, the strange retarded one with the angel face—"

"Not retarded, Ima. The word is 'challenged.'"

"Whatever. Challenged ... strange ... unfortunate ..."

"Challenged."

"So Mr. Pomerantz told Abba that this sweet child is the son of a very important Hasidic family, with a whole community of followers. And because this is a slightly degenerative family—am I allowed to say 'degenerative'?"

"You're allowed."

"Because they have been marrying among themselves for centuries, his older brothers are feeble and sickly, so there's a good chance he will be their future leader."

"The Grand Rabbi. The *Tzaddik*."

"Yes. How do you know?"

"The older one told me. Yuda-Zvi."

"Good. I see you remember his name. And as I told you, he is the son of Shaya, the charming boy you would always talk with on the stairs when you were a girl. He's not as handsome as his father, but he is very bright and devious."

"Abba ... You were talking about Abba ..."

"Yes, Abba. He was drawn to them, maybe because he missed the children you didn't give us."

"You? Give you?"

"Don't get stuck on every word of mine, Noga. I was just saying. Neither of us ever complained to you that you didn't want to have children. Anyway, Abba started getting involved with them, to kid around, play with them, and he also brought them home to tempt them with television. He would say, in jest of course, that this strange angel might someday be the head of one of the religious parties that could bring down a government, so we should get him accustomed to television."

"Nice Abba."

"Very nice. But not nice on his part to die a few weeks later, leaving me with the two little rascals who stole my key, and make you suffer now."

"No more suffering. The bolt will stop them when I'm at home, and if I discover they've snuck into the apartment, I'll whip them. I even bought a whip."

"A whip?"

"Yes, a whip. A real one, in the Old City."

"Great. Good thing you didn't buy a gun."

Noga yawns. The Tel Aviv heat and the rich food are making her sleepy, and her mother suggests she take a nap.

"Get some rest so you'll have the strength to do my thinking for me, and at the same time test the bed, though I think that if I surrender to Honi and move here, I'll bring the electric bed."

"An interesting bed, yes, although at night I divide my sleep between it and my childhood bed."

"Really! You know, me too. After Abba died, when we were both done with the narrow double bed—God knows how we managed it for so many years—and the electric bed arrived, I wasn't satisfied and started going around at night from bed to bed. I'd start with the electric, then go to yours, then wake up and move to Honi's, and from there to the living room sofa and finally back to the electric. Wandering between beds improved my sleep, and it didn't matter that in the morning I'd have to make four beds. That's another thing to consider if, in the end, I move here. In Tel Aviv I'll have only one bed."

"Like everyone else. It looks like a decent bed, and in a minute I'll try it out. But what will you do in the meantime? Even if you sit quietly and just look at me, I won't be able to fall asleep."

"So I'll leave. Maybe I'll go to the lounge and find someone to play cards with."

And she strips the sheets from the bed, puts on fresh ones, replaces the pillowcase, brings an extra pillow and cotton blanket, adjusts the air conditioner so a pleasant breeze will caress the sleeper and lowers the blinds to darken the room, all while inquiring if the guest would care for some soft music.

"No, Ima. Music for me is the real thing, not the background."

"Obviously, because you, unlike me, are a real musician. But I have been falling asleep lately to the Mozart concerto that you lost because of me. Honi gave it to me to prove what a great sacrifice you've made."

"A beautiful concerto."

"Wonderful, bright, not sad. Moves along so easily, though the flute slightly muffles the sound of the harp, and I, because of you, am interested in the harp and not the flute."

"It's just because of a particular performance, undoubtedly by James Galway, whose flute is very dominant."

"I suppose, but at least on the stage, in reality, you can see the harp. It can't be hidden. Don't worry, my daughter, you'll get to play that piece as a soloist, and others too. You're young and the world is waiting for you. Enough, I'm going, and you sleep well, and think of the assisted living as yours too, and when you wake up you can give me your opinion of the bed."

TWENTY-THREE

A T FIRST SHE DOUBTED she could fall asleep. Yes, the bed is wide, and the mattress hard enough, but the room lacks intimacy, like a hotel room, with a faint medicinal aroma. It's pleasantly cool, but the rumbling of the air conditioner is an unwelcome interference. Through the wall, from the adjoining one-room apartment, she can hear coughing and sighing, and feels sorry for her mother. Honi wants so much to move her to this confined, unfamiliar place, which is clean and respectable but nevertheless a place not her own. In her Jerusalem apartment she subdues her insomnia by means of four different beds, but here — where can she go in her distress? To the big lawn in back? Had she herself waited for a harpist position to open up at the Jerusalem Symphony, and in the meantime been content with a teaching job at the conservatory or the music academy, and had she given her husband Uriah a child, he would not have left her and there would be no need for any dramatic changes. Uriah loved her parents, but now her mother is left truly alone in Jerusalem, and it's not right to have Honi, the perennial worrier, rush back there every time there's a problem.

Filtering in from outside are the roars of Tel Aviv buses and perhaps of airplanes landing, but these somehow enable rather than inhibit her sleep. Can it be, she asks herself, that the engines of vehicles in the coastal plain sound quieter because they are free of the ups and downs of the Judean Hills? Encouraged by this horizontal hypothesis, sleep slowly envelops her. The clock on the TV cable box indicates that an hour has gone by since she got into bed. But why should an hour suffice? She is sleeping here at her mother's request, sleeping in pursuit of introspection, so she should try to extract at least one dream from the depths of her soul. Soon enough, sleep becomes her shelter. She pushes aside the pillows and buries her face in the sheet to smell a motherly scent, a smell of sweet and secure child-hood, as Jerusalem and Tel Aviv blend into one.

And so two more hours fly by on the clock, as if the cable box were generating its own time. Were it not for the soft, stubborn sound of cry-ing from the other side of the wall, the harpist might have gone on sleep-ing. Could it be that the previous tenant, who died here slowly, altered time before his death? And what's going on out there in the world? Could her mother still be playing cards? Maybe she's gambling away everything she owns? But Noga's fatigue has not been slaked, it has become hungrier, and not until she notices between the window blinds that it's grown darker outside does she force herself to get up. In a daze, she gets dressed, opens the door to the porch, crosses the garden of wilted flowers and heads for the lawn to take in the remnants of the sunset. On a pair of lounge chairs sit her mother and brother, with the grandchildren kicking a ball toward an invisible goal.

"Nougat woke up!" shout the kids, calling their aunt by the nickname inspired by candy she brings them from Europe.

"This can't be Israeli fatigue," says the brother. "In Israel you don't do much of anything. This is fatigue you brought with you from your Eu-rope."

Noga doesn't reply. She silently kisses the kids, then warmly hugs and kisses her brother and her mother, as if emerging not from sleep in a small room, but from a long and perilous journey.

Honi asks about the whip. "A real whip?" "Totally real," she says, "nearly a meter long." "It won't help you," he says dismissively. "Those *haredi* bas-tards are trained from childhood to confront the tear gas and water can-nons of the police. Your whip will only tickle them. Too bad you didn't buy a gun."

"Enough, Honi, don't get crazy," chides his mother.

Still drowsy, Noga doesn't respond and sinks into a chair her brother of-fers her. "Your bed mesmerized me, Ima," she says. "No need here to wan-der from bed to bed to make it through the night—one is enough. The cosmos is calm in Tel Aviv. History and politics don't leave it in ruins like Jerusalem. So if you want an answer regarding the experiment, I say yes,

Ima, this is the place. Move here, absolutely, we'll be relieved, and we'll help you."

Honi is surprised, excited, his eyes shining. He didn't expect such a clear-cut declaration, and so soon. He secretly squeezes his sister's hand with gratitude and turns to his mother:

"If, as you say, it's Noga who knows your heart, more than Abba and certainly more than me, then listen to her."

"Yeah," the mother sighs, "I'm listening."

"Then we can end the experiment," says Noga, "and I can leave."

"No, no, not yet," the mother says, alarmed. "The experiment was for three months, and it's barely been a month and a half. Please, children, no shortcuts. That's not fair."

Honi agrees. "We'll live up to what we said we'd do, and besides, in another ten days Carmen will be waiting at Masada for Noga to help her."

From his jacket pocket he pulls a few pages detailing the obligations and benefits of the extras in the opera to be performed in the desert. And he has tickets for himself and Sarai for the second evening, so the two of them can enjoy not only the music and the desert, but the sight of Noga as a country girl from Seville, strolling among the chorus in an embroidered dress.

"So that's the role?"

"Here, take this and read it."

"And you'll come to laugh at me."

"On the contrary, to be thrilled."

Darkness gathers, the children have lessons to do and must be taken home. Noga hesitantly asks her mother if she can stay for dinner. "Let's try," says the mother. "Dinnertime is over, but we might find something in the kitchen for a rare guest."

They manage to put together a fine meal in the dining hall from the evening's leftovers. Noga is delighted: "Even the leftovers here are spectacular. So, Ima, despite your many virtues, truth be told, your cooking was fairly pathetic, borderline hazardous. So why not, in the years that remain, enjoy some good cooking? Not just the bed but also the food is in the plus column of this sheltered housing."

"Maybe," the mother confirms halfheartedly, the other half remaining unclear.

Noga did not return to Jerusalem until ten-thirty at night, and as she walked through the Mekor Baruch neighborhood, it looked to her just as it had in her childhood. The people are the same people, what they wear is what they wore, the shops are the same shops, the streetlights have the same weak bulbs. Yes, here and there homes have expanded, adding a story and a window, enclosing a porch, and municipal garbage bins sit alongside the houses—but the dead seem not dead, and the newborns seem as yet unborn.

In her heart she harbored a hope that she would find traces of the children in the apartment, and as soon as she entered, she went to feel if the TV was warm. It was not. She inspected the rooms, even checking whether the angle of the head of the electric bed had been changed, but no alien hand had touched the mechanism. She thought about the whip, and since for a moment she didn't recall where she'd left it, she imagined that the little invaders had indeed been here and taken it. But then she remembered its hiding place and went to look for it in her parents' empty clothes closet, left lying like a desert snake in its burnt reddish skin, its long tail resting on the picture of the king of Jordan in the newspaper spread beneath it.

Since she'd returned from Tel Aviv fully rested, she sat glued to the television, surfing from channel to channel, finally landing on Mezzo and going from a concert to a dance troupe to an opera, until at a very late hour her eyelids began to droop, and musical drowsiness segued into hallucination. But instead of seeking slumber in one of the beds, she felt underneath her father's armchair for a lever that lowered the chair into a kind of bed. She doesn't stay in this bed, but climbs in her dream onto the stage before her, where the orchestra is getting ready for the second act of a concert performance of an opera. The musicians are tuning their instruments, singers are gathering on the stage. The male singers are wearing black tie, and the women wear the costumes of the characters they portray. Although this is the second act, she doesn't yet see her harp, which someone is to wheel onto the stage. Now it comes, the harp, large and majestic, but instead of being placed near a group of strings, it is moved to the brass section, next to the trumpets and trombones, not far from the drum that will drown out its sound. As she worries about the new location, a woman turns to her. "I am Carmen," she says. "Can you sing the second act for me? A grain of sand got into my windpipe."

TWENTY-FOUR

T HE NEXT DAY and the day after, the children did not sneak in. Are they sick of television, or did they find a more kosher TV? Perhaps Shaya's son devised a different way to soothe the stormy spirit of the little *tzaddik*. Either way, the threat of the whip had not been in vain, and the whip itself will eventually be put to use.

Yet she continues to hope that the children will again try to break into the apartment. In the entire building, perhaps the entire street, this is the sole remaining bastion of secularism. And even if a few scattered families secretly own the scandalous appliance, none would dare admit it.

She hopes to prove to herself that the whip is not a myth but a reality, and so refrains from locking the front door with Abadi's bolt and leaves open the window in the bathroom. "Spare the rod and spoil the child," her father would declare when she was little. He would even undo his belt to frighten Honi when she would catch him rummaging through her school-bag or chest of drawers, and demand that her parents protect her from him. But her father would drop the belt without ever waving it as a threat, because the boy would defuse the anger with sweetness and smooth talk, and beg forgiveness in an amusing performance of bowing and kneeling before his sister.

She was, in their home, an object of awe and reverence. When she was a girl it was taken for granted that no one could make her do anything against her will. This wasn't, however, out of stubbornness for its own sake, but because her boundaries were always fixed and stable, if not always ex-plicable, even to herself. Only her younger brother, who tagged along be-hind her in childhood and perhaps loved her the most, would try to shift the border and come closer.

When she and Uriah became romantically involved, Honi was thrilled, not only because he admired the future husband, but because he thought that through him he could deepen the connection with his sister. Uriah too was fond of his future brother-in-law, and when he was still an officer in a combat unit, he would come to the building in a command car and take the excited youngster on rides around Jerusalem, allowing the boy to touch the trigger of his army rifle.

But Honi's hope to be an uncle to his sister's baby was not fulfilled. After several years of marriage, her firm refusal to bear children became clear, and it was the brother, not the parents, who protested and fought in various ways for the unborn child, inevitably provoking anger. Only when Uriah demanded he stop pestering his sister did he refrain, and not long thereafter he too married, and was quick, perhaps defiantly so, to give his parents the grandchild they yearned for.

The circumcision took place in this very apartment, which to everyone's surprise had room for a multitude of relatives close and distant, of friends and acquaintances. This was after Noga's divorce, but Uriah came to the celebration and stared coldly at the newborn, who slept serenely on the knees of its grandfather, the honored *sandak,* as the *mohel* recommended and supervised by Mr. Pomerantz carefully performed the cut, his long beard brushing the tiny penis. Noga kept her distance from them, but beamed with joy at her happy brother, not least in the hope that he would now leave her be, and also because she had just been accepted as a harpist by the Dutch orchestra.

Now the apartment is empty and she is in charge. And since many possessions and pieces of furniture are gone, the space has expanded and could accommodate even more guests at a new celebration—were there any reason for one. But with her in control, and in the rising heat of summer, the lone tenant can strip off her clothes and walk naked between the rooms before dipping her body into the blue foam.

The waters of Jerusalem feel sweet, since she believes they derive in part from ancient cisterns of rainwater, as her father had taught her. So she lingers in the bathtub that stands on iron feet shaped like the talons of a bird of prey, and every few minutes she sinks beneath the foam, to the sounds of old Hebrew songs on a tiny transistor radio, mixed with an unfamiliar wailing, caused perhaps by weak batteries.

It takes a while for her to realize that the wailing does not originate from the batteries or a remix of the old songs, but rather from actual wailing through the open window, where two little feet in white socks and worn-out sandals are scrambling for a foothold.

"He's going to fall!" she screams and, naked and dripping with foam, leaps to the window and grabs the two flailing feet. Feeling more secure, the child loosens his desperate hold on the drainpipe and lets himself slide to the floor between the wet arms and breasts of the woman. Quickly she returns to the window, expecting to find his guardian behind him. But there's no one on the pipe. It twists its rusty way upward, above it only a patch of sky.

"And this time you came by yourself."

She leans over the *tzaddik*, who huddles at her feet, his sweat sour, his little hands black from the pipe. She picks him up joyfully, deftly peeling off his gray jacket and white shirt, its filthy collar embroidered with a mysterious pattern. As he struggles, she strips off his worn trousers, hand-me-downs from one generation to the next, and under them discovers a soiled diaper, which she throws in the trash, and pulls the *tzitzit* undergarment, its fringes stuck together, over his head. Naked as a newborn, the boy is propelled through the air, landing in the bathwater, and in her eyes he is no longer a boy but a beautiful little girl, whose two wet sidelocks gather into a golden mane.

Dousing him with fresh water, she diligently purifies his body, no organ escaping the hand of the confident musician, and while doing so she recalls the advice her father gave her mother, to handle the *tzaddik* with care, for he might become the leader of a stubborn religious camp that could topple a government. Sure, why not, let him topple a government, but at least he won't pollute it.

And despite her awareness of her own nakedness, she is in no hurry to cover it up. Boy or girl, she says to herself, why should I not be engraved in the child's memory? And she wraps the clean body in a big towel and carries him, light as a feather, into the living room and seats him in her father's armchair, and he still looks to her like a girl, in whose blue eyes sparkle diamonds of tears but whose little arm is outstretched pleadingly at the black screen.

Television, again? But why not? She switches on the set, hoping the symphony orchestra on the Mezzo Channel will captivate the little viewer with its rich sound. But the *tzaddik* demands the remote control, expertly changing channels, coming to a halt at the Jungle Channel and a troop of monkeys.

In which case, he's not so damaged after all.

Suddenly a frantic pummeling rattles the front door. She wraps herself in a bathrobe, firmly fastens its belt, shakes out her hair and combs it with her fingers, and only then opens the door for the pale and terrified chaperone. She escorts him to his protégé, who sits in the armchair wrapped in a big towel, transfixed by monkeys delousing one another with care.

"He's going to fall and crash if you keep this up," she scolds, not unkindly.

Yuda-Zvi says nothing. His face is red, he bites his lip, and then, in a heartbreaking gesture, he kneels before the little boy, who is not looking at him, and feels and smells the damp towel. "What is this?" he asks. "You washed him?"

"Of course."

"Why? What did he do to you?"

"He slid down the drainpipe and came in here filthy and stinking."

"So what?"

"What do you mean, so what? He had to be washed."

"How?"

"How? With soap and water. You've heard of water? You know what soap is?"

Shaya's son studies her with undisguised anger.

"And the clothes? His *tzitzit* and the shirt with the special embroidery?"

"Don't worry, it's all safe, except for an old diaper. But make sure, Yuda-Zvi, not to dress him now in those dirty clothes. Take him up to Grandma and change him."

"He has no other clothes here."

"Just take him from here as he is, wrapped in this towel, which is a gift to you. But first swear to me on your father's life, the life of Shaya Pomerantz, that never, but never, will you sneak in here again, not through the door or through the window, because if this *tzaddik* were to fall and get hurt, what would all his Hasidim do?"

"They'll find another *tzaddik*," he mumbles darkly, and measures her with a blazing look that assesses her nakedness under the robe. He's not a child anymore but a furious adolescent, who rips the remote control from the little one's hand and shuts off the TV, strips the towel from the boy and flings it with disgust on the floor, then pulls the screaming, naked child to the still-open door and, without a parting word, takes him up to the grandma who no longer knows she is a grandma.

TWENTY-FIVE

S HE WANTED TO TELL her mother the story of the boy, but then thought better of it. Her mother would not interpret the episode the way she understood it, and she did not want the joy she felt crushed by her mother's irony. And so, after a long afternoon nap, her strange elation still intact, she goes out. She decides to walk to the city center and take in a foreign film, then remembers that the movie theaters abandoned the downtown area years ago and relocated in malls, so instead she heads for the *shuk*, which she had spurned and ignored for years but has lately begun to fancy.

Evening slowly falls in Mahane Yehuda, and Noga feels a strong craving for meat soup, red, thick and hot. So she prowls the alleys in search of that underground dining room, hoping that despite the hour it has not yet been converted into the bar. But the minute she goes down the stairs, her hopes are dashed. The shutter separating the room from the kitchen has been lowered, and the long communal tables have been divided into small tables, with a boy circulating among them lighting tea lights in saucers, resembling yahrzeit candles. Next to the bar are a guitar and an accordion, still in their cases, and the two people finishing their meal are apparently the musicians.

Again her gaze is drawn to the ceiling. The black camera, real or fake, still perches in its place, though the angle of its gleaming glass eye seems to have shifted.

She turns to the candle boy.

"Excuse me, is there anything left to eat?"

"All gone, lady. Come back tomorrow."

She was about to leave when she notices, not far from the lowered shutter in the rear, the retired policeman, the stammering extra. He sits facing the entrance as if expecting someone, perhaps her.

With a small step she could withdraw and disappear into the *shuk*, but Noga senses that the veteran inspector has noticed her arrival, and that he knows she has spotted him too. Should she disregard him? Elazar sits motionless in his corner, doesn't stand up or wave. She certainly doesn't want to indulge his desire, but is it right to ignore him?

She walks toward him with a smile, but he doesn't move, doesn't seem surprised, as if they had planned to meet.

"I was thinking I could find something to eat here," she explains. "After our evening, I came back the next afternoon and had a delicious meal. But it seems they close early and get ready for another night."

"What would you like to eat?"

"Whatever . . . not much, maybe soup . . . something simple."

"If only soup, that's possible. Come, sit down."

"Meat soup," she says, unable to restrain her craving, then backs off. "If there happens to, um, b-be any . . ."

He seems shocked. "M-m-meat?" He echoes her stammer. "Right n-n-now? I d don't think they have any left at this hour. But s-simple s-soup, maybe hot, thick lentil soup. That won't b-b-be enough?"

"Definitely enough," she exclaims, blushing. "Of course . . . the meat isn't important . . . lentil soup or whatever . . . thick and hot is wonderful."

He disappears, and her eyes wander around the gray cellar, the flickering flames adding an air of mystery. The musicians, done eating, take out their instruments and start to play. The cascading notes of the guitar and accordion arouse a visceral nostalgia for her harp, and her eyes well with tears.

The policeman carefully sets before her a bowl of steaming lentil soup and two slices of dark bread.

"How did you manage that? Are you a partner here, or a relative?"

"Neither one, but a police commander, especially a retired one, has p-p-power and influence."

"Especially retired?"

"Because he still keeps his old contacts and secret information, without being subject to any r-rules."

She cautiously sips the soup, and the eyes of the eternal inspector follow her spoon as if she were a child who requires supervision. Does he understand, she wonders, that despite his power as a policeman, he cannot touch me?

"And what's happening with the little *haredim* who've been b-b-breaking into your apartment?"

"I think today I stopped them once and for all."

"How?"

She tells him about the little boy who got a thorough scrubbing.

"That was smart," says Elazar approvingly, "a good intuition. I know them, and if you, a secular woman, a stranger and not m-m-married, dared, even with a little boy—"

"But an important one, a kind of *tzaddik*."

"Exactly. So if you, a free woman with no children, t-t-took off his clothes and made him take a bath, that will f-f-frighten not only the boy who looks after him, but the parents, who will finally wise up and c-c-control his misbehavior."

"And imagine"—she laughs with embarrassment—"when I washed him, I myself, because I'd jumped out of the bathtub to save him, had nothing on."

"Naked? Better yet," he says excitedly. "You did w-w-well. And with no bad intent. You were right, no need to call the police."

"And you believe that this will put an end to the break-ins?"

"I believe it, because I know them. Now they'll be afraid of you. They'll realize that you're unpredictable. But how much time do you have left, anyway, before the end of your experiment?"

"Mine? Not mine, my mother's."

"Of course."

"Barely four weeks."

"So take it easy. And I gather that soon you'll b-b-be away, because your b-b-brother got you a role in the opera."

"A role in the opera? Ha, don't exaggerate, dear sir, just an extra—a country girl or a Gypsy or a smuggler. And as you yourself told me, with no pay, just three days at a hotel by the Dead Sea."

"Three days in a luxury hotel with a spa is fair compensation. But if you want to earn good money before you return to Europe, come and join the hospital series. They're already ac-actively interviewing ap-applicants, because they need a lot of extras, so many that they'll even take me, the eternal extra, with the face that graced a thousand films. They'll probably put me on the operating table, or in the m-m-morgue, so that my face won't show, but they need my b-b-body."

"When is it supposed to start?"

"In a week and a half. They've cleared out a huge warehouse in the Ashdod port and built a set that looks exactly like a hospital. It's going to be an elaborate series with at least twelve episodes, which will of course need a steady supply of patients and their friends and family. Since they haven't yet filled their quota of extras, I took the liberty of putting in your n-n-name. Why not earn some real money before you f-f-fly away from us? The work is on a day-to-day basis, no commitment. You can always c-cancel at the last minute. You're not angry with me?"

"Why should I be angry?"

"That I signed you up as a patient. But if that bothers you, how about just a relative of a patient?"

"No, it actually doesn't bother me to be an imaginary patient for a few days. It'll be restful. But tell me, what's your connection with the business of extras? A partner? Relative? Consultant?"

"C-c-confidential adviser, that's the title."

He suddenly seizes her hand and brings it to his lips, and she feels his relief. Is he helping her because he hasn't given up on the idea of getting her into bed before she goes back to Europe? And though his hopes are slim, she doesn't, deep down, dismiss him out of hand. But she doesn't want it to happen soon; otherwise, he won't leave her alone. Maybe just before she leaves, as a souvenir of her stint as an Israeli extra, and after all, no stuttering baby will be born as a result.

She finished the soup but didn't touch the bread. "It was excellent. You revived my soul. The battle with the little kid wore me out." And as the boy puts a saucer on their table and lights the faux-yahrzeit candle, she has a flash of suspicion that she didn't find him here by accident. That his policeman's instincts told him she would be here. And without any complaint, with a pleasant smile, she asks whether it was by chance that she found him here.

"No, n-n-not by chance."

"Really?"

"This afternoon I was on my way to your place to offer you an unusual job as an extra, for right now. When I got to your street, I saw from a distance that you were leaving the building, and I didn't want you to s-s-suspect that I was hanging around your s-s-street with any intentions. So I followed you—after all, I'm an expert in t-t-tailing people. Then I saw you were heading for the *shuk,* and from the way you walked past the stalls, I could see you weren't looking for fruits and vegetables, but a meal, at this place, because I knew you had been here once for lunch. You got s-s-slightly lost in the alleyways, and I got here before you and waited."

TWENTY-SIX

"WAITED FOR WHAT?"

"To make you a rare offer, with decent pay, in f-foreign currency, but you need to give an answer right away—y-yes or no."

"Yes or no to what?"

"To be an extra, for a few hours this evening, in a documentary now filming in Jerusalem."

"An extra in a documentary? Isn't that a contradiction in terms?"

"Absolutely. In a documentary, we expect real people and not actors and extras. But sometimes there's a p-p-problem that calls for the assistance of an extra."

"Meaning what?"

He tells her about a group of American students making a film about a professor from their university, an American psychiatrist originally from Israel, named Granot. This man grew up in Jerusalem, and as a youth was hospitalized for a while in an institution for the mentally ill, after which he went to study in the United States, where he became a prominent professor and thinker in his field. To put together this film portrait, focusing on Granot's theories and ideas, his students decided to take him on a sort of "roots" journey to Jerusalem, to meet with his elderly parents, family members and some friends, so that stories about his youth will flesh out and add color to the portrayal of his character and thinking. And of course the filmmakers hope that a few swords will be crossed and scores settled, typical of encounters with parents and relatives.

"So why do they need an extra?"

"In p-p-principle everything will b-b-be r-r-real," he stutters copiously, taking a deep breath to recover and regain control of his speech. "Except for the one important character, who was supposed to come to the shoot at his parents' home, a girl the professor was involved with in his youth and apparently was hospitalized because of her. Just this morning she canceled her participation under p-p-pressure from her husband, who vehemently objected to his wife appearing in this kind of slightly psychiatric film. But the director feels it would be a shame not to have her in it, so they decided to bring in an extra in her place, to be present at the encounter even if she said nothing, and perhaps the professor would want to say something to her, anything, because this documentary doesn't have a written script. It's all spontaneous and r-r-real."

"Very strange."

"Yes, even for a veteran like me. In any case, this afternoon the casting agency called me and others for help in finding a w-w-woman more or less your age who would be a stand-in for a r-r-real woman."

"Who is not supposed to say or do anything?"

"Of course, this is a true-life film, and no one has c-c-control or advance knowledge of what will happen."

"Which could end up as a complete fiasco."

"You're right, but you still need to give an answer, yes or n-n-no, otherwise they'll find s-s-someone else."

"How much are they paying?"

"Three hundred dollars for a few hours. Very respectable for a silent e-e-extra. Apparently their university has a lot of money, or the professor is important. So, yes or no?"

She studies the policeman's face. Is he telling her the whole story, or leaving out some important detail?

"All right, Elazar. My adventure with those two little boys unnerved me, I doubt I'll get any sleep tonight, so why not impersonate some character, a real one for once, and be well paid? But on one condition: they drive me there and back."

"But of course," he says happily. "I'll t-take you both ways, because I'm curious to see how they'll cook you into the meal."

She laughs. "And don't you, as the confidential adviser, need to be paid?"

"I don't need monetary compensation. But if you invite me for a bowl of soup before you return to Europe, I w-w-won't refuse. So let's check and make sure they haven't already hired someone."

He dials his cell phone, puts it close to his ear and speaks almost in a whisper in simple English, his happy eyes stammering too:

"It's o-o-ours. I mean, y-y-yours."

Midevening now, and Jerusalem is slowing down. In a matter of minutes Elazar drives her to the Talbieh neighborhood, which boasts the president's house, the residence of the prime minister and the Jerusalem Theatre, just up the street from the former leper hospital. For the fun of it, he circles twice around Salameh Square, then heads down Marcus Street, ending up at a long and narrow street named Lovers of Zion, lined for the most part with old, stately houses made of stone.

In the garden of such a stone house with a front porch are gathered a few people whose connection with the film is as yet unclear. Elazar whispers to her that this was once the home of a philosopher with a big white beard, Martin Buber by name, and cannot resist telling her a story about how the police were once called in because of a demonstration that blocked the street — a crowd of students, friends, neighbors and sundry admirers who had come to congratulate the professor on his eightieth birthday, and sang and shouted, floated balloons and threw their hats in the air. And when a policeman asked Buber if he needed help, he replied, in a heavy German accent, "You can best help me if you leave at once, so no one will think I need police protection."

Beside a green gate stands a camera tripod along with lighting equipment. In a large, brightly lit living room, on a well-worn sofa, in the soft breeze of a small fan, an elderly couple sit side by side, looking anxiously at a lens pointed at them like a machine gun by a tall American student, while a fuzzy microphone, affixed to a long pole held by a slender young woman, floats above them. The protagonist of the film, Professor Jacob Granot, a man in his fifties with curly gray hair in a black suit and bow tie, stands facing his parents and looks doubly anxious, both for the good name of the parents who had him put away in his youth, and for the truth itself.

As the extra enters, the filming is halted and a gentle hand separates her from her escort and guides her to an armchair in the corner of the room, and now the camera's eye is on her, lingering a bit on her facial features, then returning to the subject, the famous psychiatrist arguing with his parents.

This is an American film, and so the talk is mostly in English, but Hebrew slips in here and there. The father apparently understands the English of his famous son, but finds it difficult to reply in a language that is not his own, whereas the mother, who does not understand English but guesses its intent, permits herself to interrupt and defend her truth.

The professor has not been in Israel in a long while, and seems uncomfortable with the decline of his childhood home, moving about the room while talking and casually shifting an object or piece of furniture to a more aesthetic spot, lest his future viewers, mostly students and colleagues, regard his roots with scorn.

Now and then he stares at the extra, who stands in for the fateful figure of his youth, and there's no telling whether he's fully aware of the switch between the real and the imaginary. Can he possibly believe that this is the original woman?

The psychology students, who are well acquainted with his theories about mental disturbances in children, seek to understand from the awkward encounter between him and his parents how, out of painful and crazy youthful experiences that ended in hospitalization, such revolutionary insights arose in his mind. And contrary to a conventional scenario of such a film, the hero does not intend to settle a score with his parents, but rather to express approval of the firm hand that shook him up in his younger days.

The elderly parents, however, are gripped by a shared anxiety, fearing an onslaught of ancient blame in front of a foreign camera. The mother addresses the production crew in Hebrew, trying to persuade them of what a menace their distinguished professor was in his youth. And the father, clad for the occasion in an old suit, loosens his skinny necktie, his face waxen with shame, his eyes full of tears.

So there is no alternative but to stop filming and allow the participants to recover from their misunderstandings and find a more fitting way to deal with the hidden truth.

The room has filled up with more people, those who belong there and those who do not, and an Israeli cosmetician deftly mops beads of sweat from the burning faces of the son and his parents, and from the forehead of the extra, though she has not uttered a word. Elazar skillfully insinuates his way to Noga, whispering the encouraging news that because working as an extra in a documentary, made by amateurs to boot, is doubly chaotic, he has asked for and received payment from the producer, for who knows what will happen two hours from now—maybe the original woman will show up and Noga will have to withdraw. And he discreetly slides an envelope into her purse.

This is an independent film produced by the American psychology students, and because they lack film experience, they are assisted by students from the arts department at their university, together forming a sizable group whose work on a film biography of a man of science has included a comprehensive tour of Israel. So far, the filming and sound recording have gone well, but now, in the hero's childhood home, in the final confrontation with his parents, there is a sense that the project is tangled up in slippery truth. It will take patience to discover why intelligent and cultured parents had their beloved son, an only child, locked up in a ward for a long time, and why, so many years later, after the son has become a renowned psychiatrist, he not only bears his parents no grudge, but praises them.

This is a quandary that needs no father's tears or mother's anger, or even the explanations of a son who came from overseas, but simply a time-out to change the approach and perhaps the location, alter the angle of the camera and the position of the lights, and mostly to rephrase the questions and improve communication. To this end, the professor's wife now enters the room, an attractive American, taller than her husband, with their young son, also taller than his father. With endearing shyness they approach the Israeli grandparents, who are hard to talk to but must be loved and respected. And following the American daughter-in-law, who affectionately hugs her husband's parents, the grandson hugs and even kisses them. Then students, too, converge on the elderly couple, squeezing their hands and patting their shoulders.

Must the extra do the same? For the moment she does not move, sensing a new lethargy seeping into her bones. Her eyes close, and in her memory flows the water that washes clean the naked, beautiful little boy, who looks at her with wonder, not hostility.

A woman about her age, plump but pretty, enters and exchanges whispers with the professor. He is excited to see her, but the two do not embrace. Then the woman grows aware of the extra staring at her, and approaches Noga, leans over her armchair and quietly introduces herself.

"Have you guessed? I am the woman you are impersonating. My presence is important to this project, but my husband absolutely refuses to have me filmed, even if it's an amateurish student production that'll be screened on maybe two campuses. Look out at the garden, and by the tree you'll see my husband watching me from afar, making sure I don't get tempted."

"What's he afraid of?"

"That I'll be identified as the beautiful young girl who forty years ago was the love object of a special, unusually gifted young man—a crazy love that was so strong, in the end it poisoned her."

"Poisoned? In what way?"

"Literally. We were inseparable, together day and night, and then, out of a paranoid fear that I was about to leave him, he began poisoning my food. It was a poison he concocted himself, his own recipe. Can you imagine? It was life-threatening and I almost died, because it took forever to diagnose what was happening to me, to realize that my lover was truly dangerous. Good thing his parents, who look so exhausted now, quickly rose to the occasion. They didn't cover up what he did, but had him locked up in a mental institution for a good long time, almost a year, until his madness had passed, and by having him committed they saved him from the police, and he was exempt from army service, and after he completed his matriculation exams he went to study in the United States, and succeeded in having a brilliant career."

The extra asks an odd question: "The hospitalization was in Jerusalem?"

"Why? Are you from here?"

"In theory."

"Then you might know it was close, on Disraeli Street, the next one over. At the bottom of the street, a hospital specializing in teenage insanity, and since it was nearby, and his parents could supervise his care, they were in no hurry to have him discharged. There he was introduced to the suffering of children and young people, and probably began to develop the original ideas on which he eventually built his career."

"And you're familiar with his work?"

"A bit, from a distance. For all these years, he never lost touch with me, sent me his books and articles. But it would be an overstatement to say I understand them."

"And you have children?"

"Four. And giving birth ruined my looks."

"You exaggerate," Noga says. "Looking at you closely, it's easy to see how beautiful you must have been, and to understand why Granot was afraid you would leave him. I'm sorry I can't simulate even a little of that beauty in this film."

"Don't sell yourself short. Tell me, are you an extra as a profession or a hobby?"

"Neither. I'm an accidental extra. By profession I am a harpist, but I perform in Europe, not in Israel, and I came for a short visit to help my mother decide where to live out her old age, Jerusalem or Tel Aviv."

"And what did she decide?"

"She hasn't yet decided."

"And where did you leave your children?"

"I don't have children. I didn't want children."

"Why?"

"Maybe because I didn't want them to ruin my minimal beauty," says Noga with a laugh.

The woman stiffens. Was that a malicious remark, or did it just slip out? Crushed, she stares at the extra as if she too wanted to poison her. Without another word she hurries away, past the production crew trying to persuade the parents to move from the sofa to the cozier bedroom, and past the love of her youth, who tried to poison her and now tries to block her path, but she simply touches his gray curls with maternal affection and goes outside to join her husband in the garden.

And now what? Is my role finished too? the extra asks herself, as the living room empties out and the scene switches to an inside room, to achieve a more intimate and revealing conversation. The tripods for the camera and mixer are folded up, and the monitor and lights and fans disconnected, and within minutes she is alone in the living room of a strange house.

Good thing they paid me, she says to herself, so I can disappear without a problem. She walks out of the stone house into the long, narrow street, now emptied of people. Even Elazar, who promised to drive her back, has vanished. Would he break his promise? She decides on second thought to say goodbye to the film crew, goes back inside, passes through the empty living room and heads into the kitchen, which is stocked with plastic plates and cups supplied by the production. She opens the refrigerator, inspects its contents, pours milk into a plastic cup and drinks.

From there she walks down a dark, narrow hallway lined with old books in unfamiliar languages, and enters the bathroom, whose small window is open to the garden. The husband and wife have left, and beside the tree sit the American woman and her son, chatting with one of the students. There is a bookshelf in the bathroom too, crammed with worn-out books that refuse to find their final repose in the trash bin.

Then, to her surprise, she notices that the bathtub is an identical twin of the bathtub in her childhood apartment. The same size, the same curvature, the same rusted iron feet of a bird of prey. These were two Jerusalem homes constructed before the founding of the State of Israel, Jews living in her building, and in this one, at the time, lived Arabs, but the bathtub is the same bathtub, by the same craftsman, Jew or Arab, blessed with unusual imagination.

A plethora of toothbrushes are arrayed by the sink, as if each tooth demanded a brush of its own. She feels the weight of fatigue, opens the faucet and splashes water on her face, and with the water still blurring her vision, she goes to find the filmmakers and say her goodbyes.

Voices lead her into the bedroom, where the psychology students, with the help of the film students, have constructed a more intimate scene.

They have seated the elderly parents, wearing bathrobes, on the bed, with their son the professor between them. They have removed his suit but left his bow tie on, wrapping him too in an old robe. And so, with the camera pointed at them, they analyze the strange past in Hebrew.

The extra stands in the doorway and knows that the intimacy and candor may be impaired by her presence. As she plans her exit, a hand strokes the back of her neck.

"I thought you'd forgotten," she scolds the former police commander.

"I didn't forget you, nor will I. My daughter called, asked me to get m-m-medicine for my grandson, and I didn't think they'd let you go so soon."

"It turned out that way."

"So you got a really good deal."

"And as the agent, you deserve not just soup but a whole meal. By the way, how many grandchildren do you have?"

"One, for now."

"How old?"

"Around the same age as your *tz-tz-tzaddik.*"

He takes her home to Rashi Street and wishes her a good time at Masada. If the tickets weren't so expensive, he'd go down to the Dead Sea too.

Six voicemails from Honi await her, each more agitated and anxious than the last, all with the same message: the bus taking the extras to the opera in the desert will be leaving three hours earlier than planned.

"What were you doing wandering around at night?" he hisses when she calls him back.

"I was an extra in a documentary."

"There is no such thing."

"You'd be surprised."

But he's not prepared to be surprised. He will demand proof in two days, on the second evening of *Carmen,* since he has tickets.

"So if you can, Honi, bring me some literature about Martin Buber."

"Martin Buber faded long ago into the mists of memory."

"So retrieve him from the mists of the Internet."

TWENTY-SEVEN

T HANKS TO THE EARLY DEPARTURE, her eyelids droop repeatedly on the ride, her head bobs, and she arrives at Masada asleep. With her in the minibus are six other extras, a few of them former singers in the opera chorus, arriving today to reinforce the ranks of their former colleagues, not with their voices but with their presence.

To the women's surprise, the bus doesn't take them to the hotel but heads straight to the opera site at the base of Masada, where the sounds of rehearsal are heard.

The singers, dancers and chorus, all in street clothes, mill about the enormous stage, a wooden floor with built scenery supplemented by the natural landscape. Dirt paths run between two small hills planted with low plastic olive trees and artificial flowering bushes. The director and his assistants, wielding bullhorns, prompt the chorus members, who burst loudly into song and quickly stop. The orchestra, in its pit in front of the stage, missing some of its players, is under the baton of a young assistant conductor while the illustrious maestro, a man of three identities, gathers strength in his hotel room.

The seven women extras are greeted by an assistant director who instructs them as to their positions and movements. In the first scene, taking place in Seville, their job is to give the audience a sense of agricultural surroundings, so that while the singing of the tobacco factory workers grows louder, they as farm women will walk along the paths between the two hills, two of them with pitchfork and hoe, three bearing bushels of fruits and vegetables, and the two others, on either side, leading small wagons drawn by donkeys.

"Real donkeys?"

"Why not? In Europe they sometimes put elephants and horses on the opera stage."

The assistant director asks Noga if she would be willing to lead a donkey hitched to a small wagon carrying a few children, since no self-respecting opera production can do without children.

"What if the donkey gets wild?" Noga asks.

"It won't get wild. Its owner is sitting here on the side, and he guarantees its good behavior."

And indeed, near the hill stands a little two-wheeled cart, an elderly donkey harnessed to it, ruminating on the state of the world.

Noga approaches the animal, and as a sign of affection she gently folds one of its big ears, smiles at the owner and asks if he has a *kurbash*.

"*Kurbash?*" The man is amused by the Arabic word uttered by a Jewish woman. "No need, this is the most polite donkey in the world."

He rises and wraps the reins around her hand.

"Here, now you can take him up the hill so he'll get used to you, and I'll walk beside you."

When they are up on the hill the assistant conductor gives a sign to the orchestra and chorus, the assistant director motions to Noga to take the donkey down the hill to the stage, while on the opposite hill the other extra walks her donkey down, accompanied by the two extras carrying the pitchfork and hoe, and the remaining three carrying the bushels of fruit and vegetables—proof positive for the opera audience that the Seville of that time was most fertile and lively.

The rehearsal exhausts the orchestra and the choir. The same passage, again and again. The singers playing Carmen, the Lieutenant and the Corporal warm up their voices in their dressing rooms while three understudies perform onstage, to coordinate the movements of the chorus and dancers. The director and assistant conductor are pleased at last, and everyone is sent off to the hotel to rest, except the seven extras, who arrived late and require fine-tuning for the upcoming scenes—the entrance of the toreador, the smugglers in the hills, the packed crowd at the bullfight arena.

After the rehearsal, waiting for the minibus to take them to the hotel, the seven women flee the blazing sun into the pit, scattering among the empty chairs.

Most of the musicians have taken their instruments with them, but the big ones, impractical to carry, remain in place, among them, of course, the harp, draped in a blue zippered cover. At first Noga observes it from afar, then draws closer. A guard stands on the conductor's podium, enjoying a meal spread out on the music stand. At first she considers asking permission, but decides the guard won't care, and might take her for one of the musicians. She silently goes to the instrument, pulls the zipper of its cloak partway down and lightly touches the strings, which respond with a quiet sigh. Eight weeks have passed since she last touched a harp. She is dizzy with longing.

The guard watches her. What is he protecting, the instruments or music itself? She can see from afar her donkey standing serenely. Its feed bag of barley must be empty by now, for the donkey is not nibbling but gazing toward Masada. She too lifts her eyes to the ancient mountain, whose desolation has outlived its myth. She then completely undoes the zipper and strips the harp of its cover, sits in its shade, pulls and hugs it with both her arms and, without hesitation or tuning, as if her concert has begun, plays the Saint-Saëns *Fantaisie*.

She plucks the notes vigorously, to overpower the desert wind, and their ring in the wilderness is richer than in any concert hall. The guard steps down from the podium but is reluctant to interrupt her, as the six extras slowly awaken to the music and gather around to watch her fingers up close and her feet on the pedals.

She does not smile at them, or even look. Focused on the blue and red strings, she is amazed how precisely the melody flows through her fingertips, not a single mistake or dropped note. From time to time, by force of habit, she glances at the empty podium, as if unaware that no orchestra is playing beside her.

When she is done, her fellow extras loudly applaud. "Why are you an extra if you're such a talented harpist?" one of them asks.

"Actually, I am a harpist and not an extra," she says, and tells the story of her mother's experiment with the old folks' home.

"When will she decide?"

"In less than a month. That's how long I gave her."

Finally the minibus arrives to take them to the hotel. She shares a lovely room, with a view of the Dead Sea, with one of the older extras, a former singer in the opera chorus, and the arrangement is a pleasant one. They talk about music and life, and her roommate sings a few phrases from *Carmen* to demonstrate that her dismissal from the chorus was unfair.

The performance begins at nine, and the singers, musicians, dancers and production people have all arrived by seven. As the distant sun, setting beyond the mesa of Masada, casts delicate stripes of light on the darkening Dead Sea, the musicians tune their instruments and practice their solos. Noga, hidden behind her hillock, dressed like a nineteenth-century country girl, stands beside the donkey, now adorned with a colorful blanket, a little bell tied around its neck. The donkey's owner sits to the side, smoking, surrounded by children. "How many children do you want for the cart?" he asks Noga and smiles.

"How many can your donkey pull?"

"He can pull four, but the opera needs a couple to run after the cart, to give some energy. Look, we dressed them like Arabs from old Andalusia."

The children have been costumed with colorful scarves and embroidered blankets, and several are wearing shiny boots. And for the price of the donkey rental the man threw in various other adornments for everybody.

They finally decide on the division of children. Two will sit in the cart, three will run after it.

"Are they all brothers and sisters?" asks Noga.

"Some are, some aren't," answers the Arab.

A little before eight, a strong searchlight is beamed at Masada, and the myth returns to life. Tiny lights switch on at eight-fifteen atop dozens of music stands, as the players warm up with their instruments. In the distance, a roar of buses, ferrying the audience to the site.

At five after nine, the tall conductor with the tripartite identity—Jewish, Arab and Italian—arrives, clad in a jacket like a Protestant minister's, with a small skullcap pinned to his hair lest it fly off during his stormy performance. Noga had heard gossip in the Arnhem orchestra about his style of conducting, and today she will be able to witness the ecstasy with her own eyes.

The stage lights go on and the sounds of *Carmen* rise from the pit and flood the air, and though the music is famous and familiar, its beauty continues to astonish. The extras are given a sign, and Noga takes hold of the halter and leads the donkey, wondering if his long ears appreciate the music.

The two Arab children in the cart wave to the delighted audience, of whom they were supposed to act unaware. The three on foot hum to themselves. They cross the stage from north to south, intersecting the path of the empty cart rolling from south to north. While the tobacco workers jostle each other with female abandon, the walking donkey defecates on the stage. Outstanding, Noga says to herself as the fresh aroma strikes her nostrils. Every moment here is a gift. She will entertain her friends in the Arnhem orchestra with stories of her wonderful turn as an extra. Meanwhile, she prods the donkey to pull the cart with the children to the far side of the hill, where, amid the tempest of music and banging of drums, she detects the modest part of the harp.

The performance ended at midnight, but the participants did not arrive at the hotel until two in the morning. In the lobby, a message from her brother awaited her.

"Noga dear: Yoni is sick, and Sarai won't want to leave him alone or with Ima. I tried to sell the tickets, but sworn enemies of opera swarm all around me. So Ima and I will come tonight to see *Carmen* and the extra standing by her side, to cheer you both on and shower you with praise."

TWENTY-EIGHT

T HE NEXT DAY THE DESERT wind grew stronger, and on the opera's second evening grains of sand fluttered from the little hills onto the stage. During the first act, Carmen felt the sand scratching her throat and damaging the quality of her singing, and so during intermission, despite attempts by the production crew to lubricate her voice with remedial concoctions, and despite assurances that the evil wind would die down, she refused to continue performing her role in the second act, for fear that her professional reputation would be tarnished. In art, she decreed, there are no excuses or allowances, and she demanded to be driven back to the hotel. It would now take time to bring in the understudy and prepare the audience, not only for a change of voice, but for a different version of the opera's title character.

Honi and his mother arrived at the Dead Sea in late afternoon, and since their hotel was far from Noga's, they did not manage to see her before the performance, but the three agreed to meet for lunch the next day, before their drive home. "I do realize," Noga told them on the phone, "that you came to this opera for a donkey dragging two little kids in a cart, but try to enjoy the music too."

They did. Honi forgot to bring his binoculars, but borrowed opera glasses from the woman sitting next to him, and through smudged lenses he searched for the family extra. Once he located her, he handed the glasses to his mother, but at that very moment the donkey blocked her daughter's face and all she could see was the cart with two children.

At the intermission they decided to stay in their seats, but when the announcement came that the interval would be prolonged because of the change of cast, they joined the mass migration to the snack bar area and restrooms.

The restrooms are the portable kind—narrow but efficient booths side by side, not designated by gender, so the traffic moves relatively fast. Even so, when Honi and his mother arrived, there was a long line, and Honi brought a chair for his mother from the snack area to sit on while waiting.

The private time with his mother in the desert afforded Honi the opportunity to apply final pressure in favor of assisted living near him. Noga is scheduled to return to Europe in three weeks, so the decision must be made. But the mother, who had guessed his intentions, made up her mind not to be pressured on this outing, and not to respond to Honi's hints that the choice of Tel Aviv was a fait accompli.

As he approaches his mother to indicate that she is next in line, she points to a woman of about forty, waiting in a different line, and says, "Take a good look. Doesn't she remind you a lot of our Noga?" "How so?" he says. "The shape of her head," says the mother, "and the way she's putting her hair in a bun. Also the way she stands."

Before he can respond, a toilet stall becomes vacant and the woman disappears within, and as the line gets shorter, a well-built man, his hair flecked with gray, exits a stall, and Honi, his heart pounding, recognizes his sister's former husband.

"Uriah!" he calls out, as if afraid the man will avoid him. "Uriah!" he calls again, almost pleading.

The mother is taken aback. Just a moment ago she spotted a woman who looked like her daughter, and suddenly the ex-husband appears in the flesh. But her turn has come, and she heads for the toilet.

Honi tightly embraces his lost brother-in-law, and without asking how he is doing, quickly describes the current experiment in Jerusalem and Tel Aviv.

"Where's Noga? Is she here too?"

Honi laughs. "Here, but not with us. Onstage."

"In the orchestra?" Uriah's face lights up. "She has a job in Israel?"

"No, not yet," says Honi, and with a cryptic, slightly sheepish smile he tells the story of the extra.

Meanwhile, toilet doors open and close, and the woman who reminded the mother of her daughter exits a stall and touches Uriah with a smile, and

Uriah, with odd hesitation, introduces his wife as if she were a stranger. The loudspeaker announces the start of the second act, and the former husband abruptly ends the encounter before Honi can introduce himself to the second wife and shake her hand.

The audience, weary from the long wait, hurries back to its seats, but the mother is delayed, and Honi is afraid she may be having trouble unlocking her stall, though he's not sure which one it is. The loudspeaker issues the final call, and the unabating wind carries the sounds of instruments being tuned, as Honi rushes back and forth by the toilets calling quietly, like a little boy, "Ima, Ima, what's going on?" and tapping on doors, trying to guess where she is hidden. At last she emerges, her face washed and powdered, her hair newly combed. Her stall had a mirror that inspired her to freshen up and look pretty in honor of the new Carmen.

On the way to their seats Honi tells her about Uriah's wife and marvels at his mother's perceptiveness, but she remains blasé: "It's only natural that Uriah would find a woman who looked like the lover he left. But what did you talk about? What did you tell him?"

"Nothing, it was very quick, just a few words about our experiment—I mean yours."

"Why did you have to tell him? It's none of his business."

"No reason."

"There's never no reason."

"Yes there is. No reason."

"I just hope you didn't tell him Noga is on the stage."

"I did or I didn't," he says angrily. "I can't remember my every word. I told you, it was a brief conversation, and Uriah was the one who cut it off. Anyhow, good God, they separated nine years ago, so who cares anymore?"

TWENTY-NINE

T HE NEWS THAT HIS FORMER WIFE will soon appear on the stage has greatly unsettled Uriah, but he is careful not to betray any hint of the news to his spouse. Although their seats are in the middle section, close to the stage, he looks around for binoculars. "Why binoculars?" asks his wife. "We're not far away." "Be that as it may," he replies, "it was sometimes hard for me in the first act to tell who Carmen was, so at least I'll know in the second act who her replacement is." He asks the man sitting in front of him if he can borrow his binoculars for a moment, and as the first notes are sounded he lifts them to his eyes and doesn't put them down until the man asks for them.

He's not sure if he has managed to pick out Noga. He thought he spotted her among the smugglers who moved between the hills, dressed for the road carrying a sack of stolen goods on her back. After the binoculars were taken from him, he began to peer at a different woman. His wife was getting angry: "What's the problem? What are you looking for?"

"I want to see the understudy clearly."

"What do you care? By the way, what did her brother tell you?"

"Nothing. Their mother is moving to assisted living, that's all."

The singing of the chorus does not drown out their whispers, and they are venomously silenced from all sides.

Since they live in Ma'aleh Adumim, east of Jerusalem, and their children are at a neighbor's, they leave at midnight for home, an hour's drive. His wife, noticing his gloomy mood, tried again to find out what he was told during intermission, but Uriah denied he was told anything at all.

In the morning, after just a few hours of sleep, he drove his children to school, and from there continued to his job at the Ministry of Environmental Protection in Jerusalem, where he told his two secretaries about the opera in the desert, including the grains of sand that sabotaged the voice of the famous star who needed to be replaced with a local Carmen. At noon he went to the compliance department to find out if anyone was dealing with the trash that was building up at the foot of Masada. That night's performance would be the third and last, and before the opera's producers took off for Tel Aviv, profits in hand, it was worth making sure Masada didn't turn into a garbage dump. Nor could he stop thinking that his former wife would again be an extra on the stage, and he goes to the equipment storage room of the department and signs out a pair of field binoculars. Do I have the strength for this? he asks himself, cutting his workday short, getting home before the children do, taking off his clothes and trying to catch a bit of sleep.

He wakes up at four p.m. to find a bustling household and his wife walking around red-eyed and yawning. He immediately takes charge, and after dinner he steers her to bed to make up for her lost sleep, and promises that for next year's opera at Masada they will stay overnight at a hotel. "No," declares his wife, "the next opera, if we go, will be in a hall and not under the sky."

Uriah has mustered his nerve and decides to go to the desert. He says he has an evening meeting of senior staff with the minister of environmental protection. He will set his cell phone on vibrate and keep it in his shirt pocket, by his heart, so he can feel every jitter.

As darkness falls, Uriah heads east, gliding toward Jericho and a half-moon flanked by a trio of twinkling stars. At the Beit HaArava junction he turns south, and in less than an hour he can see the beam of light sweeping across the mountain of the ancient suicides. He has no admission ticket, and no intention of spending more money on this opera, so before reaching the main parking lot he swerves onto a dirt road and bounces along, circling the opera venue until he is blocked by large rocks. He switches off the headlights and engine and walks past the stage, planning to hide behind one of its adjacent little hills, natural or artificial, he can't quite tell. From there, he will train his binoculars on the woman who refused, despite her love for him, to give birth to a child.

As a former combat officer in the Israeli army, he strides with confidence, and the tragic mountain of Masada helps him navigate accurately. He can hear the musicians tuning their instruments. But will the security guards, if there are any, know that this man with a bit of gray in his hair isn't trying to sneak into an opera he saw last night and whose tunes he can hum, but just wants to look at one extra, with whom he has an unsettled score?

Silently he approaches the northern hill and the sound of laughing women. Now a hush, and then the audience of thousands explodes in applause for the conductor. Within a few seconds, ethereal music drifts in his direction. He inches closer, chooses an observation point and kneels down, and through the binoculars of the Ministry of Environmental Protection he observes the country girls of Seville, one of whom stands by a donkey hitched to a cart containing two little children, who wave to the crowd they are supposed to be unaware of. His heart pounds as he recognizes his former wife gripping the halter, out of context in peasant costume but still the same woman who could not be persuaded to have children with him, despite his undying love for her.

The music pulls her and the cart across the stage toward the opposite hill, and so as not to lose her, he advances slightly, careful not to enter the field of vision of thousands of eyes focusing on the stage, and thinks he has succeeded.

But from the commanding heights of the podium, the tall conductor is stupefied to spot a gray-haired man not connected with the plot, and as he dictates the tempo with crisp, stormy movements, and crouches and leaps to bring Bizet's music to life, he also threatens the foreign invader with his baton, tries to shoo him away. But Uriah does not budge. Rock solid at the edge of the stage, he tracks the country girl who crosses paths with another cart and vanishes behind the second hill. And as he is considering whether to follow her, he is seized by two young security guards and removed from the area.

"Please, sir," says one of the guards, not unkindly, "if you have no money for a ticket, then listen to *Carmen* at home. Don't spoil the magic for others."

"You're absolutely right."

For a moment the guards conspire to confiscate the fine-looking binoculars, but after the man introduces himself as a supervisor of environmental protection who has come to make sure Masada doesn't turn into a garbage dump, they drop the idea.

Before the end of act one he heads back toward Ma'aleh Adumim. On the uphill road from Jericho the cell phone vibrates close to his heart, and he says gently to his wife, "Go back to sleep. I'm almost home."

THIRTY

THE PREVIOUS MORNING, before the mother and son drove back to Tel Aviv, the three sat together on the hotel terrace, watching people float in the salty waters of the Dead Sea. They spoke about the grains of sand that had prevented the prima donna from playing Carmen after act one, and how those same grains of sand had only improved the singing of the Israeli understudy, who was showered with bravas and became a star overnight. Noga yawned and said, "Grains of sand appeared to me once in a dream. I don't remember why." Her brother and mother looked at her affectionately. She'll have to take a nap in the afternoon, or she won't have the strength to pull the donkey, who sometimes stops and will not move.

"Honestly," she asks her mother and brother, "you could actually tell it was me?"

"I tried not to lose sight of you," says Honi. "After all, I came more for you than the opera."

And the mother says, "I'm not sure I identified you, but it was nice to feel again like a young mother coming to see her daughter in a sweet costume at a kindergarten party. When you were little, before Honi was born, Abba and I didn't miss a single one of your performances, even if you had only two words to speak."

"Two words? For example?"

"Peas and beans."

"That's all?"

"And for that Abba took off time from work. But I'm not feeling young only because of you, Noga," she continues cheerfully. "It's Honi too. We haven't slept in the same room since he was ten, and last night we went out together and even slept in the same bed, so I'm asking myself why you'd want to imprison such a young mother in an old-age home."

Grimacing, Honi turns to his sister, but she smiles indifferently. He says to her, "Ima is waiting for me to have a heart attack like Abba, to be rid of my nagging."

"You won't have a heart attack," says his sister. "If, as you said, my heart is made of stone, yours is made of rubber."

"Children, enough," says the mother. "I apologize."

They resume discussing the change of singers and try to understand why the character is more important than the person who portrays it. "At one point," relates Noga, "I found myself near the understudy. I looked at her face, and though she was different in every way from the star who dropped out, I didn't really feel the difference between her and the original."

The mother, who knows her son, anticipates that he is on the verge of telling Noga about the encounter with Uriah, and she places a finger on her lips to signal him that he shouldn't. But Honi pointedly ignores her, and tells his sister about the hasty meeting and the physical resemblance between her and the second wife.

Noga listens calmly, drinks what's left of her coffee and says, "I just hope you didn't tell him I was in the vicinity."

When the mother suddenly stands up irritably, as if trying to forestall the answer, Honi keeps calm and disregards the truth: "I didn't tell him a thing. Why should I even mention you? You split up a long time ago. Who cares anymore?"

THIRTY-ONE

"MAYBE FIREWORKS, THE BEST EVER in Jerusalem, can convince you not to run away so fast from the city." A pair of old friends, both flutists who had studied with Noga at the music academy, insisted she come to a party on the eve of Jerusalem Day.

It was held on the roof of a monstrous high-rise erected on the ruins of the old Holyland Hotel, offering a fine view of the pyrotechnic bouquets launched in rapid succession from the hilltops of the capital. Many on the roof were strangers to each other and even to the hosts, who wished to prove by their generosity that they were innocent of the municipal corruption entailed in the demolition of the hotel and the construction of these hideous buildings. But in the Israeli fashion, the guests rapidly set about establishing their connections, if not from childhood or military service, at least through mutual acquaintances.

Noga stood near the rooftop railing, sipping wine, scanning silent skies tinged by a foggy, pinkish residue of fireworks. Soon enough, as always, someone would be attracted by her solitude, and on this anniversary of Jerusalem's real or imaginary reunification would expect her to reveal her connection and talk about herself. She would surely be asked why she had no children, and why she didn't live in Israel. Would she be teased if along with her music she described her work as an extra, and threw in the strolling donkey that dropped its aromatic turds at the foot of Masada to the strains of grand opera?

The unfamiliarity on the roof has given way to the singing of old Israeli folksongs that clash with the music she carries in her heart. She decides to say good night to her friends, declining offers of a ride home. Insisting on her independence, she orders a taxi.

On Rashi Street, near her mother's building, stands a man. Can it be that even close to midnight an elderly lawyer will take the trouble to stalk her? But no, it's the neighbor, Mr. Pomerantz, in a baggy white shirt, skullcap on his head, wreathed in cigarette smoke.

"At last I run into you, Mr. Pomerantz," she says, warmly greeting a man whose beard has grown white over the years but who remains handsome. "Ever since I got here I've been asking myself where you are."

"Here I am," he says with a chuckle.

"Eight weeks I've been living in my mother's place," she persists, "and I haven't seen you. And you're not sick, after all, like your poor wife."

"No, thank God, I'm not sick, and I haven't hidden from you, Noga," he says fondly, "but most weekdays I'm not in Jerusalem, but in Judea."

"Our Judea or the Palestinians' Judea?" she asks contentiously.

"God's Judea," he answers softly. "For the past year I've been teaching five days a week at the yeshiva in Tekoah so I can help our son Shaya, who has many children."

Yes, she wants to say, and I met one of them and even threatened him with a whip. But she doesn't complain.

Meanwhile, the cigarette is burning down, almost singeing Pomerantz's lips, and he quickly takes out another and lights it with the butt, which he then tramples with his shoe.

"Your father too, may he rest in peace," he says by way of apology, "liked to stand here with me by the fence at night and enjoy a cigarette, male friendship which resulted from your mother's and my wife's fear of smoke."

"Yes, you were good friends, even though my father was incurably secular."

"Enough just to say secular," he gently chides. "Only somebody in the grave is incurable. Speaking of which, Noga, have you visited your father's grave on this trip?"

"By myself?"

"What's the problem?"

"How would I ever find it? I was there only at the funeral and not at the unveiling of the gravestone."

"I'll help you find it."

"It hasn't been a year yet, and they say that after the thirty days, one must not visit the grave until the end of the first year."

"It doesn't matter what they say," he says with mild annoyance. "It's not about how much time has passed. A person who loves his father visits the grave to strengthen that love."

"True," she whispers.

"And so?"

"So?"

"If you are willing, we'll go to the cemetery tomorrow morning, before you return to your exile."

"Tomorrow?" She tries to put him off. "Tomorrow's Jerusalem Day, a parade."

"What's the connection?"

"You're right, it's irrelevant."

"So tomorrow morning early I'll take you to the cemetery," he says, and flips the burning cigarette into the air like tiny private fireworks and goes back to his apartment.

This Hasid has trapped me, she says to herself, not with irritation but marveling at how quickly he persuaded her to set the alarm on her mobile phone, so she could wait, half asleep, wrapped in her mother's black shawl, for two knocks on the door, like those of his grandson.

He stands at the door in the early morning, wearing a solemn expression, a black *kapota* overcoat and a huge hat that covers his sidelocks. Silently he leads her to a bus stop, and when a small bus arrives, perhaps public, perhaps private, they get on board, and it turns out that this special bus takes mourners not only to the entrance of the cemetery, but also to various sectors of graves, stopping on request.

"I would never have found this place. You're apparently an expert."

Mr. Pomerantz bids her to stand opposite the headstone that her brother and mother had erected at the grave. A simple stone of grayish marble, and under the dates of birth and death is engraved one line: "A beloved man who gladdened every heart."

"Lovely," she says. "Very appropriate. How come they never told me about this line?"

Mr. Pomerantz does not reply. He stands facing the grave, surveys it with approval. No one nearby. The delicate scent of flowering bushes.

"Good that you enticed me to come here," she says, immediately correcting herself. "I mean, suggested . . ."

He says nothing, nods in agreement and studies the inscription on the stone as if it were some complex text.

"Perhaps you remember," she ventures, "that none of the three of us cried much at my father's funeral. Maybe you asked yourself why."

"No," he says, startled. "I didn't ask myself."

"Because Abba died in his sleep, lying beside Ima. An unconscious death, with no fear and no suffering, and we felt that was what he wanted, and it was a good thing, and so we mourned, but we didn't cry."

He looks at her kindly but doesn't respond. He picks up a pebble and places it on the headstone, then glances at his watch, but the harpist, reunited with her lost father, seeks the good graces of her unusual escort.

"Since you've brought me to the grave, Mr. Pomerantz, maybe we ought to do something else."

"What else?"

"Maybe one of your prayers . . . so we didn't just come . . . a simple Kaddish . . ."

"For what you call a simple Kaddish, you have to be a man"—he chuckles—"and there has to be a minyan, but we can make you exempt on both counts. After all, when you used to play your instrument on Shabbat, I told you the priests would let you do it even in the Holy Temple."

"Yes," she says, blushing, "that's what you said, and that was generous and tolerant. But now I have no instrument with me."

"No." He smiles. "Not to play, but to recite the Kaddish with your voice."

"But how?"

Mr. Pomerantz produces from inside his coat a laminated yellowing plastic card with the Kaddish printed in big letters. In a clear whisper she reads it line by line, picturing herself again as an extra in that Jerusalem bar, with a camera following her among the graves. When she is done, she hands back the Kaddish, which vanishes into the black *kapota,* whose shabbiness she notices for the first time.

On the stairs of their building, before they part company, she invites him into her apartment, opens her parents' clothes closet and offers him the orphaned suit. Smiling to himself, he strokes the empty black sleeve, but politely refuses the offer. "The suit is worthy and fitting," he confirms, "and I loved and respected your father, but I suspect that the fabric is *shaatnez.*"

"*Shaatnez?*"

"Yes, Noga, a blend of wool and linen, a prohibition from which not even women are exempt."

THIRTY-TWO

A COMPLICATION OF HIS GRANDSON'S illness has prevented Elazar, Noga's driver to the film site, from reaching the Ashdod port until late afternoon. Amid the labyrinth of poles, pulleys, forklifts and cranes that glitter in the sinking sunlight, the practiced eye of the retired police commander quickly locates the giant warehouse repurposed as a fictitious hospital, which in the weeks to come will turn into cinematic reality

Standing at the entrance are several extras awaiting assignment, based on personal choice or the needs of the production. The "eternal extra" is recognized at once, but no one asks his preference.

"Elazar, you go to the morgue. Sorry, no way will your face appear in this series."

"But they'll s-s-see my face as that of a dead man!"

"And when they see you're finally dead, it'll be a relief."

Elazar sighs. "If that's your decision."

"But you won't be bored. There'll be a story line in the morgue, a medical debate about your death, possibly ending in an autopsy."

"Most entertaining."

Now they ask his companion what she would like to be: a patient or the relative of one? If a patient, chronic or recovering?

Elazar jumps in: "Patient, but not critical, just ill."

But the casting people are not about to hide such a pretty face between blankets and pillows, and so that the camera can caress her femininity, a compromise is suggested: a patient in a wheelchair, hooked up to a colorful intravenous bag.

Elazar is taken to the morgue, and Noga is led through a maze of thin white plywood partitions to an unidentified woman who asks her to change into a floral nightgown. Then she is seated in a wheelchair and taught how to operate it. Her clothes are placed in a plastic bag and hung on the chair, and an IV pole is added on, with a bag filled with blood-red fluid, its tube attached securely to her arm. From here on, she is told, she is free to go about as she wishes. They will find her when she is needed.

The night is not far off, and through the few windows, installed in the warehouse for the film production, the setting sun pours the remains of its day, a potion of copper and gold. Noga wheels herself amid medical equipment, beds and gurneys, occasionally encountering mobile cameras and fuzzy microphones. Despite its transient, improvisational quality, she finds the set to be believable and well suited to its purpose. From time to time she rolls into one of the rooms, where patients bedecked with medical devices greet the guest with friendly waves and invite her to take an interest in their imaginary ailments.

But she mainly sticks to the corridor, to check if there is a back exit from imagination into reality, and perhaps along the way to peek into the morgue and check up on the smiling policeman, missing his protective presence.

The corridor gets darker, seemingly narrower, due perhaps to some mysterious intent of its planners or merely to the evening that envelops the world. This entire huge and forbidding warehouse—it occurs to her suddenly—is a metaphor for humanity, and we are all extras in its story, not knowing if a credible and satisfying resolution awaits us at the end. If only, she sighs, it were set to the right music.

People have to press themselves against the walls to make way for her wheelchair, some of them patients, some relatives, others extras or actors, medical staff and production staff—who can tell the difference between the real and the fictitious? There are those who smile sympathetically and inquire about her disability, and others who pass by in silent sadness. But she keeps rolling along, determined to find that back exit, which suddenly dazzles her with a glimpse of the gray-blue Mediterranean.

The door leads to a small platform of facilities for workers at the port, with two sheds, one for storage and the other for changing clothes, as well as a small cafeteria, and the doorway is blocked by a large man—the retired judge, a familiar and amiable extra whose uniform, baseball cap and pistol establish him as the hospital security guard.

"What can you do?" he says merrily to the wheeling harpist in her brightly colored nightgown. "They haven't given up on me, asked me to be the guard at the hospital door, so my character will be a regular fixture in the series, a way to fatten my pension."

"No need to apologize," Noga assures him. "You're an Israeli Hitchcock. The audience can't relax till they spot his cameo. Meanwhile, our friend Elazar has been taken to the gallows. He won't be able to show his smiling face anymore."

The judge laughs. "Don't worry, the stuttering policeman will rise like a daisy from the dead and fill important roles. And you, dear Noga, have you concluded your experiment?"

"Mine? You mean my mother's."

"Yours too, because you're part of it."

"True."

"What's the verdict?"

"Mother is still up in the air, but my sense is she won't abandon Jerusalem."

"Bravo! That's how a brave secular woman should act. And you, dear?"

"In ten days' time I report for duty in Europe beside my harp, to begin rehearsals of Berlioz's *Fantastique*."

"That way, you'll be leaving Israel without appearing as an extra in a TV commercial and not just in a fictional story."

"What's the difference?"

But as the judge-cum-security-guard tries to explain the essential difference, her attention strays to the cafeteria and its customers. These are mainly men, no longer young, presumably dock workers and customs clerks, gray-haired and bald, but she imagines them as seagoing folk at a Mediterranean port, and is seized by a fierce nostalgia, as if they retained something precious that she had lost, some feeling that has no substitute.

"You're not listening."

"You're right, because I'm burned out, with no one around to explain to me how the devil I got talked into this. And you, my honored friend, where do you find the strength to hop from story to story? Your family doesn't miss you?"

"On the contrary, it's good that I'm not at home. Ever since I retired they've complained that I never stop judging them."

And as the blood of the vanished sun is soaked into the clouds, the cafeteria's lights go out to hasten the exit of the customers, a weaker light is turned on, a tall Sudanese appears and proceeds to set the chairs upside down on the tables, and in the fading twilight there emerge from the cafeteria not humans but silhouettes, headed for a rear gate of creaky revolving bars that ejects them from the port one by one. One figure remains standing on the platform as if lost in thought. Instead of exiting the revolving gate with the others, the figure turns around and heads toward the sea, past huge containers and enormous cranes, walking slowly, dreamily, alongside a gigantic, dark ship, as if hoping to draw strength from it, or inspiration. The unhurried, hesitant steps, halting from time to time, unsettle the woman watching, as if she has seen it before. Her gaze persists until the figure is swallowed in the darkness, and at the edge of the breakwater the lighthouse begins flashing its beam, three short blinks and a pause.

"What are you staring at, young lady?"

"How did the twilight in Israel become so short?"

"Become? When?" The judge laughs. "You've been in Europe too long and you forget how fast darkness falls in your homeland."

"Apparently."

"So what do you say?"

"About what?"

"About the possibility that before leaving you participate as an extra in an interesting commercial, which I've already signed up for."

"No," she protests, "I'm done being an extra. I won't be in any more made-up stories, not in commercials and not in reality, and so I am saying goodbye forever to you too, mighty watchman. You must be strict. No one must be allowed to enter and no one to escape. And now I am going to resign and give up my chair."

She mischievously pulls down the brim of the judge's cap until it covers his eyes, and spins her wheelchair around and back into the corridor, which is not as dark now, for at the far end two spotlights have been turned on to shoot a scene that calls for her participation.

Even as she rises from her wheelchair to announce her departure and request that she be liberated from the intravenous tube stuck to her arm, a young man wearing an ID tag gently seizes her arm and seats her back in the chair.

"We need you in a specific scene that will be happening soon, and then you can decide what you want to do."

"What kind of scene?"

"Permit us not to reveal it in advance, because the director wants to create a surprise, to capture an initial, spontaneous look, frightened, maybe shocked."

"Shocked by what?"

"No, please, I've already said too much, but you can be sure we won't ask anything that an extra like you can't handle. We only want your presence as a disabled patient who enters her hospital room and is suddenly agitated by an intimate scene."

"Intimate?"

"I just let slip another unnecessary word. Intimate in the broadest sense of the word."

"But wait. I came to tell you I was leaving."

"We heard you, and we're sorry to see you go, but only after we finish this scene."

"Why don't you find someone else to be shocked?"

"Because you're the best, in terms of age, looks and especially your cultured quality. You're a musician, no?"

"A harpist."

"So please, Noga," the young man sweetly pronounces her name, "don't say no."

She agrees halfheartedly. A makeup artist rushes over and cleans her face and neck of the day's sweat, and with a thin brush tries to revive lines of beauty that had faded or were forgotten, and an assistant brings her a cold beer and snack, and above her head the IV is switched from red to blue, and the young man with the tag stands behind her and wheels her expertly to the center of the giant warehouse.

"If the intimacy you're talking about is happening in the morgue," she warns, "you should know I have a good friend there."

"The morgue? Where'd you get that idea?"

"There's no morgue in this hospital?"

"I haven't heard of it, but maybe"—the young man laughs—"we'll need something like that later on, for the victims of the film shoot."

Now she is troubled and unsmiling—where have they sent Elazar? But there is no way back. Her chair comes to a halt in front of a heavy door, tightly shut, on whose other side a scene will take place, or is taking place, that is meant to frighten her.

Silence. Not a sound from beyond the door. The young man grabs the handles of the chair as if fearing a last-minute refusal. A few minutes pass, the door opens and a doctor exits, visibly upset. He is about forty, wearing a white gown and a stethoscope around his neck. Obviously an actor, not an extra.

His handsome face is serious, almost tormented, and she sees something familiar in his look, of humiliation, of passion crushed by hatred. He notices the wheelchair-bound extra in a nightgown, nods cordially and moves down the corridor. The door opens again and a man comes out, older and bearded, with an ID tag and a small walkie-talkie attached to his belt. The young man who wheeled her takes the man aside and whispers in his ear, and the older man turns to Noga, takes her hand and introduces himself as the director of the series. "I know," he says, "that you were reluctant to do the scene we're about to shoot, and I thank you for agreeing to do it. Rest assured that we won't involve you in anything undignified. Who knows, you might change your mind after this scene and stay with us for the duration."

"No. I'm sick of all this."

The director touches her arm gently, as if she were a child. He approaches the actor, pulls him aside for a confidential talk, but a sharp musical ear can overcome the distance. "She's tough," grumbles the actor. "She doesn't inspire me . . . not a bit of passion in her. All technical."

The director goes back into the room to have a tête-à-tête with the actress, leaving the actor with the extra at the closed door. The hem of his gown brushes the wheel of her chair, and he nervously plays with the stethoscope, putting it suddenly to the test. He plugs in the earpieces and smiles sheepishly at the extra, who fears for a moment that he wants to listen to her heartbeat. But the make-believe doctor wishes to examine only himself, undoing the buttons of his gown and running the disk over his bare chest. He closes his eyes as he strains to interpret the beating of his heart, but when he sees the smiling extra, he stops and mumbles, something about the chilly actress he will soon have to make love to, and then the door opens and he is summoned inside.

Deep silence. The young assistant standing behind her, quiet and attentive, grips the handles of the wheelchair. Noga's eyes close in despair. What is happening to me in Israel? she wonders. How, in just a few weeks, have I turned from a professional musician to a movable movie extra? Where will my mother and brother wheel me next in their pointless experiment?

The door opens and the director comes out and silently rolls her inside, navigating the cables, cameras, monitors and lights, stopping at the edge of the action.

"So, Noga," he calls her by name, "you're a disabled patient. You're returning to your room, to your bed. Please wheel yourself in there, just two or three meters, and stop, taken aback, shocked if possible, because in the next bed, something is happening that you didn't expect, and you definitely don't like, and the camera will tell us what you're thinking and feeling."

She does as he says, wheeling herself into a dark, scrupulously replicated hospital room with two beds, an empty one for her and a second bed, and alongside it the doctor, who can no longer restrain himself. He rips away his stethoscope, and instead of checking the heart and lungs of the half-naked patient, he brushes her sternum with his lips and kisses her breasts and shoulders, all with the complete consent of the patient, perhaps in the belief that the touch and kisses of a licensed physician will speed her recovery. As the astonished extra tries to distinguish between the lust of the actor and the lust of the man, she hears a whisper behind her: "Get closer, so they'll know you're there."

The doctor, now alarmed by his deed, comes to his senses and stands upright, his bare chest heaving inside the open medical gown. With a savage gaze he studies the disabled woman who has intruded on his passion, and with no warning, in a brisk and aggressive turn, he tears her from the wheelchair, lifts her in his arms and carries her to the vacant bed, laying her down and quickly covering her body and face with a sheet. And as she wonders whether that action was scripted or is a spontaneous move by an imaginative actor, the voice of the director shouts "Cut!" followed by the cheers of the crew.

Someone hurries to remove the sheet and help her out of the bed, as if she were in fact disabled and needing assistance. The actress—a young, slender woman with big, beautiful eyes—waves at her warmly from the next bed, as if they were partners in an adventure, and begins to dress, slowly and carelessly.

"Should we do that one again?" the cameraman pipes up.

"No," shouts Noga, "I've done my part. I don't work here anymore."

The extra's declaration halts the filming. Someone wheels in a tea cart stocked with sandwiches and bottles of juice and soda, and the hungry crew scatter around the set, eating and drinking, talking only about themselves. As Noga is having her makeup removed, the actor comes over and says, "I hope I didn't hurt you." "No," says Noga. "At first you scared me, but I also felt your fear that I would report you to management."

She is determined to get out of there and heads for the exit, but the director intercepts her, grateful for her participation. "Thank you. We got from you what we hoped and more," he says. "What were you hoping?" she asks tartly. "We were hoping for just anger and pity," he says. "And when the doctor surprised us too and carried you to the bed, we were afraid you would resist, but were happy to see you act with dignity and wisdom."

"So I'm not such an amateur after all," she compliments herself, and hurries to find her way back to the world.

The corridors that had been desolate before the filming are now filled with new extras who arrived for the evening. She is surprised that many of them are turning to her for information, then realizes she neglected to remove her nightgown, and rushes back to her hospital room to retrieve the bag of clothes on the wheelchair, but the door is locked. If she thought that by leaving she had shut down the scene, it's now clear that they can do without her, and she has to wait until one of the crew slips out for a smoke.

"What happened? Why'd you come back?" the crew member asks.

"In the confusion of illness and lust"—she laughs—"I forgot to take my clothes, which were hanging on the wheelchair."

But the wheelchair is still standing between the two beds, and will be accessible only at the end of the filming. The man takes a few steps back, and after he finishes his cigarette and crushes the butt he lights a new one. "I haven't smoked all day," he says apologetically. But the smoke doesn't bother Noga. On the contrary, she asks him for a cigarette and whether by chance he helped build a morgue.

He is happy to light her cigarette. A morgue? Not yet, but if the series runs as planned, he and his crew will need to build a believable set for those who die along the way.

Between cigarettes, the door opens and he darts inside to rescue her clothes so she can respectably enter reality. But until she can find the privacy to change clothes, she decides to try—in the guise of a patient—to solve the riddle of Elazar, still hoping to give him a personal memento before she leaves the country.

From time to time she looks behind her, as if being followed. Can it be Elazar, fired from the production, waiting for the right moment to join her? It's hard to know, because as the night filming begins, the place is bedlam, crowded with people in pajamas and hospital gowns. Her brain aches and she asks around for a ride back to Jerusalem.

"At this hour? No, it's too late," declares a production person, "and to get out of the port you have to be checked by the border police and they might have closed up by now. But why go back? The best part is still ahead."

"Ahead or not," she says curtly, "my work here is over."

"But even if you're done, Noga"—to her surprise, he too knows her name—"wait till morning, and meanwhile enjoy an excellent dinner that would be a shame to miss."

Indeed, why pass it up? He leads her to a medium-size hall, crowned by the original, huge warehouse beams intersecting at a great height. Extras sit at tables along with actors and crew members, some still in civilian clothes, some in pajamas and hospital gowns, some bandaged or wearing plaster casts—wounded soldiers, extras fresh from the battlefield, army uniforms soaked in blood. Everyone is joyful and merry, because the generous dinner is expertly prepared, and among the pots Noga finds the meat soup she craved. The happy mood of the diners around her suggests that this is not a random group of extras, but a gathering of acquaintances and friends. If this is so, she consoles herself, when rheumatism and calcification come to pass, when her rigid fingers can no longer coax true sounds from the harp strings, here in my homeland I'll always have another place to work.

Eating makes her sleepy, and she feels that the doctor who lifted and carried her to the bed also strummed a forgotten string in her soul. Best to spend the night here and leave early in the morning. She exits the dining hall and looks for a suitable bed in one of the little undefined rooms on the set. In one such room, two empty beds have been made up, and she chooses the one close to the wall. She puts her clothes under the pillow, so they will be at hand when she makes her getaway. She closes the door as best she can—insofar as a thin sheet of plywood, painted white, can be considered a door—switches off the light beside her bed and the light by the other bed too.

"Go to sleep, little girl," she tells herself in the Dutch words the flutist had taught her—just like in Arnhem when she forces herself to take an afternoon nap, to incubate, in her unconscious mind, the work she has rehearsed that morning, so that in the evening concert she can give birth to the right music.

By force of the Dutch command, she falls into a deep sleep. Despite the warm, lively sounds that never cease outside the plywood door, and although she senses now and then in her sleep that the room she has appropriated is wide open to others, who come and go, lie down and get up—the dream is still stronger than reality, and the one who carried her in his arms like an invalid and laid her down in bed and covered her with a sheet might also protect her as she sleeps from a stranger who has come in the night to lie down in the next bed.

When the first rays of sunshine filter through the giant roof beams, and silence reigns, she can see in the adjacent hospital bed a man lying on his back, his folded arms spread like wings, as if in midthought he was suddenly arrested by sleep. And because she remembers well who slept that way by her side for many years, she throws off her blanket and walks barefoot to the one who has followed her since she arrived here, her former husband, Uriah, who has turned himself into an extra.

Her heart flutters wildly as she watches the man whose hair has grown whiter since he left her. Now he has stolen his way to her in a torn army uniform and a blood-soaked bandage. And with the first glimmer of consciousness, the new extra senses the agitated gaze of his former wife and breaks out in an ingratiating smirk of apology for the terrible power of an ancient love.

THIRTY-THREE

S TRUCK MUTE BY THE SHOCK, hands trembling, she strips off the nightgown of the imaginary patient and returns to her real clothes, and without a backward look hurries to the main entrance, but finds it locked. Immediately she heads for the back door, and this immense warehouse, which last night she saw as a metaphor for humanity, is not as huge as the wheels of her chair had imagined, for within a few minutes her legs have brought her to the rear exit, abandoned now by the large security man.

At the end of the loading dock, the rotating gate dispatches her with a rusty creak into reality—at this hour, a desolate city street—yet she believes that the wave of a feminine arm will attract an early-rising driver, and until he comes she lifts her eyes to the dawning sky, to find, as her father instructed, the shining planet, her namesake, Noga.

She arrives at the assisted living facility in Tel Aviv, and since she has not often visited her mother, she must identify herself to the guard, who is loath to interrupt the morning sleep of an elderly woman. As the smell of diapers from the nursing wing blends with the aroma of breakfast pastries and coffee, Noga knocks softly on the door, which opens at the touch of her hand. It is eight o'clock, and morning light pouring through the open porch door caresses the sleeping resident.

Noga moves a chair to her mother's bedside and waits to see when her presence will rouse her into consciousness. It would seem that the notion of protected living has persuaded the mother from Jerusalem that even at night there is no need to lock doors and turn off lights, and so the entrance of an unexpected guest does not disturb her tranquility. Even when she hears the whispered words "Ima, I'm here," she is not surprised, and simply asks with eyes closed, "What did I do, Noga, to deserve a visit so early in the morning?"

"Early? You're as cozy as a bear, Ima, not locking doors or turning off lights."

"A bear?"

"A bear hibernating in winter."

"Fine," sighs the mother, "if you say so, but why shouldn't I have the peace and quiet of a bear? There are no children here who break in and watch my TV, and no Hasidim whose beliefs I must honor. That's also why I put on weight. In the city that never rests, I do a lot of resting."

"Too much."

"Okay, too much. But what's going on? Am I again to blame for something that's happening to you?"

"Indirectly you're always to blame. It seems that on top of your experiment, Honi added another experiment, just for me."

"What are you talking about?"

"First of all, please, sit up. It's hard to talk when you're lying down half asleep, and even if you stand up, you won't believe your ears."

"You're right, I'm getting up. Maybe I should first freshen up a bit."

"No, there's no time."

"In that case, I'm all ears."

"Uriah became an extra."

"Uriah?" The mother laughs. "Why?"

"To reconnect."

"To what?"

"To me."

"How?"

"Last night he sneaked in and lay down next to my bed."

"What? He broke into the Jerusalem apartment?"

"Not in Jerusalem, in a hospital."

"A hospital? What were you doing in a hospital?"

"A hospital in a new TV series. I was an extra, a patient."

"What did he want?"

"He didn't say a word. He just lay down beside me in the role of a wounded soldier."

"So why were you scared?"

"Don't play dumb, Ima. Just explain why you didn't tell me that Honi, down at Masada, told Uriah not only about you but about me too. Why on earth didn't you warn me?"

"Noga, stop. It's true I was surprised, even angry that at a brief encounter by the toilets Honi saw fit to tell Uriah, who by now is a stranger, about my living arrangements. But when I asked him if he also mentioned you, he denied it by avoiding the question."

"In other words, he lied."

"Obviously, he lied, not out of malice, but out of cowardice. Honi is a sophisticated coward. But it's still not clear why you're so upset, my daughter. Even if your ex-husband lies down in the next bed . . . Wait, are you sure it was him?"

"You're crazy."

"In any case, how strange, and just because he missed you, and without a word? And you? Never asking what he wanted, you ran away."

"Because I know."

"What do you know?"

"That it's a sign and won't be the last. And because of the childish experiment that you're prolonging for no reason, I'm exposed to him from now on."

"No, no, Noga, don't get carried away. It's not my fault that the husband who left you still bleeds for you, and don't drag my experiment into it. And it's not a childish or ridiculous experiment, and we didn't ask you to come here from Europe for no reason. It's a test not only of where to live out my life, but more than that—what the nature and value of that life will be. No, Noga, don't attack me because of the lunacy of a lover who turned into an extra."

"But I'm sure, Ima, that in your heart you've already decided. Please set me free. Let me go back to my harp."

"Don't rush me. It's my right to complete the experiment, as agreed."

"And while you're delaying, the craziness can begin. If Uriah had the nerve to follow me at night into a fictional story where I was just an extra, he won't stop there. Anyway, explain to me why your screwed-up son had to expose me to a man who I was sure had given up on me?"

"No, don't say screwed-up. Honi is your brother. Yes, sometimes he's childish, out of control. He loved and respected Uriah, and he feels guilty because you didn't want to have his child. And you know how attached Honi is to you."

"He feels guilty? Who asked him to? It's none of his business."

"But again, why are you so upset? If Uriah came and lay down next to you and didn't say a word, didn't wake you or touch you, then why all the fuss?"

"He'll be back, I know he'll be back. He'll come to Jerusalem. He knows our house well and maybe still has the key Abba gave him in case you lost or forgot yours."

"But wait a minute. He was the one who left you, not you who left him, no?"

"He had no choice. I didn't want to give birth."

"Why didn't you want to, in fact?"

"Now you ask, Ima? Now you ask?"

"Not asking, it's too late. But what could he still want from you? He already has children of his own, so what does he want? Two or three years ago he came to visit with his two children, to show them to Abba. To prove that he wasn't the one at fault."

"At fault for what?"

"That you two didn't have children."

"But why fault? Who blamed him? It was I who didn't want to, and everybody knew it. I didn't deny it."

"True, you didn't deny it. You were honest . . . No, don't cry."

"Now you're making me twice as depressed. Why didn't you tell me about his visit?"

"We didn't want you to get angry."

"Angry about what?"

"Just angry."

"There's no *just* angry."

"There is."

"And what did Abba say about Uriah's children?"

"Nothing much. Children. Ordinary. Nice. Not bad-looking. Kids. Two of them. A girl and a boy. And Abba played with them."

"Played? Why did he have to play with them?"

"No reason. Children. Why are you getting angry? What did you want him to do, kill them? Abba played with them a little, maybe to prove to himself that he still knew how to play with children. That's all. Now you're annoyed with Abba? How can you be? Abba's gone. Abba's dead."

"Not Abba. It's Honi, who has to have a hand in everything. Why is it his business? The way he used to go through my schoolbag and drawers. Why do you let him take control of everything?"

"He doesn't control anything. He thinks he controls, but you know that in the end I do what I want, exactly like you. When you were little, I learned from you how to set limits, regarding Abba and regarding you and Honi. Except my limits are friendlier, much more generous than yours."

"Tell me now, what kind of name is Honi? Who calls his child Honi? I don't know of a single person in the world named Honi, except for our Honi and the one in the legend."

"Just a minute, Noga, excuse me—we gave him that name because you asked us to."

"Me? How could that be?"

"I was pregnant, and you were in the second grade, and in school you learned the story about Honi who drew a circle and made it rain, so you asked me and Abba, if it was a boy, to call him Honi."

"Me?"

"You."

"So why did you agree? You didn't have to."

"We agreed because we were afraid you would be jealous of the baby and not be nice to him. We said, if we give him the name Noga picked, maybe there'll be peace between them, even though neither Abba nor I liked the name."

"So it comes down to me in the end."

"It was you. You liked the idea that there was a person in the world who drew a circle around himself and didn't move till he got what he wanted. And now you see how Honi is trying to draw a circle around your story with Uriah and not letting the two of you go."

"He has no right."

"Of course he has no right, and I'll speak with him and rap his knuckles."

"Your rapping never made an impression on him. I know that Uriah won't leave me alone."

"What can he want from you now?"

"The children I didn't give him."

"So stop being an extra, enough with other people's stories, and he will not find a way to get to you. From now on, stand up for yourself, in reality, with the whip in your hand."

"But I'm talking about reality, Ima. That's what I'm afraid of."

"Then I'll ask Honi to warn him to leave you alone."

"No, no. No way. Not one word to Honi."

"Why?"

"Because Honi will make things worse. Now that it's more or less clear to him that you won't move here to live near him, he'll look for a way, with Uriah's help, to tie me down to Jerusalem so I can help him take care of you."

"When did this become clear to him?"

"At the opera at Masada, when you stayed together in the hotel. It takes a while for his crafty mind to get over its illusions, but in the end he understood what I understood from the beginning."

"You two know what's in my mind even before I do?"

"It happens sometimes."

"And if I surprise you?"

"You won't."

"Tell me, my daughter, how do you manage to play such a delicate and romantic instrument even though you talk so rudely?"

"When I play I don't talk. When I play I'm not furious."

"Why are you furious?"

"About the brother you gave me."

"But your brother loves you. You know how attached he is to you. Even when he was a baby in his carriage, he would scream and nobody could calm him down. Only when you bent over him would he stop crying and start smiling."

"Except Honi isn't in the carriage anymore, and now the tears are mine."

THIRTY-FOUR

O VERCOME WITH EMOTION, she hugs and kisses her mother. "Go ahead, surprise us," she says, and hurries from Tel Aviv to the apartment in Jerusalem, bolts the front door, and though she's certain that even a former husband bleeding with love for his first wife will not dare to wriggle down a drainpipe or gutter, she checks the feeble hook on the bathroom window, unplugs the phone and takes a long shower to shed the remains of imaginary reality before huddling in her childhood bed.

She wakes relaxed. The possibility that Uriah may try to come here need not frighten her so long as she maintains the integrity of her boundaries. Even if he still has a key to her parents' apartment, now there is also the bolt, which will compel him to ask permission. What troubles her is Elazar's silence. It was he who enticed her to take part in the hospital series, and even if he didn't get the role of the dead man, he should have at least said goodbye before vanishing. True, she has been stringing him along, but really, a man his age, with a grandson, and an experienced police investigator, ought to know that patience is mandatory, even in the case of a lonely woman who will soon fly away.

How to find a man she knows only by his first name, whom she's met as an extra, in jobs that he or her brother had set up for her? Undaunted, as evening falls she strolls through the Mahane Yehuda market, stops at his favorite restaurant and describes him in detail to the waiters, imitating his stutter a bit, and they recognize the character but don't know his family name or address, only that Elazar was a former police commander, so she should inquire at the police station by the market entrance.

She had always loved this little police station, which still bears the marks of the British Mandate in the form of two stone lions that guard the front door. The years have erased the ferocity in their eyes, which seem now merely to be winking, yet they're a sweet childhood memory. Little Honi was afraid of them, and she would get him to pet their heads and stick his tiny fingers in their jaws to pacify them.

The two bored policewomen inside have never heard of a retired officer by the name of Elazar, nor did Noga's mimicking his stutter awaken their memory. If he's a movie extra, they say, she should watch more Israeli movies and catch him there.

Instead of going straight home, she takes a roundabout route through the most radically ultra-Orthodox neighborhoods—Mea Shearim, Geulah, Kerem Avraham—where she wanders the streets, stopping to read death notices on the walls alongside posters of dire warning and denunciation. When she gets back to Mekor Baruch and Rashi Street, she is shaken. Can it be the "new extra," waiting in reality by her building? But once again it's the old lawyer representing the heirs of the apartment's owner.

"So, Noga," he greets her with fatherly warmth, "by my reckoning, your mother's trial period is over, and we need to know if the right decision has been taken."

"If it has, Mr. Stoller, it's not good for you."

"How could it not be good for me?" The old man winks. "What's good for me is good for her."

"Meaning what?"

"Meaning, listen to reason and get out of a neighborhood that's getting more and more *haredi*."

"My mother, sir, is not afraid. She believes, in fact, that the *haredim* enhance her secularity."

"That's because she only talks to her neighbors the Pomerantzes, a sweet and moderate family. But the Pomerantzes are a dwindling breed, and the extremists are taking their place, people not merely bound by the strictest commandments but who also believe in devils and angels. I've got just such a crazy family interested in your apartment, prepared to pay an excellent price, which will enable us to increase the key money to be refunded to your mother. Therefore you, a rational European musician, must help your brother uproot the delusions about Jerusalem from your mother's mind."

"I can't uproot anything from her mind. She herself will decide what

to uproot and what to plant. Where are the owners of the apartment living now?"

"In Mexico, and they need money."

"So they uprooted not only Jerusalem from their minds, but all of Israel."

"My dear lady, with all due respect, who are you to criticize?"

"But I will come back here, sir. Ultimately there'll be an orchestra in Israel that will need me."

"Yes, yes, I've heard that before. Everyone promises to return, but in the
end they fly back in a coffin."

"I'll come back alive," she shouts, "you'll see, if you live that long."

"Pardon me?"

"Skip it, Mr. Stoller, I'm tired. You'll get your answer from my mother
personally. By then I'll be with my harp, rehearsing the Berlioz *Fantastique*."

"Ah, Hec-tor Ber-lioz . . ." He draws out the name, as if remembering
a childhood friend. "Yes, a wild genius and ladies' man, but what's your
hurry? The harp in *Symphonie Fantastique* enters only in the second movement."

"What," she gasps, "you know his music?"

"His and others' too," he replies with a triumphant smile. "You think
just because I'm an old lawyer who helps clear out old apartments in *haredi*
neighborhoods that I lack culture? Look around here, so benighted and
poor. What's the matter, you don't want your mother to live and die near
your brother?"

"I want that very much."

"So work on it, convince her."

He tips his hat and goes on his way.

She is shocked by the cocky sophistication of an elderly and tattered
lawyer who knows his Berlioz, and watches him fade into the darkness.
She pushes open the little gate, and with the nagging fear that Uriah has
her parents' key, she climbs the stairs cautiously, heavily, as if reprising her
imaginary disability of the previous day.

The apartment is dark, but she is in no hurry to turn on lights, for fear
that in one of the rooms, in one of the beds, lies her former husband.

THIRTY-FIVE

T HOUGH IT WOULD BE POSSIBLE for Uriah to pick out an old key tossed in a drawer, it would never have occurred to him to unlock this apartment, or come near it. When he ran into his former brother-in-law at the opera, he didn't expect, after a long silence, anything more than a brief exchange of empty pleasantries. But after Honi, with the intimacy of a long-lost relative, briefed him about the old folks' home and piqued his curiosity about his former wife's appearance on the stage, Uriah had felt that the chance encounter was significant for him but irrelevant to his present wife, so when she approached, he hurried to end the conversation.

Something had been burned into his mind, something his former brother-in-law apparently intended. And so, after failing to locate on the stage the wife he never got over, he decided to go back to the opera the next night as an infiltrator with binoculars.

And that night, after midnight, when he returned to Ma'aleh Adumim, unsettled by the extra in her embroidered costume leading dark-skinned children at the foot of Masada in a little wagon harnessed to a decorated donkey, he felt that her brother, deliberately or not, had involved him in a pointless but necessary experiment, obligating him to one more move. And since he recognized that if he were to request a simple face-to-face meeting, nothing could be said that hadn't been said many times over, he preferred that the encounter be not real but imaginary. If his former wife had chosen to show up in Israel as an extra in the stories and imaginations of others, why should he not join her as a partner?

It had not required many inquiries with agencies that booked extras. At the first agency he phoned, in Jerusalem, he happened upon a former secretary of his, who was pleased to find him Noga's name among the extras listed for a television series about a hospital.

At the Ashdod port he was not permitted entry to the film location, because his name did not appear on the list of extras. In the belief that he'd find another way in, he wandered around the port, drank beer with longshoremen at a small cafeteria, and they showed him the entrance at the far end of the warehouse. When night fell and the man standing guard left his post, he sneaked inside and began to wander the corridors, recognizing Noga as a disabled woman in a nightgown, transported in a wheelchair. But he was careful not to reveal himself before assuming the role of a new character. After asking directions he arrived at the wardrobe room, where he pretended to be an extra and the staff helped him realize his vision—the torn, filthy uniform of a soldier, which he put on over his own clothes, and for greater effect, a red-stained army bandage wrapped around his forehead. This lost soul went off in search of Noga, and found her in the dining room, but after the meal, as she looked for a bed for the night, he didn't hurry after her, and when she entered a little room and closed its makeshift door, he didn't dare follow her, but stationed himself outside like a watchman, lest some stranger enter before he did. Only after the tumult died down did he allow himself, as a wounded soldier from the battlefield and not as a former husband, to slip into the bed next to hers and again watch over her sleep as he had when they were married. And indeed on that night she had difficulty sleeping. From time to time she sighed and wrestled with the blanket and pillow until she subdued them. And if a pale ivory foot or delicate arm, familiar objects of desire, remained exposed after the struggle, he had to cover them up carefully before giving way to merciful sleep.

But in the dim first light of day, as he first noticed her eyeing him reproachfully, he realized that the character of a wounded soldier did not draw her close; it repelled her. The logical conclusion was that if he wanted to make the most of the experiment her brother had scripted for him, he could do so only by means of his real self.

THIRTY-SIX

NO ONE WAS LURKING in the dark apartment, yet her restored calm was marred by mild disappointment. Did her panicky response in that little hospital room turn him off for good? Is the "ancient bleeding love" merely a presumptuous projection of her mind on his? And if Uriah persists, how will he know his time is limited and in a few days she'll be beyond his reach? Suddenly angry, she wants to phone her brother, but realizes he'll probably make her even dizzier. Thus the best path to relaxation is to make dinner and watch a good film on television.

But her sleep is restless, as in the first days after her arrival, and she divides it among the three beds. In the morning she calls her mother and brightly announces, "I've changed my mind, Ima. I'm not putting any more pressure on you, and even if you decide to return to Jerusalem, don't cut the time short on my account. No reason you should pass up even one good meal you've already paid for, or one hour of deep sleep Tel Aviv provides you. I take it all back, Ima. Let's the three of us honor the experiment till the end. In any event, rehearsals of the Berlioz will start only the day after I get back."

"And Uriah?" the mother remembers. "You're no longer afraid of him?"

"Apparently he's given up. And even if he comes, what could he want? Just to mourn the past."

She no longer bothers with the bolt, and sometimes, when she goes out, she just closes the apartment door without locking it, and evenings she stays home, on the assumption that a man clinging to an old love would prefer to arrive in the dark. So it goes, day after day, as she counts them off before her departure from the city of her birth, dry days with cool nights. From time to time she walks around in the *shuk*, of which she's grown fond on this visit—maybe in hopes of running into Elazar, who three days after his disappearance had stuck a note on her apartment door.

When she saw the sheet of paper from afar, she laughed. Was the bleeding love making do with a piece of paper? But as she held the page, the handwriting was unfamiliar.

Dear Extra,

I haven't risen from the dead, because I wasn't there. The people at the entrance didn't know how to get rid of the eternal extra, so they sent me to a morgue that didn't exist.

Even after I realized that they had tricked us into separating, I didn't give up on you, until I saw you rolling around in a nightgown in a wheelchair, and I thought, Why get in the way of my extra enjoying herself? and I started following you from afar. But then I got an urgent call from a real hospital in Jerusalem: the sick grandson I told you about had been hospitalized and wanted his grandfather. So I rushed over there without saying goodbye, and I've been at his bedside for two days, and when he says, Saba, you mustn't move, his command carries more weight than a police superintendent's. And I'm pleased to say that there are encouraging signs, but for the duration, I'm at his side.

Nevertheless I grabbed a minute and hopped over to say goodbye, because I remembered that in the coming days you'll be flying away. And so, dear Noga, I'm done forever with being an extra. The fictions we enjoyed together were my swan song. And even if they build a morgue at the port, I'll not be there. So when you go back to playing your harp in Europe, think well of the eternal extra of the past, who sometimes got stuck when he spoke, but his thoughts were clear and pure. All I wanted from you was friendship, and am grateful that I received it.

She is pleasantly surprised by the candid and fluent text, free of hesitations or erasures. And yet she wonders, clenching her fists: How will I slake the old desire that arose in Jerusalem? Is there really nothing left for me but to wait for the flutist who betrayed my concerto?

And at night, in her disappointment, she again wanders from bed to bed until, as in her high school years, she satisfies her desire in the bed of her youth.

Morning light bathes the big kitchen of her parents' apartment, where, still drowsy, she sits in a nightgown, slowly eating a soft-boiled egg, half listening to a concert on the classical station of Israel Radio, when Uriah arrives, shaved and combed, in jacket and tie. "I was on my way to work," he explains with disarming nonchalance, "and I thought, why not say hello to her before she vanishes again."

And as if he had never pretended to be an extra in a torn army uniform, his head in a bloody bandage, or hadn't silently crept into the adjacent bed at midnight, he now stands smiling and serene, no embarrassment or apology, surveying the apartment he knows well from the years of his marriage, struck by how shrunken it seems.

"Not shrunken," she replies, calm. "Honi threw out some old pieces of furniture, so Ima wouldn't long for them in Tel Aviv at th-the—"

"The old folks' home," he says, rescuing his ex-wife from the stammer that suddenly seizes her. Not looking at her directly, and careful not to touch a thing, he is mesmerized by the apartment, drawn into the living room and bedrooms as if he were a buyer or broker and not a man come to mourn his humiliation. But Noga knows well that despite the confident façade, the jacket and tie, the briefcase that hasn't budged from his hand, despite "on my way to work," he is agitated by the uncontrollable adventure he has just plunged into.

"Yes, the old folks' home," he says, almost defiantly, as if it were the source of evil. "And for the life of me, Noga"—he is still careful not to focus his gaze—"I can't understand why your brother, in such a quick, random encounter next to the toilets, after years of absolutely no contact, had to involve me in your mother's old folks' home and the question of yes or no. Obviously, it's no."

"Meaning?"

"That she won't leave Jerusalem."

At last he looks straight at her, and a beloved face sets her heart pounding.

"And maybe she'll want to surprise you too?" She smiles.

"Me? What have I got to do with this?"

"Well, you're here."

"And all his small talk about the old folks' home was just a pretext, so he could tell me you were here in Israel."

"Why a pretext?" she says, defending her brother. "No pretext, just a simple explanation so you'd understand why your ex-wife appeared as an extra on the opera stage, and not be shocked when you saw her there."

Uriah considers this.

"But why did he need to call attention to your performance?"

"He didn't need to, no," she confirms. "It was a big pointless mistake. Honi shouldn't have mentioned my existence. Better he should have talked about the music, asked you whether or not you enjoyed act one."

He senses the irony that has evolved over many years of separation, and concedes:

"I saw no trace of you in act two."

"But I was there!" She raises her voice. "At first I was a smuggler and even carried a sack, and ended up with the chorus at the bullfight."

"And I wasn't sure if Honi was just pulling my leg."

"No, Uriah," she says, still defending her brother, "Honi wouldn't pull your leg. Not a chance. He loves you. You know how he mourned over you and got angry with me when you were compelled to leave me."

"Yes, I assumed he was serious, and so the next night I came back, because I still wanted to see you on the stage."

"What? You came back to the opera at Masada?"

"But not in the audience. I sneaked onto the stage."

"The stage? No way. Sneaked in from which side?"

"From the north, Noga, the north. I circled around the orchestra and got close to your little hill and followed one of your Bedouin kids with binoculars . . ."

"Mine?" She laughs. "How so?"

"In the cart pulled by your donkey."

"Again mine."

"Lucky kids. And what kind of extra were you, anyway? A Gypsy woman?"

"Gypsy woman smuggler in act two, but with the children and donkey I was just a simple country girl."

"And you really did look young, younger than I remembered you."

"Too bad you didn't come out on the stage. They would've found a part for you too."

He stares at her coldly.

"The conductor spotted me and got security men to remove me."

"And then?"

"I went home."

"But why? If you came without your wife, you could have waited for me and said hello."

"Why? I had more than enough of you in my life, so why look for you at intermission? I also told myself that maybe a story that wasn't ours but someone else's was my chance to understand what was still blocked. In fact, when I saw them wheeling you around in your nightgown with an IV dangling over your head, I felt what I didn't dare to feel all those years I was with you—that you, Noga, are essentially a crippled person. You have a defect, and so there's no point blaming you or being angry with you. Even when you're playing music and apparently acting normal, the sickness is nesting deep inside you. And so the question remains: why, after my decision to let go of you forever, do I come back to you again, in your childhood apartment?"

"I don't get it either. But if you can let go of your briefcase for a second and dare to sit down, together we might discover something new."

THIRTY-SEVEN

GLUM, SERIOUS URIAH SITS down in the kitchen, placing his brief-case on the table amid plates and cutlery, perhaps preparing for a quick getaway.

"If you take the briefcase off the table," says his former wife, "I'll make sure it doesn't run away."

"I keep it in full view not to forget that a whole world awaits me out there, and to remember not to be swept away by you."

"Nevertheless, it's not nice of your black briefcase to scare my soft-boiled egg."

"Soft-boiled egg? I don't remember your liking your eggs soft."

"Oh, how good that someone in the world remembers things about me that I've forgotten. Yes, I hated soft-boiled eggs. Ima didn't have the patience to keep boiling them, and the liquid yolk was like saliva. But now, on my own, I make up for her sins, and when I time it right, the egg tastes wonderful, and when the spoon taps the shell, even the chicken that laid it is happy."

Scowling, he studies the woman in the nightgown.

"I didn't learn of your father's death until I ran into Honi at Masada. But even had I known in time, I doubt I'd have come to the funeral, or even the shiva."

"Why?"

"Because I wouldn't have wanted to see you."

"But you and my father were close. I only just learned from Ima that you brought your kids to meet him, to prove that you're innocent of blame."

"That's correct."

"But who thought you were to blame?"

"Whoever."

"And now you understand that I'm also not to blame. I just have some kind of mental defect."

"True."

"And if you had understood a year or two ago that because of a psychological defect I'm not to blame, would you still have taken your children to my father to prove your innocence?"

"Yes, because the boundary between defect and guilt is not always clear."

"Would you have taken them even if you knew it caused him pain?"

"It didn't cause him pain. He was happy and he played with them."

"The fact that he played doesn't mean it didn't also cause him pain. He played with them because he couldn't kill them."

"Why kill?"

"So you wouldn't bring them again."

"I wouldn't have brought them again."

"Maybe you would have enjoyed another chance to taunt my parents. By the way, how did my father play with them?"

"He found an old doll of yours and put on a funny little show."

"And you told your wife you brought her children here?"

"I don't hide anything from her."

"You won't hide this visit either?"

"Not this visit either. The second trip to Masada, the wounded soldier at the port, all will be told when the time comes."

"When will that time come?"

"You'll know when it comes."

"Ima caught a glimpse of your wife during intermission at Masada and told Honi she looks like me."

"She doesn't look like you."

"Or reminded her of me."

"She doesn't remind."

"What's her name, by the way?"

"Osnat."

"My mother saw her at intermission, waiting for the restrooms, and not knowing she was your wife, just from a casual glance, she told Honi that she looked like me."

"She doesn't look like you."

"But my mother wouldn't just make that up. She's a smart, practical woman, and she also gave birth to me and knows me. And of her own free will she stated that your wife looks like me."

"She doesn't."

"Maybe there's something similar that you don't notice?"

"She doesn't resemble you in any way."

"You sure?"

"Absolutely. If she resembled you, why would I be here?"

"Because you still love me, even though you're the one who broke off the marriage, not I."

"True . . ."

"In which case, why exactly are you here?"

"My love is playing tricks on me."

"Who is your love? A separate entity from you?"

"Yes, a separate entity. Who tags along even after the separation from you."

"A love with chutzpah."

"Yes, separate and rebellious and cannot be tamed."

"I might tame her, take her by surprise."

"How?"

"I have a whip. I bought one in the Old City to use on the *haredi* kids who were breaking in here, but in the end I was afraid to do it. But this disobedient love of yours deserves to be whipped. Wait, Uriah, you'll see."

She dumps the remains of the egg in the garbage, puts the dirty dishes in the sink and goes to the bathroom to wash her face and put on makeup along with the appropriate smile, which she checks in the mirror. But she keeps on the nightgown that thinly veils her nakedness. She wonders where she left the whip, then remembers, but when she comes back with it in hand she finds Uriah standing sadly by the apartment door, holding his briefcase, ready to leave.

"Here," she says, putting the whip in his hand. "An old whip, a real one, which over the years beat many a camel in the desert, will now whip your love until it lets go of you."

Astonished, Uriah holds the whip. He then snaps it spontaneously to see how far it extends.

"You're insane," he declares with satisfaction, "and it's madness that needs whipping, not love." He whips the big sofa, the two armchairs, even the television, which trembles under the blow. Then he gives her back the whip and says, "That's it, Noga, enough. Everything is imaginary and absurd except for work, which I'm late for."

And as much as she feared he would come, it hurts her now that he's leaving, for this time it will be forever. When her brother asked her to join the experiment, she never imagined he would also bring in her former husband, yet now she is trying to delay him.

"Wait, Uriah. Before we say goodbye, just tell me what your job is now."

"Same job."

"Meaning?"

"At the Ministry of Environmental Protection."

"How great you're still there. I was so proud that you worked in a field that had value. Even in Holland I tell friends and colleagues that the man who left me is not only a stubborn person but a positive person."

"Please . . ."

"That's what I thought and that's what I think. That's why my love for you never fully died. Tell me, have you stayed in the same department, where you were a deputy? You haven't been promoted?"

"Now I am the director of a department."

"A department. How many people?"

"Twenty."

"A small department, but undoubtedly important."

"A department that deals with garbage, recycling, packaging . . ."

"And that's the most ethical part," she gushes. "Really important. It's the future. If only I could recycle myself."

"Too late," he quietly hisses. "The rot has proliferated."

"So why don't you let go?"

"Because I feel the pain of the unborn child."

"Then wait, and we'll make another effort to understand. If you're the head of a department, nobody will punish you for being late. Don't go. Let's talk a little longer, then you'll go . . . Just a second, somebody or something is standing outside the door. Please don't leave now."

THIRTY-EIGHT

"Y ES, THERE'S KNOCKING at the door. You expecting someone?"

"No. I wasn't expecting you either. Maybe it's your wife, coming to show me the kids."

"Don't talk that way."

"But my father—"

"Your father had the right," he interrupts angrily. "You don't."

Standing at the doorway is a Hasid, dressed in black with a broad-brimmed hat, his beard and sidelocks soft and flaxen, beautiful emerald eyes shining through the thicket of hair. With a gentle smile he proffers a glass bowl piled with fruit and says, "A little something from my mother and father to your mother. They should all live and be well."

Behind him hides a child, he too wearing black and a hat, a schoolbag on his back, his head bowed but his eyes alert.

"Yuda-Zvi!" she happily exclaims. "Here you are again."

And now she recognizes Shaya, the handsome son of the Pomerantz family, who in their youth would sometimes chat with her on the stairs with no barrier between them, in complete freedom, before he was dispatched to a distant yeshiva.

"And you too, Shaya," she adds excitedly, her face burning. "I've been living here for three months, and I even had a strange sort of romance with your clever son. But you, where are you these days?"

"I'm not far from here," he explains graciously, "on Ovadiah Street in Kerem Avraham, but during the week I teach up north near Safed, which is why we haven't run into each other."

"A shame, because your Yuda-Zvi would drop in here freely via the gutters and down the drainpipe, and bring along a mixed-up little *tzaddik*. By the way, where is he?"

Shaya smiles. "The *tzaddik*, as you call him, Shraga, he should live and be well, was sent away to Safed, to a family with the patience and heart for children like him. But here is Yuda-Zvi, coming to you to ask forgiveness, because we know what he has done. Right, Yuda-Zvi?"

"Right," the boy confesses in a whisper.

"And the fruit is for your mother, lovely fruit from the Galilee, the vineyards and orchards of Mount Canaan. Your mother phoned my father yesterday to tell him she was returning to the neighborhood, and we wished to congratulate her on her decision and give her our blessing."

"Of all of us, it was your father she told first," she murmurs, astonished.

"Maybe it was easier for her that way."

Insulted, she does not take the fruit from him, motioning for his son to come to her. The boy hesitates, looks pleadingly at his father, who nudges him forward. She clasps the child to her bosom, stares him in the eye and says, "Now do you understand that because of stupid television, you and your little *tzaddik* could have crashed to the ground?" Yuda-Zvi nods, and she strokes his sidelocks, straightens his hat, lightly kisses his forehead and eyes and returns him to his father, who watches with a smile and sways back and forth with immense devotion.

Only then does she take the fruit bowl from Shaya, placing it on top of the TV and indicating Uriah, who still stands with briefcase in hand. "Maybe you recognize him," she says. "This is Uriah, my former husband, who is on his way to work." Uriah, red with embarrassment, extends his hand, but when she extends hers too, Shaya quickly drops his hand and moves it to the doorframe, covering the mezuzah as if to keep it warm, until he and the boy depart.

THIRTY-NINE

"YOUR CHILDHOOD LOVE was unwilling to shake your hand."

"Because I was wearing a nightgown."

"Even if you were wearing a fur coat there would have been no handshake from him."

"What does he matter? You're still here."

"You just announced I'm on my way to work."

"No, today the work will be done here. We'll seat your love, that stubborn entity, between us, and together we'll set you free."

She goes into her room, puts on one of her mother's bathrobes over her nightgown, and on her way back to the kitchen she picks up the glass bowl, rimmed with a gold decoration, apparently part of a set. The fruit is unblemished and ripe—plums and apples, grapes and cherries, pears and peaches. She places the bowl between her and her former husband, and the indignity resurfaces.

"It's pretty annoying and insulting that a neighbor, a *haredi* yet, is the first to know about my mother's decision to come back to Jerusalem, and also suspicious that this man is so quick to send her a bowl of fruit."

"Maybe it's his wife."

"No, it's him, because his wife—I learned this from the grandson—is so ill she doesn't know who she is. It's him. But why? Why does he care whether Ima comes back here or not?"

"Why shouldn't he care?" says Uriah. "When I was surprised that your parents had stayed in the neighborhood, you used to claim, perhaps half seriously, that there are religious people who enhance and sweeten their neighbors' secular way of life. Maybe also the opposite is true—your mother's secular life sweetens his religiosity. When you played your harp on Shabbat, he would get all excited and prophesy that you would play in the Holy Temple."

"Fine, there's something to that. Now there's an old lawyer lurking in the neighborhood just waiting to sell the apartment to an extremist *haredi* family, and those people are specialists in making life miserable for the Orthodox who are less ultra than they are."

She sets down two small plates and on each puts cherries and grapes, a pear and a peach, along with two small knives, and says, "This, Uriah, is so we'll have the strength to work."

He looks around with mild disbelief, takes a knife and peels the pear, hesitates a moment, then reaches over without asking permission and peels her pear as well, but when he tries to peel the peach, the juice sprays all over.

"Careful, you'll stain your nice jacket. Take it off, and your tie too. You were always good at staining yourself. Anyway, what's with the tie?"

He finds this amusing, as if his ex-wife were an actress playing the wife he once had. And like a soldier who has been given a sensible order, he takes off his jacket and tie, undoes the top button of his shirt, sits down and goes back to peeling the peach.

"Strange," he says, "how the ultra-Orthodox from poor neighborhoods in Jerusalem end up in the Galilee."

"Why not? After the government built them yeshivas all over the country, they turned themselves into teachers and were in great demand."

He nods his agreement with the woman who has long since left her homeland, then eats a few grapes and a few cherries, not putting the pits on the plate but getting up and tossing them in the trash under the sink, then rinsing his hands.

"Strange"—he has grown attached to the word—"how nothing here has changed. Even the same trash can from when we were married."

"Exactly the same. But if you hadn't left me, you'd have managed to persuade my parents to buy a different trash can, one more in line with your ideology."

"No doubt. I had a very good relationship with them both."

"More than good. They really loved you. Honi especially."

"And I loved this old apartment, not just because it was your childhood home, but for itself. This is where we slept together the first time."

"And do you remember what you said afterward?"

"What?"

"'I hope we won't have a baby from this.'"

"That's what I said?"

"Yes, and that makes sense. We were so young, why be parents so soon?"

"True."

"You don't remember how I responded?"

"How did you respond?"

"'Don't worry, Uriah, we won't have a child just like that.'"

"Even then?"

"Even then I could feel the controlling nature of your love. Only you didn't want to hear the warning, and your love wasted time on me, which is why your kids are now in elementary school and not high school."

"I don't remember what you said."

"Maybe you thought it was just talk. But I don't just talk."

"Not you."

"And if you're hoping that our work today also includes making love, I'm sorry to disappoint you."

"Why?"

"Because I won't let you or me hurt your wife, even though I don't know her and you insist she doesn't resemble me in any way."

"In any way."

"But she is important to me, because I made a sacrifice for her. After you forced yourself to leave me, I knew that the heart that was still bound to me would not be able to connect with another woman. And so, although I could have waited and hoped for a position as a harpist in some Israeli orchestra, I hurried to accept the Dutch offer and disappear from your horizon, so you'd be free to heal with a new relationship. So don't think that we can repeat the past, even if I have the urge and capacity to do so."

He gets up sullenly, walks into the living room, picks up the whip from the sofa, holds it close to his face, smells it, then winds it up and places it on the television. He goes into the bedroom to look at the double bed, and is startled to discover the elevated hospital bed, plugged into the wall socket.

"What's this? Where'd it come from?"

"After my father died, my mother wanted to replace their worn-out double bed with a new single bed, but a young engineer, who took over for my father at the municipality, offered her an old hospital bed that he upgraded himself with a clever electrical system. If you want, you can try it."

"Are you crazy?"

"Why not? Back then you insisted we sleep together in my parents' double bed, not in mine."

"Because your bed was narrow, the bed of a teenager, and it was important to both of us to have a space that would calm our fear and confusion. So we made love in your parents' bed. They were abroad at the time, as I recall."

"In Greece."

"Far enough so they wouldn't surprise us."

"I wasn't afraid of being surprised, but of violating my parents' intimacy. I washed and ironed the sheets, but two spots of my blood managed to stain the mattress, and I couldn't get rid of them, so I had to flip the mattress over."

"And let's assume that your parents, without knowing it, had sex on the proof of their daughter's virginity — maybe that was nice for them, unconsciously I mean."

"So now you're getting into my parents' unconscious."

"By logical deduction. I, for example, wouldn't care if I slept on a mattress where, unbeknownst to me, were buried signs of my daughter's virginity."

"How old is she now?"

"Six."

"Then you have time."

"I hope. Anyway, if even in the beginning you had your doubts about having children, I, as a young man, swept away by love, might have interpreted your hesitation as a teenager's fleeting radical protest against the state or against the world."

"The state?"

"In the hackneyed sense that if Israel was going downhill, better not to have children here."

"I never said that and never thought that. And even if I was sometimes too radical for your taste, I could have given birth to radical children who would aid and abet my radicalism."

"In other words, the future here is not secure, is full of danger."

"No." She raises her voice. "Who am I to presume to know what will be here in the future? Who am I to decide if the danger is real or exists only in newspaper articles? My parents conceived me during a terrible, shocking war, and still the two of them didn't presume to know. Oy, Uriah, you won't get free of a disobedient love if you keep rehashing old stuff."

He smiles, and she knows, as in times gone by, that tough talk on her part doesn't deter him; it makes him want her more. He cautiously leans over the bed and tugs one of its levers, listens to the buzzing motor, watches the pillows rise. Then he turns to her and gently says:

"Then there's no point in discussing your music."

"Of course not."

"Still . . . it's very important to you."

"In the right proportion. But there's nothing about music that precludes having children."

"So I shouldn't even try to complain again about your harp."

"No. It makes me angry."

"Why?"

"Because there's no truth to it. We talked about the harp so many times, one could write a book about it. I never saw myself as a tormented artist whose life is enslaved to her art. Bach had twenty children, and that didn't prevent him from writing a new cantata every day. In my case all the more so, because I don't write music but just perform it."

"Bach didn't give birth to them or nurse them or take care of them. His wife did that."

"You're being clever to escape."

"From what?"

"From the slavery your love wanted to impose on me."

"On you or on me?"

"No difference. To enslave me, you wanted to be enslaved to me."

"But you could always have gotten free."

"Only so long as we didn't have children."

"Why? If you wanted, children or no children, you could have gotten free of me."

"No. Because in your anger and humiliation the children would have become hostages, and you would have harmed them."

"Harmed them? But they're my kids too."

"As revenge because I abandoned you . . . I took pity on them by not giving birth to them."

"But what could I have done to them?"

"Medea slew her children as revenge on the husband who abandoned her."

"That's mythology. What could I have done?"

"Maybe thrown one of them from the roof, and yourself too."

"I can't believe that such a thought ever occurred to you."

"From the moment you began to call me Venus and not Noga, even as a joke, I understood what a dangerous place your love had reached."

"Didn't you tell me that your father always told you to look in the sky for the planet that belonged to you?"

"But who asked you to follow in his footsteps? No, I didn't want to be Venus, not for you or for anyone. I was born in this apartment with neighbors around me for whom the only myth is simple, old-time religion. I wasn't named Noga after a planet in the sky, but for a grandmother who died a long time ago. And I chose the harp not because I wanted to play in the Temple, but because not many people play it, so I knew I wouldn't have much competition. But a young woman from a modest home and neighborhood, a pretty woman but certainly not beautiful, a reasonable and rational woman but not unusually talented, turned for you into a figure of adoration, a religion."

"Religion?"

"Your own private one."

"And in this religion there is no room for children?"

"They are in danger."

He gives up, shaken and perhaps gratified by the blow she landed on him. He points to the electric bed, its sheets tangled, and asks almost in a whisper whether in the months she has lived here by herself this has been her bed.

"Not the only one. At night I wander from bed to bed."

"And last night?"

"Last night I slept in this one too."

"Will it bother you if I lie in it a bit?"

"But a minute ago, when I suggested you try it, you asked if I was crazy."

"I was wrong, Noga, I was wrong."

And he takes off his shoes and lies on the bed on his back, fiddling with the levers until he finds a comfortable position, tucks his fists under his graying head and closes his eyes, his arms like a pair of wings spread on either side.

FORTY

D OES HE INTEND to fall asleep now? she asks herself, moving a chair to the head of the bed. So as not to spoil the odd serenity that has come over her guest, she speaks in a low voice, but precisely, as if playing a musical score. A mere four days now separate her and her orchestra, and the desire to clasp the harp to her heart is so strong it hurts.

"After all, we kept reexamining ourselves. When your mother was still alive, we ended up discussing it frankly with your parents. A confused and fruitless conversation. Because how could your parents express understanding for what I did if I had a hard time explaining it to myself? And because of their anger and pain, you sprang to my defense, you were afraid your parents would start hating me. But they didn't, not only because it's hard to hate me, and not only because they already had three grandchildren from your sister, but because they couldn't imagine you leaving me, and in order not to poison your marriage, they decided from the outset not to hate me."

She presses the point. "Why didn't they believe you were capable of leaving me? Maybe because your parents, whose marriage was full of bumps and bickering, grasped the big difference between them and their son—your ability to love passionately, a love that to this day can't die and simmers between us, amazingly enough, even at this very moment."

"Yes," he mutters, his eyes still closed, "which is why I overcame my indecision and came here."

"You vacillated but you came. And even if we've analyzed our separation so many times that not one but two books could be written on the subject, nevertheless, after years of no contact, after you've remarried and had children, you go searching for me in the desert and sneak in as an extra in the uniform of a wounded soldier. So we need to clarify if this is just stubborn love or something else."

"It's something else."

"Yes, so perhaps today it'll be something else, something new. But you should know that if you surprised yourself when you came here, you didn't surprise me. I waited for you. My mother can testify that I told her I knew you wouldn't be content with playing the wounded extra, that you'd have the nerve to come to this apartment, that you might still have a key. I do know you. But even if you hadn't dared to come here this morning as yourself, you should know that in my mind I am still in conversation with you. And I have thoughts that haven't yet been expressed."

"Those two books notwithstanding."

"There may be the need for a third, a thin one, like a book of poetry. In Europe, when I thought of you—at rehearsals, or at concerts, since there are works with long stretches where the harpist has nothing to do except sit on her hands and count the measures while other players were making music—your image would suddenly surface, and I would reconstruct you in my mind, or recycle you, if that word better fits your ideology."

"Both words fit."

"And I'd be drawn back to the beginning. That party in Rehavia, how you insisted on walking me home through the Valley of the Cross, and at midnight, near the monastery, the way you kissed me. That wasn't the first time I kissed a man, and certainly not the first time you kissed a woman, but you managed to make it momentous, because the next day, after my classes at the academy—which in those days, you remember, was near the prime minister's house—without our having made plans, and I hadn't mentioned my class schedule—you, in your army uniform, waited for me on your motorcycle with an extra helmet—"

"They had just passed the helmet law—"

"Of course, the law. And later on, during the intense courtship, you quickly learned not only my class schedule but also the times of the private piano and recorder lessons I gave around town, the addresses and the names of the children. Little by little you collected the names of my friends, male and female, and my relatives, and you tried to become friendly with them.

Not to mention my parents, and especially my brother, who truly fell in love with you. After all, you're talented, with a quick mind, and when you make the effort, you're not devoid of humor. From the beginning I felt you were destined for greatness. Don't be offended, but when you told me you were now head of a department, I felt a twinge of disappointment that you were not head of the whole thing. If it were up to me, I'd have appointed you long ago."

"With total objectivity."

"Total. From the minute we began our courtship you proved yourself, to me at least, to be a smart and efficient manager of transportation and errands and shopping, including active participation in clothes shopping, and dispensing advice at every opportunity on what to wear and what not to wear. And so your love was enthralling, but it began to tie me down. Not your occasional jealousy, which was only natural — mine too — because without it, love life isn't genuine. But you, with warmth and tenderness, began to swallow me."

"Swallow?"

"Siphon me inside of you."

"Sounds even worse."

He moves the levers and the bed slowly rises, tilts him to the side and sets him on his feet. With a troubled look he leaves the room and wanders through the apartment as if seeking refuge. Finally he brings a chair from the kitchen, sits down facing her and mutters, "This book ... the third one ... the thin one ... is indeed turning into poetry, less and less understandable."

"Be patient," she says softly, "and it will become accessible, especially to a man as intelligent as you. Even before we got married, when we lived in Jerusalem, in the apartment near the museum, and you were on your pre-discharge leave from the army, you said I came to you spoiled or lazy, from a home that was too loving, and for this dubious reason you cheerfully took upon yourself most of the chores — cooking, paying bills, cleaning, shopping — so I would be free for music, studies, private lessons and of course performances. I sometimes think that the seed of failure was planted during that period, when you had plenty of time to learn about your lover mentally and physically, not only so you'd know how to live with her day to day, but to gently appropriate her into yourself."

"Appropriate—another annoying word."

"Is there a word that won't annoy you? Assimilate? Internalize. There, a moderate word that won't annoy you. You tried to internalize me, and that way I wouldn't be a burden on you. I would enrich you."

"Not internalize or assimilate." He gets up and begins pacing around the room. "Precisely the opposite. I was only trying to protect you."

"Protect me?"

"Look, Noga, just as I sometimes surface between the notes when you're listening to other musicians play, in long and boring meetings you sometimes poke through the tedious talk of other people, and despite the fact that I have my beloved wife and children, to whom I am devoted with all my heart, I, like you, reconstruct you sometimes in my mind. And even when I reaffirm for myself, over and over, my decision to leave you, it's natural that I'm occasionally curious about what's happening, and if the harp is still alive."

"The harp?"

"Yes, the harp."

"The harp is alive and playing."

"Because once I came to understand that this instrument was not a compromise, not a steppingstone to another instrument, but an expression of your inner essence, possibly meant to fulfill a mission that you believe was given to you—"

"That's surprising, Uriah, that's a new one—"

"See, I can also contribute something original to the thin book. The minute you told me, Noga, that your instrument was the harp, it added to your charm, but I was also worried about the harp—I mean about you—I mean me. In other words, the question arose, how to integrate the harp into my life. Because from that very first kiss I knew the die was cast and I wouldn't let you go until you became not just my lover but my wife, and so the harp would need to be included in that love and commitment."

"Naturally. And I must admit that regarding the harp, you proved to be a partner and honored your commitment."

"On the outside, Noga, so as not to hurt or demoralize you. It was out of my love and devotion. Because, to be perfectly honest, I didn't believe in the harp, nor did the sound do much for me. I also didn't think—you'll forgive me—that you had a special talent for it. All this, and also the trouble caused by its shape and weight. I always had to be ready to move it from place to place, even a few centimeters. And add to that the hassle of the big old unpleasant car we needed for it. And how bored I got when I had to go with you to far-off places, to all kinds of ceremonies at out-of-the-way schools or community centers, dozens of kilometers round trip to play for ten minutes for a pitiful fee, just so you wouldn't lose faith in yourself and would feel like an artist in demand."

"That's the new contribution to the thin book?"

"That's just the beginning."

"Everything you've said up till now seems trivial coming from a man who claimed I was his heart and soul."

"Trivial and easy for a devoted lover like me, whose love added power to his muscles when he had to carry the harp up and down the thirty-two steps of our apartment in Jerusalem, before we moved to Tel Aviv and found the noisy flat on the ground floor."

"But on the ground floor it was much easier, because we could move it from there in its harp cart."

"Only relatively so, compared to our place in Jerusalem. Even when the harp would roll in its cart straight from the apartment, I always thought that if it were a baby, it would be easier and nicer for me."

"Maybe, but at least my harp didn't cry at night."

"Is that a joke?"

"Your new and original idea has now become stupid."

"Be patient," he says, softly repeating her words, "and it will become accessible to a person as intelligent as you. And so, after you were rejected by every Israeli orchestra you applied to, I didn't want you to lose self-confidence, so I didn't criticize. But I was bitter inside and even angry that you had picked an unconventional instrument, heavy and clumsy and lonesome and unwanted in many works of music. An ancient instrument, religious, ritualistic, even mythological, which you were maybe attracted to because of the Orthodox people who lived around you in your child-hood."

"The Orthodox around me didn't play any instruments."

"Precisely. And so you decided to play instead of them, or for them, with a type of instrument that fits their tradition and maybe also their dreams."

"Oh, Uriah." She laughs. "That's not only new, it's ridiculous. I can't believe a thought like that ever entered your head."

"Wait, wait." He touches her lightly to hold her attention. "You asked me to write in the thin third book, so be prepared, as in poetry, to expose the truth concealed in absurdity. After all these years we've been apart, I see you still have that sweet, fragile, delicate, girlish quality that stole my heart from the minute I met you. And though your hands have grown stronger and your fingers are flexible from playing, I still ask myself how you manage on your own, in a foreign country, with your heavy and cumbersome instrument."

"It became less heavy and cumbersome after I separated from you. And you, even if you wheeled it and lifted it, and even if eventually you understood how to tune it, don't think you knew all about it."

"Not about *it*, about *you*, because from the first moment you were my musical instrument. So now when I remember that Hasid who didn't mind that you played on Shabbat because he hoped you would someday play in the Temple, a story you told me over and over—"

"Yes, I admit it, I sometimes repeat myself, but that's how I hold on to a childhood that was good and happy, as opposed to your gloomy child-hood."

"Forget my childhood now and listen. Your story is not just another charming childhood tale to remember fondly, but a story with a meaning that I always sensed without being able to put my finger on it, until I saw your excitement just now when your childhood sweetheart brought you a little boy and some fruit. This was the one you talked to on the stairs, hour after hour, in total freedom and openness."

"And if I was once in love with a gentle boy who was open to the world, whose face was still bare and smooth—"

"So perhaps it was for him that you decided to devote yourself to an ancient and ritualistic instrument his father couldn't give him."

"For him?" She laughs. "After such a long separation you've come up with a new jealousy? And by the way, since you insist on going back to my old story, why leave out its bizarre ending?"

"What ending?"

"His father told me that to play in the Temple, the girl would have to turn into a handsome lad."

"No, Noga, I couldn't forget the ending of that story, which you also clung to. But what I'm asking now is whether you sometimes toy with the possibility of turning into a handsome lad?"

"Why would I?"

"So as not to give birth to a child."

"No. Absolutely not. Though I didn't want a child forced on me, I wanted a child born out of the thought and will and agreement of its two parents."

"And that's why you secretly aborted the child that came by accident."

"Secretly, because I didn't want to hurt you."

"But that hurt me more."

"Because you were looking for pain and insult. And for many long months after you learned about the abortion, you decided to punish me and yourself and deny your sexual desire. But you didn't succeed in denying it, just in poisoning it, and when you got tired of denial it was too late. Your poison also poisoned my desire."

"I poisoned it because I was never able to get a simple admission from you: 'Yes, I am guilty.' You, Noga, could be the foreman of any jury and cast blame on anybody else with complete confidence, but you always exonerate yourself."

"Jury?" she exclaims with amazement. "Wait, where'd you get that idea? Your deep attachment to me scares me sometimes. Listen, Uriah, if you don't want to destroy your love, then go to work and take it with you, but don't try to destroy me on its account."

FORTY-ONE

S TARTLED BY THE LAST WORDS she blurted out, knowing from experience that he will be hurt and defensive, she looks with suddenly rediscovered compassion for a way to retract them. But Uriah turns abruptly away, quickly puts on his shoes and with a grim expression goes to get his jacket from the kitchen chair, shakes it out and puts it on, takes his necktie and goes to her old, familiar clothes closet and opens it, seeking a mirror.

She follows him.

"No," she says gently, "you don't need the tie."

He looks at her coldly.

"Listen to me, it's for your own good. Ties never looked right on you. They make you look uptight and bossy, especially now that your hair is turning gray."

"Tell me," he says as he fumbles with the knot, "why is that any of your business?"

"Why not?"

"Why not? Why not?" He imitates her mockingly. "Maybe why yes."

"It's only natural."

"How I look? My look is no concern of yours. I don't need your indulgence or anything else from you."

He yanks apart the tangled tie and starts over.

"Listen to me. There's a problem with that tie in particular. I saw it the minute you walked in. Not only does it not suit you in principle, but the color clashes with your shirt."

"The color is fine."

"Yes, but not for you, which is why I always had to help you. Can't be that your wife didn't also see this tie doesn't match, unless she was busy with the kids."

His hands freeze. The tie dangles on his shirt.

"Don't talk about her, it drives me crazy."

"Don't go crazy. You didn't come here to go crazy, but maybe to reconcile. And I'll help you reconcile and take my share of blame. But please, lose the tie."

Suddenly he surrenders, as she knew he would, pulls the tie from his neck and stuffs it in his pocket, but she pulls it out. "No," she says, "let me fold it properly."

And she straightens and folds it, hands it back to him.

He rejects her extended hand. "No, you keep it. So something tangible will remain and not just an imaginary book of poetry, and if somebody here turns into a handsome lad after all, why not have a tie handy?"

A smile crosses her lips, and for the first time she has an urge to touch him. "Just a second, before you disappear," she says, blocking his way to the door. "Since you brought up the story you'd patiently listened to countless times—now is your chance to take a look at the protagonist, the childhood harp that started my passion for playing."

"That harp? The little one? The old one?"

"I thought my father got rid of it years ago, but it turned out he stashed it in storage, and Honi and Ima, who found it when they were clearing out the apartment, thought this poor old harp might be just the thing to comfort me while I was far away from my orchestra."

"And did it comfort you?"

"How could it?"

"Then why look at it?"

"You don't have to, but since you talked about it, and you've never seen it, here's your chance."

"My chance?" He turns red with insult. "For this childhood harp I've made a fool of myself running after you? No, I'm here only to mourn my child that you aborted in secret." He shoves her violently out of his way, opens the door and disappears down the stairs.

FORTY-TWO

Now, WITH THE DOOR closed after him, pain and disappointment are all that remain. Noga hurriedly removes the old bathrobe and the nightgown and takes a long shower, then phones the assisted living facility with news of the fruit offering in honor of her mother's return to Jerusalem.

"Fruit?"

"From Mount Canaan."

"Who brought it, Pomerantz himself or one of the grandchildren?"

"Shaya, who refused to shake my hand."

"Why should he shake your hand? He was in love with you, but marrying him was the furthest thing from your mind."

"Still, I was insulted. We were good friends."

"Only on the stairs, so why be insulted?"

"True, no point in being insulted by him, but I can be insulted by a mother who informs a stranger about a decision that her two children are eagerly awaiting."

"Honestly, Noga, were you really awaiting my decision after you claimed that you know better than I do what goes on in my mind?"

"Nevertheless, there's a family protocol that must be observed."

"You're right. But since I couldn't surprise you by the decision, I decided at least to surprise you with the way I announced it."

"And you succeeded. And Honi?"

"He'll hear it from me this evening, nor will he be surprised. The assisted living was an experiment, the three of us committed ourselves to three months, and we stood honorably by our commitment."

"Given no choice."

"You should eat the fruit so it won't spoil."

"We already ate some."

"You've started referring to yourself in Jerusalem by the royal 'we'?"

"Not quite. Uriah actually showed up, and I served him some of your fruit."

"Unbelievable."

"Believe it."

"And this time he appeared as himself?"

"As himself."

"So this time, at least, he didn't want to scare you."

"Not even as a wounded man did he want to scare me. He wanted sympathy."

"And as himself?"

"As himself, after all these years, he still mourns for the child we didn't have."

"But he has children of his own. I saw them, hugged them."

"Still, he won't give up on the child I didn't give him."

"And on you?"

"Not anymore. It's the child, not me."

"So listen to me, Noga. Listen to what a wise woman has to say to a beloved daughter, hear me out and don't interrupt. Give him that child, give it to him, and that way something real from you will stay in this world, not just musical notes that vanish into thin air. Make an effort, then go back to your music. Give birth to a child, and I will help him raise it."

"He doesn't need help. He'll take the child home and raise it with his children."

"And his wife?"

"I know him. He'll persuade her, or force her."

"If so—I'm out of breath—listen to me, I'm begging you. Don't dismiss this out of hand. It's a wonderful idea, it's profound, and at the last minute it also turns our failed experiment into a surprising victory. Stay a little longer in Jerusalem, until it happens, and instead of outrageous payments to an old folks' home, we'll survive handsomely together in Jerusalem, owing nothing to anyone. Now that you are used to Jerusalem, and not afraid like your brother of the neighborhood Orthodoxy, stay with me a while longer. And Honi and I will participate with love and devotion in this experiment, which this time will be yours. You won't have to work, not even as an extra, and if in the meantime some harpist retires, or gets sick or dies, you could—"

"Enough, Ima, enough delusions."

"Why delusions? Today, with Abba no longer alive, these aren't delusions. I swear to you on his soul that he was the one to blame, only he. With some weird confidence he succeeded in scaring me, and I bet you too, that you were likely to die in childbirth. I bought into it, but now that he's gone, we have, you and I, the freedom and the ability to understand the reality by ourselves. And I'm telling you, you're forty-two years old, and this is the last moment."

"The moment has passed."

"What do you mean?"

"I have nothing in me to give life to a child, even if I were to succumb to Uriah."

"In what sense? In what sense? Noga, my darling, in what sense?"

"In the simplest sense. My period, Ima. My periods stopped."

"Why didn't you tell me?"

"Why would I?"

"So I wouldn't keep torturing myself with false hopes."

"I'm telling you now so you won't torture yourself with false hopes."

"But I will torture myself, because I know that even when it seems like the end, it isn't the end."

"Tell that to my body, Ima, not to me."

"Then the time has come for me to speak directly to your body without your interference."

"That would be wise and helpful, because the body, and not just the soul, sometimes needs a mother's words. But hurry, because the day after tomorrow I have an early flight out of here."

FORTY-THREE

ONLY NOW, AFTER THE PHONE CALL with her mother, does it register that the encounter with her former husband rattled her so much that it's hard for her to be alone in the apartment, and she hurries to the workers' restaurant in the *shuk* and sits facing the entrance to see who comes in. But Elazar doesn't appear, and the black camera on the ceiling is inert, the angle of its lens unchanged since her last visit. On her way back she buys some spices, to season the farewell meal she plans to cook the next day for her mother's homecoming. But in the apartment, instead of napping on a blazing afternoon in one of the three beds that will soon no longer be hers, she changes from her sandals into sneakers, shaking out the sand from the Judean Desert, and makes a return visit to the little police station.

In the dimly lit station sit the same bored policewomen, and what was unknown in the past about the man who hurriedly broke contact remains unknown in the present. She gently pats the heads of the Mandatory lions, faithful to their post after so many years, and walks down Jaffa Road toward Zion Square, to see the building that, if memory serves, long ago housed the conservatory. But the original building, whose studios had been connected by an outdoor portico accessed by shiny stone steps, has vanished, and instead of asking passersby who won't know the answer, she goes up Ben-Yehuda Street, the heart of the Jerusalem Triangle, to the street named for the British king whose son gave up the throne for the love of a divorcée, and walks past the circular synagogue en route to the Gymnasia, her high school. She sits down in front of a café and looks at the wide steps leading into the school, where sometimes the principal himself would stand to chide latecomers. It was here, as a freshman, that she became serious about classical music and learned to appreciate what she was playing, and after school hours, in a classroom with chairs inverted on tables, she learned to distinguish the unique sound of the harp amid the energetic fiddling of the other strings.

Her thoughts keep returning to Uriah, a married man and father of two, who mourns and yearns for the child not born to him. But what's the value of such yearning if he lacks the patience and curiosity to look for just a moment at the childhood harp that, he insists, was the source of all his woe?

A week after she'd arrived in Jerusalem, she visited the Academy of Music, which in her day was in the process of moving from its home near the prime minister's residence to the campus of the Hebrew University at Givat Ram. There she met two of her former teachers, who were happy to know that her love of music had not merely endured but flourished. First off, she wanted to know if there was a harp available for her to practice on from time to time. But her teachers didn't think it dignified that she wait around between lessons so she could play a student harp. Take some sheet music and play in your imagination, they said, you're enough of a professional to do that. Now, as she is about to leave Jerusalem, she is drawn back to the academy's previous building, for another look at the spot where an enraptured young man waited for her, helmet in hand.

Since Lovers of Zion Street is not far from there, she continues on to the home of the parents of the youth who tried to poison his girlfriend so she would never leave him. Unlike that busy night of filming, the house is silent now. Only an old mother is visible through the kitchen window.

She walks downhill to the end of Lovers of Zion and over to the parallel street and stands before the gates of the former mental hospital, now a church, where the parents had installed their son to pacify his demons, thereby enabling his illustrious career overseas.

This journey on foot does not tire the harpist. On the contrary, it gives her pleasure. Her flexible sneakers add spring to her step, and the advent of the Jerusalem evening tempts her not to head home but to go on to Emek Refaim for a look at the first rented apartment she lived in after getting married. Was it really thirty-two steps that Uriah had to carry the heavy harp up and down for her? Old streets have been widened and familiar buildings renovated, so she cannot find the place at first, and when she does it looks different, but she's sure the number of steps is the same. She can't find the light switch on the stairway, so she climbs in darkness and counts. And yes, these are difficult stairs, steep and angular, unlike the friendly stairs in her parents' building, where, when she'd get home from the Gymnasia, a gentle, handsome Orthodox boy would be waiting for a heart-to-heart talk.

Twenty-six steps and not thirty-two lead to the door of the old apartment. In which case, she thinks, scowling, why does a person who always prided himself on his precision need to add six stairs to embellish his suffering for the sake of her instrument? She heads back down, again counting the stairs, to double-check the number.

The gathering dusk prompts the lighting of the street lamps, and the colors of fruits and vegetables glisten in the storefronts on Emek Refaim Street. Baby carriages cross the street in midblock and hold up traffic. Men look at her for long moments, and she imagines herself again as an extra, only this time without a camera or director or story—standing by herself and for herself. She would like to further explore this pleasant, secular neighborhood, but she needs to start packing her bags and prepare for her departure, and the light rail is far away, so she hails a taxi and asks the driver on the way home to stop for a moment in the Valley of the Cross. But the driver doesn't know where he can stop in a valley paved long ago with fast roads, yet he does know where the monastery still stands, and how to approach it.

"Exactly. Get as close as you can, stop for a bit, then continue."

And he does, and for a few minutes she and the cabbie look at the old, dark monastery, a little light burning in its tower.

Did I forget to shut off a light? she asks herself as the taxi turns into her street and she spots a light in the apartment—or could it be the little *tzaddik* misses me?

As she enters the kitchen, Uriah stands up. His face is tense and tormented, and the fluorescent light intensifies its pallor. The jacket he wore in the morning is gone, in its place a faded but familiar sweater.

"Wait," she says. "Before you apologize—"

"Explain," he corrects her.

"You should know that I just got back from our rented apartment in the Greek Colony, and I counted the stairs twice that you complained about this morning, so you should know that it's not thirty-two steps but twenty-six."

"You forgot to add," he says calmly, "the stairs inside the apartment."

"Inside the apartment?"

"Beyond the front door there were six more steps."

And in a flash the six interior steps come back to her, padded with old carpeting, and small pictures on the wall that she believed added a special charm and enhanced their marital intimacy.

"Yes, you're right. I forgot."

"Not by chance, not by chance," he mutters. "But it's unimportant, and I only wanted to explain—"

"Don't explain. I knew you'd hold on to the key my parents gave us, and had no doubt you'd be able to pick it out among all your other keys. Which is why I told my mother three days ago, 'Uriah won't need to ask permission to come in here.'"

"But I wanted to ask permission, only you weren't here. So I thought I'd simply leave the key."

"And stay around to protect it."

"Only because this morning I promised to let you know when the time had come."

"Which time?"

"The time I would tell my wife everything I hid from her."

"And what did she say?"

"She cried. The anger and shock dissolved into a long cry."

"And you?"

"I cried with her."

"You're an honest man. You're a faithful husband. It's a shame I lost you so easily. But how did you explain to her the fever you've been running ever since Honi told you I was here?"

"I said I'd given you up a long time ago, but was furious about my unborn child."

"Yours, or ours?"

"It doesn't matter anymore. Any child of yours, wherever he comes from—I'm taking him."

"But what would such a child give you, if you're not a part of him? You already have your two children."

"He will give me what will be in him of you. It doesn't matter what—a birthmark, a dimple, the shape of an ankle, maybe a smile, hair color. Little things, physical and mental, that you might not even be able to identify, but they are precious to me, which your music had stolen from me."

"The music?"

"The playing."

"And what did your wife say about this child?"

"She cried."

"And didn't say anything?"

"No. But I know that if she believes that this would quell my fever and restore my calm, she would be ready to adopt a child of yours to raise along with our kids."

"And that way she would merge herself with me."

"Perhaps."

"But there is no such child, and there won't be one. You understand. You know."

"I know and understand."

"It's too late."

"I know that too. Actually I feel it."

"If you know everything, why did you come?"

"To return the key to your mother and keep my promise to tell you that the time had come and I didn't hide anything from my wife."

"And you still didn't think to look at my childhood harp, which you ran away from this morning, and which Honi will throw away tomorrow or the next day."

"Wrong again. I took off the cover and looked at it, to try and understand its power."

"And did you?"

"I saw a unique and unusual instrument, a primitive *shaatnez*, a hybrid of harp, guitar, banjo and more. I can see why your father, who knew nothing about music, wanted to get it for you, not in a music store but an antiques shop. It can't make music now, many strings are missing, and those that are left are loose and bent, so how could I understand why it enslaved you?"

"You can't. And neither you nor I can resurrect the dead, so go back to your wife and don't torment her anymore with the illusion that you can turn back the clock."

FORTY-FOUR

Since the residents of the old folks' home in Tel Aviv include some very old ones, soon to depart this world, the management tried to provide the healthy and charming lady from Jerusalem with a pleasant and comfortable stay, so that she might cast her fate with the residence and enhance its image. But as it became clear that the little perks and luxuries, the lectures and the concerts, had not produced a decision in favor of Tel Aviv, and that the popular lady would soon be leaving, everyone was sad, and Honi, feeling guilty for his mother's decision, at the last moment spread idle promises of a repeat experiment. Thus their arrival in Jerusalem was delayed, and the savory lunch prepared for them by the daughter was turned into a half-eaten dinner.

Honi wears a look of dejection. "Don't worry," says his mother, "you won't have to rush here for every little inconvenience. I'm surrounded by plenty of poor Orthodox people who'll be happy to take care of me for a few pennies."

"And for the same nickel they'll bring you back to religion."

"Not me. Abba and I managed to hold our own, and God made us stronger in the process."

As her three heavy suitcases are hauled to the apartment one by one, she makes a tour of the three big rooms and marvels: "What's this, Noga? Was I really such a good mother that you spruced up the apartment for me?" "Yes, you were great," says Noga, "because you always made me feel free." Tears gleam in the eyes of the old woman, whose emotions are usually blocked by irony. As Noga smiles at her mother's tears, her brother storms through the resurrected apartment, grousing about the weak lighting and checking out Abadi's bolt. "This is not a bolt," he sneers. "It's a parody of a bolt. If you had a dog here, that would stop the bastards."

"Au contraire," the mother says, laughing, "a dog will appeal to them a lot more than Israeli television."

"No need to worry," says his sister. "No more kids. Shaya personally brought his son to apologize."

But Honi stands firm. "It all depends on Ima not tempting them again."

"I am not responsible for the temptation. It was your father. He hoped that the television would make them secular."

"A futile hope."

"Of course, but when I saw how they wore themselves out running up and down the stairs out of sheer boredom, I began to feel sorry for them."

"Beware of pity," pronounces Honi, fixated again on the lights. "We have to change all the bulbs," he says, poised to take his sister's two suitcases down to his car.

"Wait a minute," scolds his mother, "relax, what's your hurry? This is the last night, this is goodbye. If you need to get back to your wife and children, have a safe drive home, and we'll call a taxi to take Noga to the airport."

Honi objects. He is the one who waited at the airport three months ago and will be the one to take her back there and be responsible for her until the last minute. The flight is at five in the morning, and Noga should get there around three — so no taxi, just him. That's what he promised himself.

"If that's what you promised," says his mother, "you can relax. Instead of taking Noga now to your place in Tel Aviv and going back to the airport in the middle of the night, act logically and get a little sleep here. Even if I turned down protected living in Tel Aviv, I still need, at least on the first night, a protected home in Jerusalem."

"Protected from what?" Honi asks.

"From loneliness and sadness."

A pleasant calm settles on the old apartment, and Noga takes the fruit bowl from the refrigerator, sets out three plates and small knives and says, "Here, children, let's polish off the Land of Canaan, but without the blessing." And they peel and eat the remaining fruit, duly impressed by the beautiful, delicate glass bowl, especially the gold decoration at the rim. Honi says the bowl is fragile, should be handled carefully, and he gets up to wash it in the sink, where it falls and shatters and his fingers drip with blood.

"Was the bowl included with the Pomerantzes' fruit?" he asks his mother, licking his wounded fingers, "or do we have to return it?"

"Let's consider it included, since you broke it, on purpose."

"Not really on purpose, but I also didn't want Pomerantz to be too happy you're coming back."

"Don't be a child," Noga says. "Stop sucking your fingers. You can't re-cycle the blood. Run cold water on them until we find a bandage."

But the mother has forgotten what's in the apartment and what isn't, and they have to dig through drawer after drawer to find some ancient Band-Aids.

The bleeding is finally under control, but the shirt and pants are stained, requiring immediate attention, and Honi stands in his underwear before his mother and sister, who dismiss his embarrassment: "We've seen you na-ked before, no problem."

Be that as it may, he's cold in the Jerusalem evening, and his sister lends him a big shirt, his mother contributes an old bathrobe, and he sits com-fortably, a man dressed as a woman, reminiscing about himself as a child, and instead of complaining again about his mother's failed residence in Tel Aviv, he envisions the fast train of the future that will zip between the two cities in twenty minutes flat.

"Then you can come here every time I sneeze," his mother teases.

And so the evening goes. They are still in the kitchen, and after they've carefully picked the shards of the bowl from the sink and eaten a bit more of the meal Noga prepared, the talk turns to the past and concentrates on the virtues and flaws of the father who died nine months before, and Noga recalls the rainy night she saw her father shuffling from room to room like a humble Chinese man.

"Yes," the mother confirms, "in recent years when he would get up at night to use the bathroom, he would turn into a different character on his way back to bed—Chinese or Indian or Eskimo, or somebody disabled or paralyzed. We once saw a wonderful short film called *Aisha*, about a woman of ninety-six, all bent over, who would lean on a pail as she walked, and he was so impressed that he tried imitating her in the dark."

"But why?" Honi is shocked, hearing for the first time about his late father's nocturnal habits.

"To amuse himself and me."

"And you were actually amused?"

"At first, out of surprise, then I reprimanded him."

"Hardly reprimanded," Noga recalls. "'That's not Chinese, it's Japanese,' she would tell him, as if Ima really knows how the Japanese walk. Then he'd look bewildered and take even smaller steps."

And she jumps up and charmingly mimics her father's steps.

The chatter flows freely and merrily as the night slowly embraces their camaraderie. They drift on to relatives and absent friends, and even Uriah's name comes up, but the two women are careful not to let slip one word about his performances and visits, and it would appear that Honi has not only accepted his failure to move his mother near him, but that the failure has lifted his spirits. He walks from room to room in his mother's robe, planning how to renovate the apartment, to put money into it now that they've been spared the expense of the old folks' home. And as he puts together a list of what to replace and what to fix, and especially how to improve the lighting, he arrives at the emptied clothes closet and rocks his father's new black suit back and forth on its hanger.

"Take it," urges his sister, "don't be stubborn. Take it before Ima throws it out. You might need it someday."

"That day will never come. Who wears suits like this anymore? Abba only had it made so he wouldn't be conspicuous in the neighborhood."

"Maybe in the future you'll also need to not be conspicuous here."

"Me?" he shouts. "Why?"

"So they won't throw stones at you."

He pauses, unsure if she is joking. Then, in a snap decision, he frees the suit from its hanger, folds it into a small bundle and declares that he will personally donate it to charity.

The family is getting tired, and as the mother is still confused in her apartment and has not begun to unpack, the temporary tenant who is leaving Israel indefinitely has to act the efficient housewife. She changes sheets, spreads out blankets, arranges towels, but her brother's wet, blood-stained clothes she cleans with only partial success before tossing them in the dryer, which rattles the dimly lit Jerusalem flat with a vaguely menacing roar.

"Yes, we must get some sleep," says the mother after her daughter has finally finished packing her bags. She urges her two children to turn out their lights, but because it's hard to part from the daughter, whom she'd hardly seen during the three experimental months, she subverts the sleep agenda and has Noga join her for a midnight cup of tea. "Come, you'll sleep on the plane," she says to her daughter, "and I won't wake up till the afternoon. Honi must go to bed. In two hours he has to drive you to the airport." But Honi is lured by the spontaneous tea party. "No worries," he scoffs, "from Jerusalem to the airport at two in the morning takes half an hour, tops," and wrapped in the old robe, he joins his mother and sister, but instead of tea he makes himself a strong Turkish coffee.

Now, as Noga studies her brother's weary face, her heart melts and her anger fades. Nonetheless, she is careful not to mention Uriah's bizarre appearances, lest her brother think he made it all happen. So they sit, warm and drowsy, refusing to let sleep come between them. "Children," the mother suddenly declares, "please don't be upset that I failed the test. On the contrary, be happy about the failure. Now, with no insane maintenance payments in Tel Aviv, here in Jerusalem I feel like a wealthy woman. And as a wealthy woman, even old Stoller will have to respect me and make do with the piddling monthly rent until my dying day, which will be many years from now—being rich, I will have a greater will to live. And as a rich woman," she goes on, "I will not only phone you, Noga, every day, but I may even come to visit you in Europe, to listen to your harp. What do you say?"

"Shh . . . she's asleep," says Honi.

Indeed, the harpist hasn't held out, and as she sits at the table her eyes are closed, her breathing is heavy, and her head droops and nods. Her brother and mother stand her up gently and lead her to her bed, lay her down and cover her. "Even one hour of sleep will help," declares Honi, "so she won't be confused and get on the wrong plane."

Now, in the quiet of night, the mother is very much tempted to tell her son the Uriah story, but loyal to the promise she made to her daughter, she restrains herself and goes to take the pants and shirt from the dryer, their bloodstains warm but undiminished. The time passes quickly, and at two in the morning, it's difficult to wake the sleeper, and lest she stumble on the way to the car, her brother and mother help her down the stairs, put her in the front seat and fasten her seatbelt. Only then, in the chill of the coming dawn, does she open her beautiful eyes and kiss her mother and whisper, "Now that you're rich, you can have free protected housing in Europe with me."

The car sails away with the windows open, so the summer night breeze will rouse the sleepy woman. In the airport, despite the bloodstains on his clothes, Honi insists on steering his sister through the check-in process, including the baggage inspection. And because it's hard to say goodbye, he holds Noga's boarding pass in his hand, so he can accompany her to the place where he will be told: Stop.

It's hard for her too. She knows she is returning to a foreign orchestra, free of any obligation other than her music, while her brother remains in a country that never ceases to be a threat to itself, saddled with a demanding family and a lonely mother who insists on growing old in an old apartment. When Noga takes the boarding pass from him, she wonders: Why not give him some hope that she, for one, is not so lonely. After all, she was not only an extra here, but also a woman who was wanted and loved. Standing by the doorway of the security area, she gives her brother a quick rundown of what happened since the intermission at *Carmen* in the desert, the story of the former husband who invaded the opera stage and then turned himself into a wounded extra, before daring to appear as himself in their childhood apartment to demand the child who wasn't born.

Honi doesn't seem surprised, as though it was he who thought up the convoluted story she is confiding to him, and as she keeps talking, he is careful not to stop her, just to take her arm gently and move her from place to place, so she will not block the flow of passengers to the metal detectors, or notice the tears that fog his eyes.

FORTY-FIVE

AFTER NIGHTS OF WANDERING among beds, the sleep she'd hoped for on the flight to Amsterdam was unsettled and spotty, and in the morning, on the bus from the airport, her eyes were fixed on the great green fields and the plentiful water, as if she were visiting the Netherlands for the first time.

Three months ago, the landlord's son helped her carry the two suitcases down the narrow, winding stairs, but today she does without his help, to avoid a long conversation with the landlady, who will be curious to know the outcome of her mother's experiment with assisted living.

Her attic apartment consists of two rooms, small but comfortable. And since she has lived there for quite a while, it's easy to spot any changes that took place in her absence. The three houseplants stand in place and have been tended properly, and the kitchenette is sparkling clean. But there's a whiff of suspicion that the landlord's son, or possibly her friend the first flutist, took advantage of her absence and came to sleep, alone or otherwise, in her bed.

So she rips off the sheets, shoves them in the washing machine and, before putting on new ones, lies down on the bare mattress and tries, eyes closed, to make orderly sense of her memory of Israel. But the passion for her instrument propels her instead to the musicians' café by the concert hall, where after a couple of double espressos her mind is fixed on the waltz in the second movement of Berlioz's *Fantastique*.

As it turns out, it is not this piece that awaits her, but another one, richer and more complex. This is the news about to be delivered by Herman Kroon, the orchestra's general manager, who is happy that "our Venus" has returned, and clenches between his teeth, unlighted, the pipe Noga bought for him in the Old City, trying to get a taste of the Holy Land. Before telling the musician about the program change, he is curious to know what the elderly mother has decided, Jerusalem or Tel Aviv. Where is it better to live out her old age?

"Jerusalem," the harpist says quietly. "My mother returned to her old apartment, and I knew that would happen."

The man's face brightens. He is a Flemish bachelor of seventy-five, tall and nattily dressed, who after his retirement from the cultural affairs department of the city of Antwerp was chosen as administrative director of the Arnhem orchestra. When his tenure in Holland is over, he too will likely return to his old apartment in the gray Belgian port, and is thus encouraged by the decision of a distant, unfamiliar widow of similar age.

Noga asks about the response to the Mozart double concerto that was stolen from her.

"People still love Mozart," says Herman with an evasive smile. "Mozart is easy for them."

"I wasn't asking about Mozart," she says sharply, "but about reactions to the performance."

Herman remains evasive. "Your loyal friend Manfred is a virtuoso, and so Christine, whom I brought in from Antwerp, did the best she could not to get in his way. Don't be angry with her. She is surely not to blame."

"Not her," whispers Noga, deciding to leave it at that.

Only now is she struck by the silence around her.

"Where is everybody?"

"The orchestra is playing tonight in Hamburg. They'll be back tomorrow, and rehearsals begin in three days' time."

"And we'll start with the Berlioz?"

"No, Noga, here's good news for you. The *Fantastique* has been canceled."

"Canceled?"

"That's right."

"And that's what you call good news for me, Herman? Why was it canceled?"

"Because we've played it so many times. Also, we don't have the budget to double the timpani again and add three more contrabasses and bring all the noisy toys the Frenchman required to describe the torments of his love."

"And what's instead?"

"Instead of Berlioz we chose another French piece, something mature and subtle, and this is the news that will please you personally. Instead of the little waltz for harp in the second movement of the *Fantastique,* you and Christine will have the full dialogue between the wind and waves in Debussy's *La Mer.*

"*La Mer!*" she rejoices. "Oh, Herman, you're so right, this is wonderful news, consolation for the three months I didn't play with you. The harp is almost the main player."

"The two harps."

"Of course. Both of them."

He admires the pretty musician's dimpled cheeks as she glows with happiness. Taking a wad of tobacco from a box on his desk, he tamps it into the twisting pipe from Jerusalem, but has difficulty lighting it.

"This is a young and modest pipe," he pronounces, taking up his old pipe, which readily responds. "But I won't give up on it."

"Where did you get the idea to replace the Berlioz with Debussy?"

"You won't believe it—from very far away, the management of the Kyoto orchestra. While you were in Israel we got an unexpected offer from our embassy in Japan for an exchange of orchestras with Kyoto, and when we mentioned Berlioz, we sensed a polite hesitation, because the *Fantastique* had been in their repertoire the previous year, so they came up with an original notion, expressed in an inspired fashion. Here, listen to what they wrote us: 'You, the Dutch, have wrestled with the sea and succeeded in taming it and even conquering it to some extent, whereas for us Japanese the sea brings destruction and death. Therefore kindly perform Debussy's *La Mer* for us not only as musicians but as experienced conquerors of the sea, and maybe through your performance we too can learn how to contend with the sea that surrounds us.' Strange, no?"

"Strange and profound."

"Yes, well, Debussy's Impressionism was inspired in part by Japanese art, and on the cover of the original score of *La Mer* from 1905 was a huge wave, a tsunami, by the Japanese printmaker Hokusai."

"I didn't know that, haven't seen it. When's the picture from?"

"Hokusai lived from the mid-eighteenth to the mid-nineteenth century. There were devastating tsunamis then too, it would seem."

"Wonderful," says the harpist, "wonderful. *La Mer* is a piece that will lift my soul. When do we leave?"

"In ten days' time. Dennis returns tomorrow from America, and will rehearse the orchestra and conduct the performances. And so, our Venus, your vacation is over."

"It was hardly a vacation, but if you insist, you can call it one."

"I won't insist if you tell me exactly what happened," says Herman solicitously. "But vacation or not, now it's back to work. First of all the music library, to organize the scores for the various instruments, and at the same time check on Debussy's *Danse Sacrée et Danse Profane*."

"The *Sacred and Profane Dances* for harp and strings!" she shouts. "Herman, I am beside myself, I'm so happy. You mean I can be a soloist in Japan?"

"For now these are ideas—they still need to be discussed. But if you were upset about the Mozart you missed, here are two Debussys to console you."

Herman reaches for the Jerusalem pipe.

In high spirits, she hurries to the library and finds the score of *La Mer*: a pocket-size version with small print. She skims rapidly through the three movements: "From Dawn to Midday on the Sea" to "Play of the Waves" to "Dialogue of the Wind and the Sea," and happily confirms that both parts for harp are rich and varied, sometimes in unison, sometimes in conversation. She rushes back to the orchestra's main office and gets the key to the basement storeroom. The heavy instruments in storage—the bass drum, xylophone, two contrabasses and an enormous tuba—cast shadows in the sparingly lighted room. Her harp had made the trip to Germany, but the second harp, the old one, stands cloaked in its pinkish case. With great care she uncovers it and begins tuning the strings. It's not easy to tune the elderly harp, whose presence is needed in but a few compositions along-side the first harp, but she doesn't give up until all forty-seven strings are proven ready.

This harp, built in the nineteenth century, was a gift to the orchestra by a provincial gentleman who thought he was donating an antique of great value, which was not the case. Despite its regal frame, painted several times over in reddish gold, the wood is quite ordinary, and worms that feasted on it over the years have left little holes that sometimes muffle its tone. But now she holds it close to her heart and for a full hour warms up her fingers with fast and slow glissandi, also improvising her own little melodies. Only after she is warmed up and her yearning has been satisfied, her thoughts turn to her mother, alone in the Jerusalem apartment. Will the new "wealth" she acquired in her imagination help her acclimate without regret to the solitude she chose?

Noga exits the basement and walks out to the street as night slowly falls in the Netherlands. A fine European rain sweetens the air. She goes back to the musicians' café, where the owners greet her fondly. Her sojourn in Israel to assist an elderly mother has raised her stock in the eyes of the Dutch; they all have parents or relatives whose dilemmas of old age will involve them, or already do.

"She returned to her old apartment in Jerusalem," Noga announces triumphantly.

Only natural, declare the restaurant owners, and a longtime waiter offers his approval: "Hard to give up Jerusalem."

Noga corrects him: "It's easy to give up Jerusalem, but Tel Aviv is too expensive."

While she enjoys some of her favorite foods, she entertains the woman proprietor, who has sat down beside her, with tales of her adventures as an extra.

"And you didn't play for three months?"

"Only once, for just a few minutes — in the desert, by a historic mountain covered with ruins."

That night she phones Jerusalem, but there is no answer. She calls Honi to ask about their mother. He knows nothing, hasn't called her since they parted the night before. "If she insists on Jerusalem, she should enjoy it however she likes," he snaps. "You and I have done our part."

The next day she works for hours at the music library, organizing all the parts in the piece. She makes sure no instrument is left out, carefully marks the cues and phrases for each one. At twilight she returns to the orchestra's office, carrying in her arms a sizable bundle of scores, and sees the weary musicians get off the bus that has brought them home from Germany and help each other unload instruments from the truck that followed. She watches from afar as her harp is slowly wheeled to the storeroom, but does not yet approach it. Everyone is glad she is back. The aged flutist overflows with affection and calls over a tall, pale woman with hard eyes and a bitter smile. This is Christine, her understudy. Belgian, from Antwerp, French by tongue and temperament, awkward in English and Dutch.

"Your harp, it has a strong sound," she informs the Israeli. "I tried to play it gently."

"Thank you," says Noga, extending her hand to the woman, whose belly, under a light pastel sweater, signals early pregnancy.

"And what is happening with your mother?" asks the harpist who took her place in the Mozart.

"Yes, what did she decide?" chimes Manfred.

Other musicians, despite their fatigue and eagerness to get home, want to know what an old mother in faraway Jerusalem has decided.

These Dutch people have no other worries, Noga thinks, chuckling to herself. Their wars ended seventy years ago, and they glow with self-satisfaction. They knew when to give up their colonies in Southeast Asia and have been spared the new wave of terrorism. The euro is stable, their economy is strong, and unemployment is low—so all they have left to worry about is my mother.

"She decided to stay in Jerusalem," she tells the musicians gathered around her, "which I expected all along."

In the evening there is still no answer in Jerusalem, and the daughter leaves a voicemail message: "Where's the new heiress?" She immediately phones her brother, who spoke with the mother in the afternoon, and reports that now she's complaining that because of the experiment they imposed on her, she barely saw her daughter in those three months. From now on, will she have to meet her only in films?

Her mother calls that night. Yes, she's been spending time in town, with friends in cafés, going to movies, but the Uriah story has stayed with her. "Your visit, Nogaleh, still hovers over me like a dream. You were in Israel for three months and I barely saw you. I did learn from you to wander at night from bed to bed, but my sleep is hardly sound.

Noga tells her about the change in repertoire, the trip to Japan and about *The Sea* of Debussy, which in French sounds identical to *la mère*, the mother. "So in Japan," she consoles her mother, "I'll be playing you on my harp."

"At least that," sighs the mother, ending the conversation.

FORTY-SIX

I N THE MORNING SHE GOES to the music library, where she finds a score of Debussy's *Sacred and Profane Dances.* She makes a photocopy and gives it to Herman, who says not a word and places it in a drawer. In the evening, the orchestra members gather at the concert hall for a briefing about the trip to Kyoto. In fluent English, the cultural attaché of the Japanese embassy in The Hague provides information about their lodging near Doshisha University in Kyoto, and shows impressive slides of the auditorium and the temples of the holy city and environs. Four concerts are scheduled for orchestra subscribers, and three more are planned in two southern cities—Kumamoto and Hiroshima. Finally, since the musical director has not yet arrived, the administrative director of the Arnhem orchestra goes over the specifics of the repertoire, which will include Beethoven's *Emperor* Concerto; a rotation of Haydn symphonies 26, 92 and 94; the *Melancholy Arabesques* by Van den Broek, for it is important to include a contemporary Dutch composition; and, of course, as requested by the Japanese, the orchestra will perform *La Mer.* The Japanese pianist who broke her arm playing tennis in Berlin has recovered, and will make her own way to Japan, where there will be two rehearsals of the *Emperor,* a piece both she and the orchestra know well. The orchestra has also played the Haydn works in recent years, so four rehearsals in the coming week should suffice. The focus will be on Debussy and the *Arabesques,* which is a complex and difficult piece, but is fortunately only eight minutes long.

The principal conductor and musical director, Dennis van Zwol, strides into the room, straight from the airport, and is greeted with polite applause. He is a bald, chubby man of about sixty, with blue, froglike eyes, a strict and erudite musician whose ample sense of humor softens his pedantic demeanor. He ascends the stage in jeans and a red sweater and sits down beside Herman, surveying his musicians with amusement. When he spots the harpist, he waves to her warmly. So, she whispers to herself, why not, he's friendly, likes a good joke, and they say he also loves receiving gifts.

The next morning the rehearsals begin. There are no parts for the harp in the Haydn symphonies, so she sits in the hall and watches. After a short break, some of the strings leave the stage, and their places are taken by percussionists, including a few playing strange instruments. The conductor calls for a young composer, a man of around thirty with a ponytail, to take his place on the podium, to lead the first encounter with his provocative cacophony.

Van Zwol chooses to sit next to Noga in the auditorium and inquires about her vacation.

Blushing, she insists on repeating what she said to Herman: "It was not exactly a vacation."

"Then what was it?"

"Something complicated and surprising. I myself still don't understand what it was."

"And your mother?"

"She decided to stay in Jerusalem."

"And you are satisfied with her choice?"

The question reflects an unexpected sensitivity, and she tries to offer an appropriate response.

"From this distance, what good would my worrying do her?"

The conductor nods sympathetically, and she elaborates.

"My father died nine months ago. He and my mother were inseparable, dependent on one another, and who knows if they enjoyed that or whether their devotion had become oppressive. I think the sudden freedom my father granted my mother is exciting for her, and she may be afraid to curtail that freedom with the rules and activities of a retirement home."

Van Zwol nods gravely even as he winces at the wild sounds emanating from the stage, which are interrupted by the tapping of the baton as the young composer attempts to explain to the players ideas that gave birth to his music. Although it is Van Zwol who will conduct this piece in concert, he does not intervene, in order to give the musicians the chance to experience the new composition through the passion of the composer himself.

He meanwhile drums with his fingers on his knee a different, hidden melody that enters his mind. And she again says to herself, Really, why not?

She turns to him, blood rushing to her face. "Maestro, I brought you an unusual gift from Jerusalem, something you might find useful."

"A gift?" He is surprised. "Oh, my dear Venus, I do have a weakness for gifts, but on condition they are inexpensive and small and just symbolic, because that way I am not obligated to give gifts in return."

A quake of anxiety seizes her as she leans over and produces the whip from her bag, wrapped in a shawl of her mother's and tied with string.

He recoils. "What is this?" he asks. "It doesn't look like a small gift." But his lust for gifts overcomes his resistance, and he carefully undoes the string and shawl, releasing the strong scent of leather that has whipped the bodies of many beasts.

"What is this?" The conductor is shocked.

"It's a whip I bought from a Bedouin in the Old City, a whip that tamed and drove camels in the desert, and I thought, Maestro, that it might also be good for taming and driving us musicians."

The froggy blue eyes of the Dutchman light up with great amusement, and he raises the whip to his nostrils.

"I don't believe it . . . You thought about me all the way in Israel."

"Why not? I'm a musician in your orchestra."

"True. And you thought I need to strengthen my conducting not only with a baton but a whip?"

"In a symbolic way, Maestro. Only symbolic. It's a symbolic gift, the kind you like."

"Marvelous," he murmurs, and extends the whip along the empty seats to measure its length, apparently tempted to whip something or somebody.

"But why symbolic?" he asks, studying the pretty harpist warily. "Why only symbolic? Why not whip someone who ruins the tempo or misses notes or comes in at the wrong place?"

She is alarmed.

"No, no, Maestro, it's a symbolic whip, only symbolic, otherwise the musicians will blame me."

But the maestro continues to marvel.

"Where did you get the idea to bring me a whip?"

"As it happened, I bought it for myself, to protect myself from the neighborhood children who were breaking into my mother's apartment to watch television, which was forbidden in their homes."

"Television is forbidden? Why?"

"Because according to our religious people, it corrupts values and draws the children away from Torah studies."

"Yes," rhapsodizes the Dutchman, "your religious people have it exactly right. Television is evil and corruptive, and you did well to whip their children."

He clasps the Bedouin whip to his breast like a beloved infant.

"Symbolic ... symbolic," he mutters, "and I have the urge to whip this young man on the podium who is driving our orchestra crazy with his music."

She laughs. "No, no."

With great feeling he takes her hand and lifts it to his lips, gathers up the whip, takes it with him to the podium and embraces the young composer, who has just concluded his *Melancholy Arabesques* with a blast.

"Bravo," he says, "but it still needs polishing."

The percussion players vacate the front of the stage for the string players arriving from the wings. The two harpists take their positions behind the harps, the timpanists tune their drumheads, the other percussionists strategically arrange their instruments, the French horn players remove their slides and shake out the spit, the oboists and bassoonists choose the right reeds and adjust them. Gradually they all finish leafing through the scores, and quiet descends on the stage.

The conductor taps the music stand with his baton and begins the little lecture he likes to deliver when starting a new piece.

"At the end of the nineteenth century, France lost a war to Germany but won the culture war. Paris became the capital of the European artistic avant-garde, the city where the painters Manet, Monet, Renoir and Degas created Impressionism, while French poetry thrived in the Symbol-ist vein.

"Claude Debussy, born in the year 1862, was revolutionary in his style and became the greatest painter of music and a leader in the Impressionism of sound, though he complained that 'imbeciles,' as he called them, cate-gorized his music as Impressionist, confusing painting and music. Debussy established a new concept of tonality in European music. With his fertile imagination he rebelled against the strong German influence in classical music and turned to exotic areas of influence, taking non-European scales and musical colors from the Far East, also borrowing from Spanish dance, and experimented boldly with instruments that seldom had central roles in classical music, writing, for example, complex parts for the harp."

Van Zwol points his baton at the two harpists and smiles broadly.

"Symbolism in literature also influenced Debussy," continues the con-ductor, "and he wrote program music, giving symbolic and literary titles to his compositions, and strove with elegance and sensitivity to evoke the complexity of nature and humans, first and foremost to fathom the soul of woman."

"We would like to have more specific details," says Ingrid, a beautiful French horn player. "Also personal ones if possible."

Laughter and applause.

The conductor raps his baton.

"If we start recounting Debussy's romantic adventures, we won't get to the first notes of the piece today, nor do I wish to be responsible for cor-rupting decent Dutch men and women with racy French anecdotes. That's what the Internet is for, answerable to no one. So suffice it to say that he was quite the adventurer, and that his tonal instability may have derived from romantic instability. He switched women easily, cheated on them un-conscionably, and one of his wives shot herself in despair in the Place de la Concorde and survived only by a miracle. But all this proves that for him, woman was the ultimate creation, an eternal grail of love and desire, even when no longer young and pretty. She is the purpose of art."

The musicians, women and men, nod in agreement.

"Debussy died at the age of only fifty-five, at the end of the First World

War, as German cannons battered Paris with their last remaining shells. And so his funeral procession took place in empty streets, although he was, in my view and that of many others, the most important French composer of the twentieth century, whose influence continues to be felt to this day."

"How, exactly?" demands a white-haired cellist.

The maestro laughs. "I see you don't want to play today, just talk."

"We want to have a better understanding of what we're playing," several voices chime in.

"Fine, fine, you're right, because in recent years this orchestra has not played Debussy, and this is music that requires particular precision. It's not easy or simple. A complex and dreamlike harmonic world, scales of whole tones, atonal passages, glittering transitions. His repetitiveness is unsettling. In short, ladies and gentlemen, we are not lounging in a beach chair and looking at the sea, but entering the depths, and the Japanese want an answer from us—what to do in the next tsunami."

"Just so it doesn't swallow us too," interjects a veteran oboist, and everyone laughs.

"No," the humorless first violinist assures her, "we shall not perform on the east coast of Japan but on the west coast, the one not exposed to the Pacific Ocean that still yearns for the moon that was born from it."

The conductor silences them with a tap of his baton.

"Now let's get to work. And since this is a serious and difficult piece, I will be more of a taskmaster and less of a comedian, nor will I limit myself to mere criticism. Rather, I'll do some whipping, since I just got a whip as a gift."

He picks up the Bedouin whip, extends it and waves it cautiously above his head.

Pandemonium. The orchestra goes wild. Shouts from every corner. "Not fair!" howl the string players. "Your whip only reaches us and not the winds and percussion!"

"Why won't it reach them?" asks the conductor. "It will. I'll step down from the podium and whip any faraway offenders."

A bold cellist asks, "Where did you get the whip?" She rises from her chair and comes over to inspect it.

I hope he doesn't give me away, Noga thinks, cringing. Damn, what a mistake I made.

But Dennis van Zwol, the incorrigible joker, cannot conceal the provenance of the gift. "Beware, friends," he declares, "the whip arrived from the Holy Land. Our Venus gave it to me as a gift, to strengthen my standing with you. You know the Israelis, don't you? They are new Jews, swift and strong, who don't hang up the whip as a wall decoration, like us cowardly Europeans, but use it to straighten out anyone who angers them. So beware —from now on, I too am a new tough Jew."

The Bedouin whip merits an enthusiastic reception, as bows, trumpets and woodwinds are waved at the harpist, who reddens with emotion. Finally the musicians calm down, and deep silence engulfs the hall.

Van Zwol closes his eyes, presses his palms together. After prolonged introspection he lifts the baton delicately, as if all musical wisdom were hidden within it, bids the timpani to beat the first sounds, then signals the two harpists, their hands poised on the strings. Christine is to strike the first note with the left hand, and immediately thereafter, Noga, the first harpist, is to enter with her left hand, and though both are playing the same melody, they are to remain an eighth note apart, in strict time. But the conductor quickly stops them, for it turns out that Christine is unaware that her harp, not the other, is supposed to stress every note in the opening bars.

"Pay attention," he warns her in French. "Sharpen your accents."

He gives a sign to start over, then again stops. He feels the accents are not emphatic enough.

Noga studies Christine's face as she groans under the weight of the conductor's reprimands. Her face is pale and severe; luminous golden hair streams to her shoulders. From time to time she veils her face with her hand, as if banishing a painful thought. She has come to the rehearsal in a long, baggy dress that covers her long body, and the little bulge, which at their first meeting seemed to Noga to hint at pregnancy, has vanished. Over and over Christine stresses the accents requested by the conductor, but she cannot seem to satisfy him. Noga hides her head behind her harp, fearing that the conductor will move her from first harp to second, to achieve the sound he insists upon. Finally he resigns himself and motions to the orchestra to play a few more bars, then harangues the clarinets and bassoons to produce exactly the soft sound his inner ear is seeking.

"How can you not feel," he says, by way of explaining his mood, "that here the composer has planted the melody of a mysterious sea nymph, the song of a melancholy mermaid, which from now on will evolve as a motif in the depths of the music." It is clear to the orchestra that they are in for a rough patch, and although the piece is not long, merely twenty-eight minutes, they will spend many hours rehearsing picky nuances, to realize the vision of a conductor who has decided to turn *The Sea* into his new flagship.

When the rehearsal is over, Manfred is quick to complain to Noga: "That whip you gave him drove him out of his mind."

She grins. "It's okay. He's still got enough mind left over."

Manfred invites her to dinner, and she declines. She's still recovering from the sojourn in her homeland, but not to worry, they'll have ample opportunity in Japan.

"We'll have to wait till Japan?"

"Why not?" she says, and asks about Christine — who she is, how well she played the Mozart, why she looks tormented.

The flutist doesn't know much. In the Mozart double concerto she played with precision, but the notes lacked luster and emotion. He hasn't noticed her distress, just her reticence, maybe because her French is hostile to Flemish and English, and her accent is funny. He hasn't really delved into her story. He's not interested in silent married women, only in unattached and talkative ones, like the one who stands before him.

"Christine is married?"

"It's hard to say. More or less. In any case there is a man in her life. He was at all the concerts, sat in the front row, apparently not out of love for music but out of concern for her. He would arrive from Antwerp, sometimes in his work clothes — a dockworker, or immigrant, or refugee seeking asylum."

"Where's he from?"

"I didn't ask — it's none of my business. The world today is intermingled. We even have an exotic woman from the Middle East, where people still ride innocent camels and prod them with whips, who became the first harpist of a civilized orchestra."

He puts his hand on her shoulder and says, "By the way, you got prettier in Israel. You have color. What do you people eat there?"

"Fruit. Beautiful, juicy fruit."

FORTY-SEVEN

FOUR DAYS BEFORE LEAVING for Japan, at the morning rehearsal for the farewell concert in Arnhem, the orchestra plays a Haydn symphony and Noga goes up to the balcony to hear it from there. Seated below her in one of the front rows is a man dressed in overalls, presumably the workingman Manfred had mentioned. Christine is not sitting next to him, but her scarf is lying on his lap. The man intrigues Noga, and worries her as well. She goes to the other side of the balcony to get a better look—a well-built man, his face somber, suspiciously eyeing the onstage activity. When Christine enters the hall, still in the long baggy dress that conceals her curves, he stands up and holds her. He seems to want to take her out of the hall, but she refuses, sinking into one of the seats, hiding her face.

Later, as they begin the Debussy, Noga senses a strong smell of perfume that seems intended to mask another smell, perhaps of vomit. While the musicians tune their instruments, she asks Christine how she feels. "I'm fine," says Christine, straining to smile. "I felt dizzy and a little nauseous." She searches for the right words in English, then adds, "But that is expected now," and it is clear that she regrets the explanation, and in her embarrassment, despite the drumbeats, she misses the conductor's cue for her first note.

So she's pregnant after all, decides the first harpist, who again notices that little round bulge under the folds of the long dress. But why is she disguising her pregnancy? Is it for fear that the orchestra's medical insurance will not cover her trip to Japan?

The rehearsal does not go well. The music is halted after every few bars by an angry baton. The beautiful tone achieved with great effort in previous rehearsals has gone tinny, the fluid transitions feel rough. "What's going on?" shouts Van Zwol. "What the devil happened? This isn't Debussy's

La Mer, it's a muddy tsunami that will repulse the Japanese. Remember, people in the Far East understand music no less than we do. And they pay us a lot of money and bestow a great honor on our humble municipal orchestra by inviting us to such a prestigious city. So please, wake up, concentrate. If you don't, I'll replace the whip with a machine gun."

Sometimes a wrong note by an unidentified instrument spreads through the orchestra. Van Zwol is aware of such an error, yet in the flurry of playing cannot locate its source. But Noga can. The second harpist did not press the pedals in time, and the error spread to the strings and undermined their precision. Noga tries to alert her neighbor to the mistake, but Christine's anxiety and weakness only compound the blunder. The conductor finally locates the problem, stops the music and returns to the beginning so the piece can regain its honor.

When the rehearsal is over, Noga inquires if the dizziness and nausea have waned, and asks about the pregnancy.

Christine is at the start of her fourth month. Your first pregnancy? Almost, essentially, not counting a youthful abortion many years before, no connection to her present partner. And with curiosity mixed with vague anxiety, Noga persists: "Is he your husband?" "Almost," she says again. "Not really. We'll have to wait for the birth to make the marriage official along with the citizenship."

"He's not a citizen?" probes the Israeli.

"He is almost. He has a work permit as a port traffic controller."

"And he'll go with you to Japan?"

"To Japan? No, on the contrary, he wants to prevent me from going."

"Prevent?"

"He is concerned about the pregnancy on such a long trip."

"Explain to him that you are essential, that there's no *La Mer* without the dialogue between the two harps."

"He understands, I did explain, but he doesn't care. That is why I am in despair. He is here to sabotage the trip."

"Have you informed Dennis or Herman about his objection?"

"Not yet. If I told them, they would find another harpist to play, even in the farewell concert tomorrow, so I am waiting."

"Christine," Noga says calmly, straining to suppress fear and anger, "if you delay telling them till after the concert, it will be too late to find a replacement for the Japanese tour. In fact, it's already late. It's not fair to hide from the orchestra that your husband doesn't want you to go."

"He's not my husband."

"That's irrelevant. Whoever he is. If you keep silent, they won't be able to find a new harpist for such a long and difficult journey. You must let them know immediately. You are putting the whole repertoire in danger. Without the second harp there is no way to perform the piece."

"That's right."

"Which is why you should do the right thing."

"Perhaps . . . perhaps in Japan," Christine says despondently, "you can play Schubert or something else instead of Debussy. There are enough suitable pieces in the repertoire of this orchestra without a second harp or even a first harp."

"No, no," shouts Noga, "no Schubert, no Mozart, no Beethoven, no nothing. We will play *La Mer*. That's the piece the Japanese are waiting for, and we will perform it."

"So what should I do?" agonizes Christine.

"Tell Dennis and Herman immediately that you are not going to Japan."

"But perhaps I will go after all."

"How?"

"Perhaps I can convince him that nothing will happen to the baby . . . Perhaps you will help me . . . Perhaps you will explain to him that without the second harp Debussy is lost."

"All right, I'll try, I'll help you, and so will other women players. We'll look after you on the trip. But first you must inform Herman and Dennis, otherwise I will warn them."

"You cannot go in my place."

"I will go if you don't. Because you must not steal this unique piece of music from the rest of us. *La Mer* is also *la mère*, the mother, and you of all people, being French, must understand the significance of the connection between the two words. I left my elderly mother in Jerusalem, and that's why I want so very much to play her on my harp."

"To play your mother?" Christine is dumbfounded. "I don't understand."

They are now standing in the lobby of the concert hall, and musicians walking by seem to sense the tension between the two harpists and walk faster. The man in the overalls emerges from the auditorium and hurries to his partner. From close up, he looks handsome and sensitive, yet the hand he extends to Noga is rough, hard. His skin is dark and his hair curly, but his sparkling eyes are blue as the sea, possibly strengthening his claim to citizenship. He positions himself between the two harpists, suspecting that the Israeli is trying to persuade his girlfriend not to forgo the trip to Japan.

"What's happening?" he asks his girlfriend in French.

"What should be happening?" she answers coldly, dismissively.

Convinced now that the first harpist is the one obstructing the withdrawal from the tour, he switches to English, so Noga will understand, and asks Christine to do exactly what Noga had just insisted on, which is to go to management immediately and inform them.

Christine merely shrugs, but Noga, realizing that she and this man are in agreement, intervenes. "You're right," she says, "Christine must tell them now, otherwise they won't have time to find a replacement."

Strengthened by the ally he had assumed was an obstacle, he moves quickly. Gently but firmly he puts his arm around his partner's waist and steers her toward the office.

Expecting to be met with anger, Christine considers asking the Israeli to accompany her, as if hoping that the dialogue between the wind and the sea could be played by one harpist alone. But as they approach Herman's office she decides that Noga's presence would make matters worse. She also insists in French that her partner wait outside, and enters quietly to bear the bad news that might wreck the repertoire of the tour.

Slowly the guardian of the pregnancy begins to relax. First he stands by the office door, trying in vain to overhear the conversation inside. Then he sits down on a bench in the hallway, stretches his legs, sees no one around but Noga, takes a single cigarette from his shirt pocket and sticks it in his mouth. But before he can light it there is the sound of rapid footsteps in the corridor, and Dennis van Zwol arrives in a panic, summoned by management to deal with the incipient dropout. Identifying the progenitor of the bad news, he knocks the cigarette from the man's mouth with the flick of a finger and growls in French, "No smoking!" Turning to Noga, as if she too were responsible, he says in Dutch, "Tell me what's going on? What's the story here? What was she thinking?" He doesn't wait for an answer but disappears into Herman's office to fight for the integrity of the repertoire.

Noga looks at the boyfriend, who retrieves the damaged cigarette from the floor, shreds the paper and collects the tobacco in his hand. Without a word or a glance at the harpist, he sits back down, determined to guard Christine's pregnancy at all costs. Now Noga takes a closer look. His dark skin is velvety smooth, his thick curly hair is black as coal, and the northern blueness of his eyes blends the world into one country. Her heart is heavy. From the speed with which the conductor was summoned, she gathers that it will be hard, if not impossible, to find a harpist at the last minute who will be able to get ready overnight for such a long and distant journey. After so many exhausting, exhilarating rehearsals, Noga thinks with a pang of despair, will Debussy be forced to cede his place to some same-old Schubert or hackneyed Beethoven?

And now her memory conjures a movie extra, a disabled woman in a wheelchair waiting outside the closed door of a room that masqueraded as a hospital room. There too, beside her, stood a stranger, a handsome actor whose bare chest gleamed under a white gown. An imaginary doctor whom she would soon be directed to surprise in the midst of forbidden lovemaking, and he, spontaneously, would pluck her from her wheelchair and, with a mixture of anger and pity, carry her in his arms to her sickbed and cover her, as if to blot out the shame he had brought on himself.

But now there is no director to tell her what to do. She has no choice but to direct, produce and write her own script—to give voice and movement to her thoughts so that her harp will play a piece of music whose beauty floods her soul. She gets up her nerve and approaches the man in overalls, who sits on the bench with his eyes closed and head tilted back.

"Excuse me, sir, may I have a few words with you?"

He opens his eyes.

"I wanted to tell you that although I respect your concern, you are going too far. Now you are not only making things harder for Christine, but for the entire orchestra."

He tenses but doesn't interrupt.

"Millions of pregnant women," she says, raising her voice, "travel, fly, go about in the world, and nothing happens to them."

"It takes all kinds," he says offhandedly.

"After all, our Christine will not be asked to climb mountains in Japan, or dance in discotheques. On the plane she will rest. Others will lift and wheel her harp, so she will only need to put her fingers on the strings and play."

"I know," he snaps, "but still."

"In general," she insists, "the female womb is far stronger and steadier than men imagine, and pregnancies have survived wars, poverty and famine, even concentration camps."

Now he is irate, but remains calm.

"Yes, I also sometimes pay attention to what goes on in the world, but Christine is not in good health and not young, and it was not easy for us to get pregnant."

Although Noga is rebuffed at every turn, she believes that the fate of the sea is in her hands alone.

"You should also know, sir," she says, sitting down next to him on the bench, "that in our orchestra there are women who have given birth to children and have a lot of experience, and we have a violinist and an oboist who are grandmothers and were present at the births of many babies."

With an ironic gesture he salutes the mothers and grandmothers, but does not yield.

"I have respect for them all, but what can they do if she starts to bleed, or if to save the pregnancy she has to stay in bed for a long time, and in a strange and foreign country?"

"Why strange? Maybe foreign in culture and language, but otherwise everything in Japan is modern and rational, often more so than here in the West."

"You have been there?"

"No, but everyone knows that about Japan. Besides, Christine will not be alone. We will all be with her, look after her."

His patience runs out.

"But there will be visits to temples and flights to Hiroshima and other cities. Christine is a fragile woman and not young, and this pregnancy is important and precious for us. We cannot take chances."

But Noga won't give up. She has not played a concert for three months, and she is desperate to perform in front of an audience.

"Excuse me, sir, can you tell me your name?"

"Saharan."

"May I ask where you are from? Where you were born?"

"In Iran, in—"

"Tehran?" She tries to be helpful.

"No, in a place you never heard of."

"Then please," she implores, "please, sir, trust me. I personally pledge to be with Christine at every moment of the trip. You were at the rehearsal, and perhaps you noticed the dialogue between the two of us, two harpists who have not only a professional partnership but also a human one, so it's natural for me to take personal responsibility for her well-being."

"Who are you, anyway?" He tries to get to the root of her stubbornness.

"What do you mean, who am I?"

"Am I allowed to ask a question?"

"Of course."

"You speak with such confidence—how many children have you given birth to?"

"How many children?" She smiles uneasily and gets up from the bench. "How is that relevant?"

"Why not? After all, you are asking me to trust you."

She shudders.

"I haven't yet given birth, but . . ."

And to her surprise, he is not surprised, as if he anticipated her answer, but instead of puncturing her arrogance, he studies her with interest and asks gently, "Why? Because you couldn't?"

"No. I could, but I didn't want to."

Now he won't let go, as if her promise to watch over his partner's pregnancy has exposed her to the same blunt challenge voiced by Elazar, the eternal extra, at their first meeting, though now in a foreign language: "How do you know you could, if you didn't want to?"

"I know . . . I know." She holds on to the scene that is disintegrating in her hands. "If I want to, I can have a child."

"Of course, and we shall all pray for his health," he graciously promises, in his name and in the name of his partner, who at the moment is being badgered by her bosses. "Meanwhile, until your wish for a child is awakened, respect our wishes, for we need our child, and no music has the right to stand in the way."

As he speaks, his fist springs open and flakes of tobacco scatter like sand. Since he is loath to kneel down before her and pick them up, he stands and brushes them aside with the toe of his shoe. And to indicate that the conversation is over, he strides to the end of the corridor, opens wide a small window, lights a fresh cigarette and expels the smoke into the world.

FORTY-EIGHT

B EFORE THEIR DEPARTURE, the orchestra played a farewell concert for the residents of Arnhem, with tickets for sale at a token price. As a replacement harpist had not yet been found, a frantic request was dispatched to Kyoto to find a musician who could assume the part of second harp in the work by Debussy, but since no reply had arrived, the orchestra held an urgent rehearsal of Schubert's Ninth Symphony, the "Great," a piece they'd played dozens of times, so if necessary they could plug the gaping hole in the program. Noga's trip, and that of her harp, was assured, but it was not clear whether she would have the chance to perform. Will she be reduced to a mere extra in Japan too? She asks Herman to take from his drawer the score for the *Sacred and Profane Dances* for harp and string orchestra, hoping a way might be found to compensate her with a public performance of this work.

On the morning of the concert Noga tried to decide what to wear onstage. Should it be the black silk dress, whose hem nearly reached the floor but which left her neck, shoulders and arms bare, or should she go with a delicate black pantsuit, purchased in Israel, which she felt accentuated her slenderness and flexibility? She was tilting toward the elegant black silk, befitting the formality of a concert to which notables had been invited. But her shoulders seemed bulky to her compared with the younger women players', so she combined the two outfits: to hide her shoulders and arms, she will wear the jacket of the pantsuit over the long silk dress.

But is the black of the two outfits the same black? She didn't feel herself competent to judge this, so she enlisted her landlady, a great admirer of her tenant, to view the combination and render an opinion. And the landlady, whom Noga had invited to the concert, was adamant. Even if the Dutch black does not clash with the Israeli black, Noga must wear only the long dress and leave her shoulders and arms exposed. Yes, she too noticed that they had thickened a bit during her vacation in Israel, possibly the result of hearty meals and juicy fruit, yet at the same time, perhaps from the desert sun, they have a rosy golden sheen not easily acquired in the Netherlands. So why conceal an attractive body that will blend with the beauty of the harp?

It was impossible to exclude Christine from the farewell concert, despite the anger directed at her, and she too turned up that evening in a long black dress, albeit of slightly threadbare wool. The appearance of the two harpists in their long dresses encouraged interest in a complex piece of music.

During the intermission Noga asked the conductor if there had been an answer from Japan. "Not yet," said the maestro, but with cheerful optimism promised that the entire Japanese army had been deployed to find a substitute. "We will not give up the sea after we polished every one of its waves." Indeed, the Debussy was received with surprising warmth and enthusiasm at the farewell concert, even though it was not an audience of the usual music lovers, but of municipal workers and members of trade organizations, including transit employees and industrial workers, plus excited high school kids and German students from across the border. And since the printed program, distributed free at the door, explained why *La Mer* had been selected for the Japanese tour, the Dutch were flattered that such a large and strong nation as Japan, whose technology had conquered the world, was in need of inspiration from a small, modest people in a spiritual and artistic contest with a cruel sea.

Knowing that the farewell concert would be attended by the general public, some receiving free tickets, Dennis van Zwol asked the musicians to play the Haydn symphony at an especially sprightly tempo, but with the Debussy he would allow no compromises. During the many exhausting rehearsals, the orchestra had perfected various refinements, and any deviation from them would ruin the musical flow.

Having gotten past her torment over leaving the tour, Christine was newly serene. She no longer bothered to hide her pregnancy, and under the long wool dress that smelled slightly of camphor, the bulge that would force the Belgians to grant full European citizenship to her partner was clearly visible.

The dialogue between the two harps was executed flawlessly in the concert's second half. Sometimes the first sang out and the second answered, sometimes they sang in unison, till the second subsided and the first went on to trill another phrase. The breathtaking glissandi played by the two evoked the sparkling foam of the waves, cresting and ebbing. The conductor was focused on them, and they felt his constant presence. Since the harpists sat on a riser above the other strings, the eyes of the audience were fixed on them even as they rested, waiting for the moment when the two women, with perfect timing, would tilt their gilded, regal harps toward their hearts and spread their fingers on the strings.

The cheers at the conclusion of the Debussy were loud and long. Backstage, a chattering crowd of friends and relatives said their goodbyes to the musicians. Christine was upset and parted from Noga in tears. She too had yearned to travel with the orchestra instead of returning this very night to a small apartment in Antwerp with the knowledge that perhaps until the birth of her child, and perhaps thereafter, she would have no opportunity to perform. Moreover, it was reasonable to assume that an orchestra that had been dealt so severe an inconvenience would never again invite her to play. The father-to-be showed up at the concert not in overalls but in a suit and tie, and interpreted the musical struggle between the wind and the waves in his own fashion, perhaps as a port worker.

He studied Noga with a friendly look, and at the moment of parting dared to hug her, feeling the chill of her bare shoulders. She sensed he bore her no grudge over the words they had exchanged, and thought of telling him about the dear father who feared the death of his daughter in childbirth. But was this man the right audience for such a strange confession?

FORTY-NINE

Only after she returned from the concert to her apartment did Noga begin to fear that the following day, amid the rush of preparation for the long journey, she would not have time to say a proper goodbye to her mother. It's late now in Israel, but she knows that the lonely mother would be pleased to wake up and hear her voice. But the phone rings in Jerusalem with no reply, giving rise to a new worry. Were we too hasty to rule out assisted living? She calls her brother, a sound sleeper, and her sister-in-law Sarai, who tinkers with her eccentric paintings into the wee hours, answers and reassures her: "Your mother hasn't vanished. She's here, sleeping in the kids' room. She arrived two days ago, supposedly because she missed the children, but it's really because she's worried."

"About whom and what?"

"Hard to know," Sarai says. "Maybe herself, maybe you."

"Me? About what?"

"Not clear. Maybe your trip? I'll wake her up. She'll be happy to hear your voice, and you can find out what's eating her."

"No, no, don't wake her," says Noga, flustered. "I only wanted to say goodbye, but if she'll still be there tomorrow morning . . ."

"She'll be here, she'll be here. She doesn't seem in any hurry to go back to Jerusalem."

"In that case, I'll call before we leave for Japan."

"Japan . . . Japan . . . ," sighs the sister-in-law. "Wonderful. I envy your freedom."

"Don't exaggerate. It's not about freedom, it's just a path to the music I'm starving for."

"But you at least have an orchestra to help you satisfy your hunger. I'm all alone here, wrestling at night with my unfulfilled artistic ambition."

"But you have your children to make you happy."

"They don't always make me happy, and even when they do, they're not relaxing."

Noga is sorry that her work as an extra didn't leave her more time to spend with her sister-in-law.

"Maybe after we get back from Japan you can come for a little vacation here and leave Honi and Ima to look after the children."

"Thanks. But so long as your mother doesn't let go of Jerusalem, she won't really be able to help us."

After she hangs up, Noga finds it hard to fall asleep. Lacking an extra bed to seduce the elusive slumber, she swallows a sleeping pill, hoping to awake refreshed, ready for the trip to a distant land where she may or may not be called upon to perform.

Under the influence of the pill she plunges into solid sleep, and in the depths she meets her father, who since his demise has appeared in none of her dreams, but here he is, lying innocently in the electric bed, unaware that it was built after he had died. But is this the childhood apartment she had been assigned to protect? The waves of the dream wash over familiar furniture and kitchenware, lingering on the cumbersome television that won the hearts of the little boys. Yet the flat has undergone a major upheaval: the living room has expanded and her childhood bedroom has shrunk, and a thick, tangled tree she has never seen thrusts its branches through a window that never existed.

The father is pale and silent, and though he slowly turns the pages of a newspaper, it would seem that death discourages reading. Nevertheless, he doesn't look pained or depressed, as if death had been a difficult but successful surgery, and is relieved because further death will not be necessary. Would it be right, wonders the dreamer, to exploit the gift of his resurrection to bid farewell to him too before her trip? She heads into the kitchen to ask her mother whether saying goodbye to a living-dead person would add to his pain, except the kitchen has relocated to some unknown corner of the apartment, and in its place is a small, dark bathroom, its window bolted shut. A pale woman, immersed in reddish foam, lies in the bathtub, her eyes closed, not her mother but a total stranger. The eyes of the woman open wide. She is young, though apparently the owner of the apartment.

In the morning her mother phones, apologizing for calling so early.

"You were looking for me last night, so I'm calling before you vanish in the distance."

"You did well. It's time for me to get up. But what's going on? Only a few days in Jerusalem and you're back in Tel Aviv. Do you actually regret not sticking with the assisted living?"

"Regrets are also part of life," says the mother evasively. "But not to worry, my daughter, we won't draft you again for any experiment."

Noga provides her mother with details of the orchestra's trip to Japan. She spells out the names of the cities letter by letter and, for emergencies only, tells her how to get through to her cell phone with an entry code, and of course reminds her of the high cost and the time difference. But she doesn't mention the second harpist who dropped out at the last minute and the possibility that the whole trip might be in vain.

"Good," says the mother, "this way I'll be able to keep track of you at all times."

Now the daughter wants to know how old she was when they moved from the apartment where she was born to the one where she grew up.

"How old?" her mother asks. "Why?"

"No reason."

"You know me, no reason is not a reason."

"Let's say because of a dream."

"You have time to dream before a trip like this?"

"It was a dream that didn't ask permission."

"How can I give you an exact answer if I'm not sure how old you are now?"

"You're not sure? Ima!"

"Yes, it is odd, but I just want to confirm you're forty-three."

"Why three? Where'd you get three? Not even two, and that's two months away."

"Not even two? So why do you think of yourself as a hopeless woman?"

"Hopeless? In what sense hopeless?"

"I apologize. In no sense. I already told you that the Uriah story is eating me up inside. But I'm not saying anything. Okay, forty-two. So if we do the simple math, when we moved from Ovadiah Street in Kerem Avraham to Rashi Street in Mekor Baruch—in other words, from the apartment where you were born to the one you grew up in—you were all of five, five and a half. When we moved I was already pregnant with Honi, who was born in the new apartment, which by the way was never new and never will be. But why are you digging into the past? What happened in the dream?"

"You and Abba always refused to show me the apartment where I was born, even though you described it as beautiful and special, with a view."

"Yes, a wide-open view, from more than one window. But I'm sure that with so many births and so much new construction in the area, nobody has a view anymore. Yes, it was a very nice apartment, in a neighborhood that changed since then, became blacker than black, the usual story."

"If it was such a nice apartment, why did you move?"

"Why, why, all these whys because of a dream?"

"Why not?"

"All right—we moved because your father insisted."

"Why?"

"Again why? What was in that dream that upset you so much?"

"Abba was in it, for the first time since he died."

"Ah ... Abba ... It's about time. In my dreams, this week alone he appeared three times."

"And said something?"

"No. He can only speak if we give him something to say. So far in the dreams he's only an extra, standing up."

"An extra in a dream? Good one."

"You see? Sometimes I also have great ideas."

"Absolutely. Sometimes too many. But still, why did you leave the lovely apartment?"

"You really insist on knowing."

"Because you're avoiding the answer."

"All right. The young landlady, who lived on the same floor, died suddenly, and the husband quickly remarried, so the new wife could take care of the baby."

"There was a baby?"

"I just said, she died in childbirth."

"You didn't say that."

"Sorry."

"But what did Abba care if the landlord found a wife to take care of the child?"

"Ask him when he comes to visit you again in a dream."

"Now you're hiding something."

"Because it was a long time ago, and complicated, and if I go into detail you might miss your flight."

"Don't worry about my flight. It suddenly occurs to me that I also saw this young woman in my dream, the dead one."

"You didn't see anything. You were five years old then, or five and a half."

"So that was how Abba started having those strange delusions!"

"Could be. You knew him. The humor, cracking jokes, his little comedy routines, it all came so naturally to him, unless of course something bad happened. Then he would get scared and imagine the worst. And since I was also pregnant when the landlady died, he insisted that we leave the apartment and move someplace else."

FIFTY

THE CHARTERED JAPANESE AIRCRAFT looked old, but the cabin was spotless. Most of the instruments were stowed in the belly of the plane along with the musicians' luggage, except for the flutes, clarinets and oboes, which would easily fit in the overhead compartments. A few violinists who deemed their instruments priceless received special permission to keep them in sight during the flight. There were only twelve seats in business class, which were reserved for the conductor and his wife, as well as Herman Kroon, the deputy mayor of Arnhem and his wife, the Japanese cultural attaché who initiated the trip and the young composer Van den Broek. The remainder were allotted to senior musicians, most of them not young. Noga was seated, of course, in tourist class, beside a contrabass player, Pirke Wisser, a plump, middle-aged Dutch woman who, it turned out, was a grandmother.

Just after takeoff, at three in the afternoon, one of the pilots came out of the cockpit and with the help of a digital display briefed the passengers about the flight, which would first head north, not east, since the polar route was shortest. Thus now, at summer's end, the sun would shine during most of the flight, and only an hour or two before landing in Japan would they encounter the starry night sky.

Winging over the North Pole struck some of the musicians as a bold, even presumptuous undertaking for an older airplane, and there was macabre joking that the orchestra's crash into a giant iceberg would be a boon for Arnhem, not merely relieving the municipality of a budgetary burden, but obviating any costly search for bodies and instruments. For some musicians, fear of flying is intensified by such black humor, and there are calls for self-control and silence. All are exhausted following the festive farewell concert, and since the sun will stand still in the heavens, it's best to lower the shades.

Crammed in her seat beside a round window, the Israeli harpist floats above white lakes of ice, pondering her interrupted dream. Will her imagination manage next time to chat with her silent father, the extra? Now that the dream has been interpreted, will she be able to dream it again? She smiles sadly at the grandmother beside her, a tall, stout player in whose hands the contrabass seems like a violin that grew up and stood on its feet. The Dutch woman smiles in return, and is well aware of her neighbor's concern. Yes, based on many years of experience with the orchestra, she believes that someone will be found in Japan to play second harp. "Everyone in the orchestra," she says, "especially after such demanding rehearsals, is determined not to forgo the Debussy."

Meanwhile, the Arctic Ocean gets bigger and whiter, and the words of the older musician do more to allay her concerns than the promises of the conductor and the administrative director, and Noga asks if she'd like her to pull down the shade on the midnight sun. "Light never bothers me," the grandmother replies. "I can sleep peacefully even when the grandchildren read or play by my bed at night." Grateful for her reassurance, the Israeli inquires as to the number and ages of her grandchildren. "Only seven for now," answers Pirke Wisser, and Noga asks to see pictures, but this grandmother does not carry pictures of her grandchildren to faraway places; they are engraved in her mind. Instead, if the harpist would like, she can tell some amusing stories about them.

Feeling warm and secure alongside the grandmother, Noga leans her head on the glittering window and slips into a cozy nap, until someone touches her gently. The elderly first flutist, her occasional lover, seated up front with the notables, would like to introduce her to the conductor's wife, who wants to thank her.

"Thank me for what?"

"For the whip you brought her."

"Brought *her*?"

"What you give to her husband belongs also to her."

On most of the tray tables in tourist class dinner is being served, a combination of Japanese and Western food. "Wait," she says as Manfred pulls her from her seat, "I'm hungry." "Don't worry," he says, "up there wonderful food is waiting." And he leads her down the aisle, opens a curtain and escorts her into business class, redolent with alcohol fumes, where the inebriated conductor, in stocking feet and short pants, greets her cheerfully and introduces her to his wife, a loud and pretty American, also rather tipsy, who gives the harpist a big hug. It turns out that the maestro's wife is more excited by the idea of the whip than the whip itself. For the gift of a whip to an orchestral conductor is not merely, in her opinion, an amusing stroke of brilliance, but a call to action. So she intends to show the whip to conservative conductors who are wary, like her husband, of postmodern, experimental music. A whip, not a waving baton, can prod the unwilling, among players and conductors both. She points to the young composer Van den Broek—cocooned in a blanket, like a corpse shipped home from the battlefield—and says to Noga, "Here, for example, you have a talented young man who gave the world original, melancholy arabesques, but everyone, my husband most of all, is still plotting how to cut some of its eight little minutes."

Amused by her remarks, Dennis and Herman don't try to justify themselves, and Manfred hands his friend a glass of wine, vacating his seat so she can sit down and sample the luxuries of business class. She is excited to be included in such lofty company and sips a little wine, but is reluctant to try the food, and still standing in the aisle, she turns to the conductor to plead the case for her harp. Will it be possible to find another harpist, without whom Debussy cannot demonstrate his genius in Japan?

"Why, dear Venus, do you worry so? If we don't play the Debussy in Japan, we'll play it when we get back to Europe."

"That's true, Maestro," she says, her voice quavering. "I know we'll play it in Europe, but it's important to me to also play the piece in a distant land for a foreign people with an ancient culture. Remember too, Maestro, that for three months in Israel I didn't touch a string, and when I returned, you all made me so happy with a piece you chose not only for the Japanese but for me as well. Because as we all know, *La Mer* is not only 'the sea' but 'the mother,' and no doubt a Symbolist composer like Debussy was aware of this and also intended to make a connection between the two. So this piece will connect me with my mother, who chose to stay alone in Jerusalem, a complicated city that gets more so all the time . . ."

Unexpected tears flood her eyes, and the conductor's wife offers her a paper napkin, seizing the moment to speak for her husband.

"Don't worry, we'll find you a partner, but it will have to be an experienced player. There's only one rehearsal before the concert."

And the maestro, with a loving smile, confirms his wife's words.

Now, in the presence of his colleagues, Manfred unabashedly throws an affectionate arm around his friend, and she knows that her tears arouse not only his compassion but his lust, and again he urges her to sit in his seat and eat his meal. But she declines, saying she has a seat of her own.

Meanwhile, the captain's voice is on the loudspeaker, announcing that at this very moment the plane is passing over the North Pole, and everyone is invited to take in the view and preserve it in their memory.

But to remember what, and how?

For in September the North Pole is no longer lit by full sunlight but by a hazy, weak sun stuck at the horizon, neither rising nor setting. The barren, frozen land at the top of the world is wrapped in a dark twilight that blurs the view. In strangely fearful silence the passengers are riveted at the windows, searching for a marker, a structure, a flag or just a pole, to engrave the sight in memory.

Manfred gives Noga his window seat so she too can get a good look at the crown of the world. Her eyes aren't focused on the earth but at the sun, which sits on the horizon like an overripe orange. Might the planet Noga be found nearby? Her father would tell her to look for it just before sunset or sunrise, but who knows what sunrise and sunset are here?

"Maybe the planet . . . Venus . . . is out there," she whispers to the flutist.

"Where?" he asks. He turns to the flight attendant and requests permission to enter the cockpit—perhaps from there it will be possible to locate Venus. They gingerly step into the darkened cockpit, cradled in polar twilight, and amid greenish dials and glowing levers they are welcomed by little bows and the soothing smiles of angular eyes.

The two pilots ferrying a European orchestra to the Far East are accustomed to such requests, and they rotate the phosphorescent radar to locate the desired planet, and direct the attention of the two musicians to a solitary disk glimmering on the horizon, loyal to the sun that stubbornly stays put twenty-four hours a day.

"Venus," say the two young pilots, pronouncing the sweet name of the ancient goddess. After the sun leaves the North Pole to allow a long night to spread its wings, this planet will vanish as well.

FIFTY-ONE

W HILE THEY WERE on the plane from Europe, Osaka was struck by a mild earthquake, the airport was closed, and they circled in the air for an extra hour before receiving permission to land.

The night that blackened the world after they passed the North Pole did not last long, and before landing in Osaka the sun had fully risen. After clearing passport control, the players of the large instruments were asked to retrieve them and check that they had weathered the flight safely. Escorted to a large hangar that reminded Noga of the faux hospital at the port of Ashdod, the musicians descended on their instruments, banging the drums and plucking the big strings. Noga at her harp happily executed long, liquid glissandi that delighted the baggage handlers, who gathered around her and thanked her with friendly bows.

The musicians were then transported in three buses to Kyoto, the city of temples, where rooms awaited them at the handsome guesthouse of Doshisha University. Two musicians would occupy each room, and since Noga did not wish to validate her relationship with Manfred, she quickly suggested to the sturdy grandmother Pirke Wisser, her neighbor on the plane, that they share a room. The contrabassist hesitantly agreed, warning the Israeli with Dutch candor that she was likely to snore. "That's all right," replied Noga. "My parents, who slept their whole lives in a narrow double bed, taught me that snoring bothers only someone who doesn't like the snorer, and I like you a lot."

The hosts decided to impress their guests right away with a visit to the Temple of the Golden Pavilion on the shore of Mirror Lake. Despite their fatigue from the long flight, and the pole that confused day and night, most of the musicians accepted the offer, and at a soft, radiant afternoon hour they embarked on the tour, accompanied by Dutch-speaking Japanese guides, who divided the orchestra members into five small groups, to enable each one to ask questions without trying the patience of their companions.

The orchestra was first taken for a view of the golden temple from afar, to marvel at its holy reflection in the waters of the lake. The sight is spectacular yet intimate. The solitude of the temple on the edge of the lake, the harmony of its three-tiered structure, the radiance of the gold leaf that covers its walls, the gentle shingled roofs shading the balconies that surround each story, convey the warm humanity of a private villa converted long ago to a Zen Buddhist temple. Although the pavilion is familiar from photographs, its living, organic presence, in a thick green grove with a botanical garden, arrests the visitor. Indeed, explains the guide of Noga's group, its official name is Rokuon-ji, or Deer Garden Temple. It was built in the fourteenth century, and survived a devastating civil war in the fifteenth, only to be burned down in the mid-twentieth century by a monk who lost his mind, and reconstructed thereafter.

Burned down and reconstructed? The musicians react with wonder at the fate of a temple that looks so calm and serene, as if nothing had befallen it since the day it was built.

The group's guide is petite and bespectacled, and speaks Dutch with an accent that Noga has difficulty understanding, but she is drawn to her nonetheless, for she seems to be well educated. Unlike the many tour guides who mechanically recite names and dates, she tries to widen the scope and compare Japan with other nations.

To better understand the Dutch, which is native to neither her ears nor the speaker's lips, Noga moves closer to the slender woman, who looks like a student who skipped several grades at once. At a quiet moment, as the group walks around the lake to the temple, Noga asks her a question that arose in her mind at the sight of the temple: What is the religion of the Japanese people?

"The religion?" The guide smiles and pauses to evaluate the questioner. "Here is a surprising answer for you. According to a recent poll, seventy-five percent of Japanese people do not define themselves as having a religion, and until the middle of the nineteenth century there was no word in Japanese for the concept of religion."

"Seventy-five percent?" The Israeli is stunned. "That many?"

"Yes, because when a Japanese defines himself as religious, it means he is a member of a religious sect, and that can also be a Christian sect. So when seventy-five percent define themselves as not religious, it means first of all they are not members of any sect, yet eighty-five percent identify themselves as Buddhist."

"Eighty-five percent Buddhist!"

"And ninety-five percent believe in Shinto."

"How can that be?" Noga protests. "These are two different religions!"

"Of course they are different. The Shinto ceremonies connect the person to the ancient gods, the Kami spirits that must be appeased, especially when a child is born or at a wedding, whereas Buddhism, which is universal and not only Japanese, is also connected with death, and a person who dies is given a Buddhist name."

"The dead have a Buddhist name?" asks the harpist uneasily.

"Yes, the death rituals are done in the Buddhist way."

"Meaning what?"

"Meaning that a Japanese can honor and perform, even in the same temple, ceremonies of two religions, and add a ritual from a third faith, without perceiving it as a fault or contradiction. We are polytheists," stresses the tiny tour guide, "believers in many faiths, and therefore here in Japan a person is not asked what his religion is. It is entirely a personal matter. After the Second World War, the victors forced us to completely separate religion from the state—that way all the religious fanaticism is uprooted. The Japanese are loyal only to their emperor. That is enough for them."

"Enough for you too?" asks Noga.

A mysterious smile crosses the lips of the guide. "For me too," she says softly. "Why not."

"That's good," concludes Noga.

The rest of the musicians in the group have long since left the two behind. The air is sweet and the light soft, and the scene is one of silent dignity. Other tourists, not orchestra members, walk quietly beside them. The pair walk side by side, and Noga wonders about the age of this intelligent guide, who seems ageless.

"I'm not Dutch, but Israeli," she discloses. "So what you told me about the religious chaos in Japan is very appealing."

"It is not chaos," the guide says, rejecting the definition with mild annoyance. "It is tolerance. It is freedom."

"Of course, tolerance, freedom," Noga hastens to correct herself, but adds with a sly smile, "if not with regard to your emperor."

The guide shakes her head with suppressed anger, but does not respond.

"Because with us," Noga persists, suddenly switching to English, "in other words in Israel, there is one religion, but everyone bends it his own way."

The guide smiles politely, clearly eager to get free of Noga. But Noga for some reason feels the need to tell her about herself.

"I am a harpist," she says, "but I didn't find work in Israel, so I play with this orchestra."

They approach the pavilion, where the entire orchestra has gathered. They may not enter, for the inside of the temple is off limits to tourists and visitors, open only to a select few. On a low hill nearby stand the managers of the orchestra with their local escorts, and it occurs to Noga that they are waiting for her. Indeed, with a brusque wave of his hand the maestro signals her to come, his face beaming with the promise of good news.

Along with them, slightly hidden, stands a short old Japanese man, his white hair in a braid, wearing a long gray robe and wooden clogs. On his back is a blue pack that resembles the traditional pillow of Japanese women.

"And so," says Dennis van Zwol, pointing to the old man, who bows deeply before the harpist, "we told you not to worry, and we were right. Tomorrow at the concert you will have a partner whose reputation precedes him. A harpist of the highest caliber, who served as a soldier in the world war, and since then, for many years, was a harpist with the Kyoto Symphony Orchestra and also a teacher at the conservatory in Tokyo. A few years ago he went back to live in the area where he was born, to be near his family. This is an area that was damaged in the last tsunami ..."

The conductor turns to the cultural attaché for help with the name.

"Fukushima," says the attaché.

And when the old man hears the name of his area, he bows to the conductor.

"Yes," the conductor goes on, "Fukushima, which is where he was found. He speaks only Japanese, but neither you nor I will have any problem with him, since he has played *La Mer* by Debussy a number of times as first harpist, and he no doubt knows the part by heart."

The little old man bows again at the sound of the French composer's name.

"So he'll be playing the first harp part?" Noga asks anxiously, her eyes fixed on the old man, who now and again bows his head.

"No, no, you are the first harpist, and he is the second," the conductor says. "He has not come here seeking fame, only to help. He has come from far away, two days of travel, and he is a simple and modest man, as you see, and also adorable."

Everyone smiles at the word "adorable," and the cultural attaché translates the adjective for the old man, who erupts with laughter, his mouth nearly toothless. Again he presses his palms together and distributes bows in a semicircle to the entire group.

"And what is his name?" asks Noga. "I should at least know his name."

"Ichiro Matsudaira," says the attaché, and the old man who hears his name spoken bows once again.

He just might bow to us while playing, thinks Noga, wondering if she should extend her hand to him, but thinks better of it and instead bows deeply and recites her name: "Noga, which means Venus."

And the old man whispers reverentially, "Venus," and bows heartily in return.

At the conclusion of the bowing a monk emerges from the temple and admits only the maestro and the Japanese harpist, and the rest of the group heads into the garden.

FIFTY-TWO

As noga prepares for the night in the room she is sharing with her seatmate from the plane, her mobile phone startles her. Her brother Honi, his voice as clear and sharp as if he were next door, wishes to know if the flight went well.

"Is it you who's concerned, or did Ima lay her worry on you?"

"I don't worry about someone who knows how to take care of herself, but Ima is here with me, and she misses the sound of your voice."

"Ima is still with you in Tel Aviv?" she asks, astonished. "Why, what happened?"

"Ask her, but I doubt you'll get a reasonable answer. Anyway, before I hand you over to her—in one word, how was the flight to Japan?"

"We flew over the North Pole."

"And what's happening there?"

"The sun. It never sets."

"And Japan?"

"Pleasant and strange, but it's only the beginning."

"Anyway, take care of yourself. Here's Ima."

The mother's voice, soft and tentative, seems to have changed.

"Something happened or is happening in Jerusalem that makes it hard for you to go back there?" the daughter asks bluntly.

"Yes . . . I mean, no . . . nothing special . . . and if there is something, then it's not clear. But don't worry, because I realize I'm a burden here and I have to leave, that's clear to me, so you don't need to remind me from Japan. Not to worry, I won't stay, it's just that all of a sudden it's hard for me to go back to Jerusalem, somehow because of you."

"Because of me?"

"Because ever since you left I can't stop thinking about you ... that dream ... and on top of that Uriah's visit. But wait, first you. What's going on with you?"

"Everything's fine. Tomorrow is the first concert in Kyoto, but it's not worth going into at length in an overseas call to my cell. It's very expensive, also for me—"

"Please, don't worry about the money. I already explained to you that after my release from assisted living I'm a rich woman, so please, send me your phone bill, just don't stop me now."

"Okay, talk, even though it's late here. But please, don't talk about me, talk about you. What's bothering you all of a sudden?"

"About me is about you, and about you is about me. After all, it's you who promised to play me on your harp, so I'm also playing you, in my heart."

"Lovely. In other words?"

"The dream you told me about is disturbing, painful."

"It's a dream, Ima, only a dream."

"Right, only a dream, but your visit in Israel also seems like only a dream. You were here three months and I barely saw you."

"Because you and Honi asked me to look after the apartment."

"Right, but you looked after it too much, and I was stuck with that pointless experiment in assisted living. But it's okay, our intentions were good, and with the same goodwill your visit flew by."

"But Ima, what's going on now? How'd you get stuck at Honi's?"

"Stuck, that's the right word. You know me, this is something new, because I don't get stuck anywhere. I got stuck here because I'm afraid to go back to the apartment, because maybe Uriah made himself a copy of the key and he'll surprise me there."

"Uriah? Ima, why Uriah?"

"You weren't fair to him. I'm telling you straight. If you're playing me on your harp, listen to what the harp plays back. You weren't fair. If you loved him, and you did love him, you should not have aborted his child."

"Ima, just drop Uriah, he is irrelevant now, he came and went and won't come back, he has a wife and two kids and he doesn't need me, and certainly not you."

"No, it's not that simple. Don't think that everyone else is an extra, without a mind of their own or power of their own. You were wrong . . . I don't want to make you angry now, before the concert, but if you think you're playing me, you should pick some better notes . . . That's all. I shouldn't have let you run away from Israel before explaining to me what's going on with you."

"I didn't run away, I came to help you decide. Honi asked me to."

"Honi has one story, I have a different story . . . Don't worry too much about him. He's fine, and tomorrow I'll set him free and go back to Jerusalem. What time is it there? Morning?"

"Morning? Why morning? We're in the Far East, not the West. The sun went down here hours ago. Now it's late, eleven at night. I'm staying in a room with an older woman who doesn't understand Hebrew, but would surely like to go to sleep."

"An older woman?"

"From the orchestra, a contrabass player, a grandmother, a good woman—"

"A contrabass player must be a big strong woman."

"She actually is as you imagine her, but skinny and delicate people can also play the contrabass, in fact any instrument. Here, for example, the second harp will be played tomorrow by a tiny Japanese man."

"Tiny Japanese man?"

"Really tiny. A little old man."

"So you'll have an interesting challenge, the dialogue with him. Good thing you're sleeping tonight in the same room as a big strong woman who's a grandmother—it will give you confidence, as if I were sleeping beside you. Tell her hello from me, and that she should protect you."

"Ima, what's with you? Why protect me?"

"Because I still think Uriah won't give up on the child you didn't give him."

"How?"

"Maybe he'll come again, this time to me."

"To you? Why? In what way are you responsible?"

"I'm responsible because I gave birth to you. I'm responsible because I didn't know how to guide you in life. The least I can do for him is sympathize."

FIFTY-THREE

THE SNORING THAT THE CONTRABASSIST had warned of in advance indeed disrupted Noga's sleep. At first she tried to muffle her ears with a pillow, but it was no match for the snores. With no alternative, she left the room in hopes that the snoring might wake the snorer. The guesthouse was dark and silent, with a dim light in the stairway. She went down to the dining room but found it locked, and the front door was locked as well, but a rear door turned out to be open, with trees whispering in the park beyond.

The night is pleasingly cool, and she is drawn into a thicket of trees whose overcrowded roots have emerged from underground to twist around the trunks. Along the paths are bushes decorated with tiny light bulbs, apparently left over from some celebration, that calm her nerves with their childish innocence. She steps on, bathed in the sweet, familiar fragrance of fresh-mown grass. From the middle of the garden comes a murmur of human voices, borne on a bluish cloud of harsh tobacco smoke, recalling the cheap cigarettes Uriah was addicted to in his army days. She follows the smell and the voices, arriving at a handsome wooden gazebo, in front of which are gathered a dozen or so young men and women, most likely students from the university, smoking and talking, and planted among them, to her astonishment, is the little old man who came from afar to be her partner. He sits on a bench, barefoot, his legs folded under him. He wears the same gray robe, with the same pack tied to his back. But his white braid is unraveled for the night, and the mane of hair framing his face gives him the look of a sweet old Japanese woman from an American movie about World War II.

He is half asleep, half listening to the youngsters, with a small pipe stuck in his mouth. The young people, noticing the foreign woman heading their way, fall silent. But she is no stranger to the old man, and to demonstrate this she stands before him and bows deeply, in the spirit of their meeting a few hours earlier at the Temple of the Golden Pavilion. But the old man merely nods his head, apparently failing to recognize her as his partner. Is he a blind musician, improvising the part of second harp? She feels a sudden pang of anxiety, but doesn't press the issue. Touching two fingers to her lips, she offers an excuse for her presence: the craving for a cigarette. The young people oblige her, and rather than say thank you, she delights in local custom and bows to the whole group, cigarette in mouth, as if she were a soloist onstage before a cheering audience. She then walks back to the guesthouse, filled with the scent of simple tobacco that reminds her of Uriah.

The room is still, but the snoring grandma has woken up and turned on her small bedside light, waiting to apologize to the neighbor. To be honest, she hadn't imagined that her snoring would startle and drive away the Israeli, who has evidently long grown accustomed to sleeping alone. Now she will not fall back to sleep until Noga has soundly done so. As reinforcement she offers Noga a dependable sleeping pill, whose effect is impervious even to cannon fire. "A whole or just a half?" "Whole," says the harpist. "Half the night is gone, and tomorrow's a big day."

The little pill is indeed a mighty potion, and the sleep is so deep that her dreams lie dormant. And when she opens her eyes she finds herself alone in the room, her neighbor's bed meticulously made, and morning fiercely shining through the folds of the window curtain. It is nine o'clock. Eight hours of pure sleep, which instead of alertness have produced a thick blur. Noga smiles, thinking, This sweet grandma could have killed me so she could snore to her heart's content. She rises sluggishly, washes slowly, her head spinning, limbs heavy, and before making her bed she rushes just in time to what's left of the breakfast buffet. The many hours of sleep did her no good, and the visit to the park seems like an illusion; she's not even sure if the cigarette was lit or not. Since the rehearsal at the concert hall is called for one p.m., most of the musicians, encouraged by eager guides, are making a quick tour of two more temples. But the Israeli does not seek further holiness—she has more than enough in her homeland. She returns to her room, where instead of making her unruly bed she slips back into her nightgown and huddles like a fetus, no longer from fatigue but from feelings of illness and pain.

At noon Manfred arrives to wake her. What's going on? carps the flutist. They will only be in this jewel box of a city for four days, so what's the point of sleeping? She looks at him sadly and doesn't reply. Her roommate is astounded: there's no way a little innocent sleeping pill could depress somebody quite so much.

"Little but not innocent," Noga mumbles feebly in English. "But it's not depression, it's memory." Without adding a word, she banishes Manfred and goes to the bathroom, and is terrified to find two blood spots on her nightgown. Could her period conceivably be coming back, or is this a symptom of something more serious? She washes out the nightgown, rubbing the blood spots with a bar of soap, struck by a sensation of death.

The Kyoto Concert Hall is splendidly modern, resembling a giant shoe. The heel is a round structure containing the main hall and its rectangular lobby. At the back of the stage rise the lofty pipes of the organ, silvered and gilded, in the manner of the Concertgebouw in Amsterdam. Most of the instruments have been brought onstage, and her harp has been joined by a black one the likes of which she has seen only in old photographs. "Is this the house harp?" she asks the Japanese cultural attaché, who explains that this is the private harp of the elderly Ichiro Matsudaira, which he brings with him to every performance. The rehearsal begins with Symphony No. 26 in D Minor by Haydn, a dramatic, tempestuous symphony, which an ensemble of the best players performs with vigorous precision. As they play, Herman Kroon and a woman violist, who Dennis believes has a uniquely sensitive ear, prowl about the hall to verify how its acoustics respond to a foreign orchestra. It turns out that what sounds right and good in Europe also sounds right and good in the Far East.

Next in turn, after the Haydn symphony, is Beethoven's *Emperor* Concerto, and most of the musicians who had not been part of the previous ensemble come to the stage. Only Noga and a few percussionists stay seated in the hall. She has installed herself in the first row to get a better look at the Japanese soloist, on account of whose arm, broken in a tennis game in

Berlin, Noga had been robbed of the Mozart concerto. This is a short, dark young woman in jeans and a lightweight blouse, her hands quick and dexterous, and it would seem that her self-confidence flourishes here in her homeland, for she asks, even in rehearsal, that the house be completely dark, to compel the few listeners to concentrate on her alone.

Her playing is powerful, fast, virtuosic, but uninspired. From time to time the conductor halts her racing tempo, trying to reach a compromise, not always with success. "She's a well-known kamikaze," Herman whispers to Noga, "who turns music into a suicide mission. But don't worry about her, tonight they'll love her, because she was born in a small town not far from here to a poor family, and when she studied music she supported herself as a waitress and babysitter, and soared to the top on her talent alone. Many people here still remember her from the beginning of her career, and whoever doesn't can read about it in the program. The Japanese, unlike us, don't just flip through the program, they read it from cover to cover. And besides," Herman goes on, "let us not forget that this is the *Emperor*, and for the Japanese that's not Napoleon but *their* emperor—beloved, mysterious, revered, the bedrock of their identity."

Little noises in the darkness. Noga turns around and sees the elderly harpist feeling his way inside, a small stick in his hand. She wants to exchange a hello with him, but fears he will again find it hard to recognize her. No matter, she thinks, soon we'll sit shoulder to shoulder and he won't be able to deny me.

The glorious metallic tones of the piano are suddenly accompanied by the acute contraction of her lower belly, like a knife blade turning in her gut, and though she tries to distract herself from the pain, it won't let up. The young Japanese woman is galloping like a wild horse that has thrown its rider, and the conductor is trying to slow her down with the help of the wind instruments. Noga has seen her share of young and brilliant soloists who after a few years sink into anonymity. Soloists of age sixty or seventy are less abundant than these youngsters. Personal life experience, the broader and deeper the better, is the key to fresh interpretation of the tired, crowd-pleasing classics.

The pain increases, her muscles strain. "Excuse me," she whispers to

Herman, and goes out of the hall in search of the ladies' room, which is tucked someplace far away, and she only finds a large door with the stenciled image of a person in a wheelchair, crowned by one word in Japanese. Does this suggest anyone, male and female? If she had access to the chair she occupied as a disabled extra, she'd roll right in, not as a man or woman, but just a human. In the absence of such a chair, does her distress confer permission? There is no one in the corridor to tell her what is and isn't proper, so she cautiously opens the door and enters.

She finds a big, wide stall, immaculate as a doctor's office. At one side is a diaper-changing table big enough for twins or even triplets. She unzips her pants and discovers that the same bloodstains that she removed from the nightgown have reappeared on her panties, larger and redder than before. Something is wrong with her body. Her periods are long gone. What are the odds of a return visit?

A loudspeaker tucked in the ceiling plays the music from the hall, and while she is convulsing miserably in a public washroom, the notes of the *Emperor*'s finale cascade from a piano above her head. In a few minutes the conductor will exchange a few more words with the soloist before moving on to the second part of the rehearsal. But Noga doesn't budge. She waits for the pain to subside, or at least to make its intentions clear. Very slowly she tries to regulate her breathing. The new blood spots cannot be removed right now, and will alas accompany her to the stage, but with all her might she will strive to control the pain, hoping it will actually intensify her performance.

The *Emperor* is finished. According to the program, the time has come for the *Melancholy Arabesques* of Van den Broek. In which case, she has eight whole minutes to recover and calm down. Lucky for her that in the end they didn't cut anything from the already short piece. She waits for the opening shriek of the piccolo, and now, here goes, the third time she's heard these insane arabesques, this one through a little speaker in the ceiling, and quite miraculously, what had earlier sounded chaotic and gratuitously provocative seems cloaked in a kind of decadent beauty. Yes, despite his disdainful objections to this work, the maestro has succeeded, perhaps under the influence of his wife, in shaping it to shock listeners without repelling them.

Her eyes are glued to the clock, and at the fifth minute she gets up, straightens her clothes and quickly applies makeup before the mirror to conceal her pallor, and as the Dutchman's demanding arabesques flow to a finish, she feels a vague flowing within herself. Could this be a vestige of the old abortion? It's crazy just to raise the possibility.

She returns to the hall precisely as the young composer rushes with excitement to embrace the conductor, whose interpretation, in the end, was an improvement. Her new partner is already sitting on the stage, tuning his harp. She walks over slowly and bows slightly to him, and now he does recognize her, but instead of returning the bow he surprises her by extending his hand.

Sitting close to his black harp, she can examine it thoroughly. It looks large and unwieldy, owing perhaps to its extreme age, or in contrast to its tiny player. At the top of the harp there is no portrait of an angel or embossment of a gold crown, but the face of a black bird. The Japanese has his score open, and from the folds of his robe he produces thin gold-rimmed glasses and places them on his nose. At least he won't be playing from memory, Noga consoles herself as she begins to tune her strings. The harpist, her very old new partner, listens with concern as she works, without a word or suggestion—just his tiny hand trembling at every twitch of a string, then relaxing when it reaches its proper pitch.

The musicians who have played three pieces in a row and gone out for a break now return to the stage. Ingrid, the French horn player, walks past Noga and senses her distress. "Is anything wrong?" she asks, placing a soft hand on the Israeli's shoulder. "Yes," Noga decides to admit. "If you have a little time after the rehearsal, I will need your help." "Of course I'll have time," promises the musician, "as much as you want."

The words are spoken sincerely. Ingrid de Monk is a beautiful young woman who protects herself through generosity of spirit. Well aware of the attraction, envy and confusion that her beauty can arouse, she tries to dull her glamour by means of simple, rumpled clothes, and also tries to be as helpful as possible to anyone who needs help. From her husband, older by a number of years, a family doctor at a rural clinic, she has acquired useful snippets of medical knowledge, plus a little toolbox containing pills and ointments, bandages and tape, a thermometer and blood-pressure gauge, pins and needles and buttons, and even a makeup kit. She carries this box, dubbed the "Wonder Horn" by her fellow musicians, not only when traveling, but sometimes to long rehearsals, possibly as a sort of penance for the gift of beauty bestowed on her.

Dennis van Zwol takes the podium and waits for the absolute silence that enables the sounding of the first note. To Noga's astonishment, the Japanese harpist has removed his wooden clogs and is poised to press the pedals with his tiny, wrinkled bare feet. The conductor turns to the two harpists, readies their entrance with a finger of his left hand and then, with the baton in his right hand, gives a clear sign for the timpani to stroke the opening beats, and the old man plucks the first note with a stunning power that Christine could never accomplish, and Noga joins him an eighth note later, plucking rapidly and without accents. Side by side, in partnership and dialogue, with four swift hands and quick, precise pressure on the pedals, the two summon the wail of the wind and the sparkle of the waves from the music of Debussy, convincing the strings and woodwinds, and the percussion in their wake, that they are in fact sailing together on the wide-open seas.

And with love and devotion to her instrument Noga is able to conquer her pain. Inspired by the fierce virtuosity flourishing in the fingers of the old man, whose black harp seems entwined with his body, she discovers that her own instrument has a tone and resonance she had not known or imagined, and these tempt her to pluck its strings with all her might, nearly to uproot them.

The maestro settles down, and instead of waving his arms and jumping, he closes his eyes, and with soft, nonchalant hand motions he lets the orchestra guide its conductor, who sails alone in a simple sailboat, trusting the music not to drown him or betray him, but land him safely on the shore of his desires.

When the last note disappears and silence conquers the hall, the administrative director cannot contain himself and leaps from his seat with the cry of "Bravo! Bravo!" while Dennis's wife rushes from her seat to the stage and bows emotionally to the entire orchestra.

And the conductor sighs and says, "What a pity this is just a rehearsal."

FIFTY-FOUR

S EVEN HOURS REMAIN until the concert. Some of the musicians run off to see a few more temples, but most, including her roommate Pirke, go in search of culinary delicacies. Only a few, Noga among them, return to the guesthouse. Her nightgown is still damp, and the morning's blood spots are still visible. She will need to find a stronger detergent, but where and when? She takes off her clothes and examines with dismay the new spotting on her panties, then wraps them in a bag and buries them deep in the trash. For a moment she deliberates whether to take a shower or immerse her suffering body in the bath. The dream of the woman with her eyes closed, floating in the reddish foam, was frightening yet seductive. But no, it's too soon. A person must not wallow in her own blood.

After her shower, she curls up under the blanket in a clean, flimsy nightgown, hoping that if the bleeding stops, the pain will too. All is quiet at the guesthouse. The musicians are wandering from temples to restaurants, refreshing their souls before the concert. The warm, clear sounds of a clarinet playing an old folksong waft from a room on the top floor. No, she is sure, these cannot be the signs of a monthly period. Hers ended a good while ago, and why should it return? No, she knows that this is something else, new and serious, plotting against her in this strange and distant land to put an end to the freedom she has allowed herself.

She does not hear the knock at the door, and when her eyes open the French horn player is hovering over her, blushing shyly, here to keep her promise, to which end she has brought her Wonder Horn box.

Ingrid wears no makeup, her clothes are baggy, but her natural beauty triumphs over self-imposed restrictions, and now, with the two of them alone, close to each other in a small room, Noga knows she has no further need to lift her eyes to the sky at dawn or sunset to find the planet whose name she shares, for that planet had descended to her room in the form of a young Venus, a musician in her orchestra, who will try to interpret her pains in order to relieve them.

And since Venus is also the wife of a doctor who between concerts tutors her in medicine, she unflinchingly rummages through the trash to examine the bloodstained panties. She confidently determines that the stains are evidence of menstruation and nothing more serious, and even if her periods had stopped, they have not, on the strength of her age and health, lost their right to return. And the French horn player bolsters her diagnosis with stories of women who visited her husband's clinic.

"How old is your husband?" asks Noga, basking in a new serenity.

"Forty. Ten years older than I am."

"And children?"

"Just one for now. Age five, staying with my parents at the moment."

Noga closes her eyes and asks if there is something in the Wonder Horn that will lessen her pain but won't knock her out like the sleeping pill the contrabass player gave her at midnight. Ingrid produces a small bottle and shakes out two golden pills, deciding after a moment's thought to leave the bottle with her patient, to guarantee her peace of mind for the whole Japanese tour. And from the bottom of the box she removes a few sanitary napkins, since the blood flow will increase.

"The main thing, our Venus, is that you stay as sharp and confident as ever. Because in the last rehearsal, if I'm not mistaken, there was a bold new sound, a sort of wailing from your harp strings, or possibly the strings of your fellow harpist."

As she closes the lid of the Wonder Horn and leaves to get ready for the first concert on Japanese soil, Noga wants to tell her, No, don't say "our Venus" anymore, you should all just call me Noga. But she is not sure the time is yet right.

The concert hall glitters with bright lights, and along with subscription holders and paying customers are local elders and dignitaries who have been specially invited. Dennis van Zwol has passed up his light, flexible Chinese jacket, much in vogue among conductors, in favor of his old tuxedo, with an artificial lily pinned to its lapel. The male musicians have donned their black suits, and the women have endeavored to look their best. In honor of the orchestra the French horn player has elected not to conceal her beauty. She has let down her hair, adorned it with an orange flower and polished her horn to a dazzling golden sheen. In the wings, before taking the stage, everyone marveled at the metamorphosis in the Japanese pianist—in the morning she had looked like a student or waitress, and in the evening had turned into a woman of mystery in a cherry-colored silk kimono and silver high-heeled shoes that greatly increased her height.

"Listen," Herman alerted the musicians before they went onstage, "don't expect a long wave of applause, because the Japanese are restrained. Don't be demoralized if the audience response seems moderate."

But the audience response to the Haydn symphony was actually wildly enthusiastic, and the *Emperor* was awaited with tense anticipation. The house lights were turned off, contrary to typical concert procedure, a hush fell over the crowd, and the soloist entered to the sounds of applause and roars of joy. No doubt the family of the pianist, residents of her home village, friends and teachers, and perhaps her former employers from her days as a waitress and babysitter have not missed this chance to witness her greatness. For she is a local girl who has been away a long time, and her return is cause for celebration. Who knows how many have come to the concert just for her?

Perhaps for this reason, in the first movement she slowed the galloping tempo of the rehearsal. And from the start of the second movement there has been a dramatic change. Her playing has become soft and dreamy, as though the emperor were napping in his chamber and the piano had come not to hail him but caress him. And the slow, soft caress has unsettled the percussionists sitting backstage with Noga, so the waiting musicians have decided to fortify themselves with strong drink before the cafeteria and bar are swamped during intermission. The harpist was invited to join them, but declined, and remains alone backstage in her long black dress with her neck and shoulders bare, waiting for the blood to flow, and to her surprise also yearning for the accompanying pain.

Then a side door opens and into the darkened backstage space comes her partner, the elderly harpist Ichiro Matsudaira, who has replaced his gray robe with a magnificent colorful one, a samurai sword embroidered on it in red silk thread. His braid is neatly combed, and seems for a moment to be a bit blacker. He approaches her with tiny steps and bows deeply. It would appear that in the afternoon rehearsal he came to appreciate her playing. This musician is essentially a teacher and not a competitor, and therefore he can be happy about every student or partner who is likely to surpass him. And as Noga stands up to bow her thanks in return, she feels the bursting flow that soaks the sanitary napkin given her by the good Ingrid, and despite the pain that seizes her, she feels relief. This is indeed her period, no doubt about it.

The wrinkled old man studies her with interest. Soon they will sit onstage side by side, a golden harp beside a black harp, to give sound and color to the sea.

So I was right, she tells herself, when I told them all that I knew I could have a child but didn't want to. I was right, and the proof now pours through my body. Ima, Honi, where are you now and what time is it? Has Ima returned to Jerusalem, or is she still afraid to be alone and clinging to her son? And suddenly an uncontrollable weeping rises from deep within her. It cannot be that the mother who gave birth to me thinks I am lost. And the little old man sees the tears and trembling shoulders of the first harpist, half a century his junior, and he seems overcome with compassion, for he stands up, and with small, delicate steps, like those with which her father would amuse his wife at night, he floats to her and gently bows.

Haifa-Givatayim, 2012–2014